The Woman of the House

ALICE TAYLOR

The Woman of the House

BRANDON

A Brandon Paperback

Published in 1999 by
Brandon
an imprint of Mount Eagle Publications Ltd.
Dingle, Co. Kerry, Ireland

First published by Mount Eagle Publications Ltd, 1997

10 9 8 7 6 5 4 3 2

ISBN 0 86322 249 8

Cover illustration: John Short
Cover design: Public Communications Centre, Dublin
Typesetting: Red Barn Publishing, Skeagh, Skibbereen, Co. Cork
Printed by The Guernsey Press Ltd., Channel Islands

To Gear
for your encouragement

CHAPTER ONE

THERE WAS NO key for the front door of Mossgrove, nor had there been for as long as Kate could remember, but her grandfather had fitted a large iron bolt to stop the door shuddering on stormy nights.

The east wind would whip up along the valley and blow in underneath the heavy door, shaking it in its wooden frame and rattling the brass knob. With the first rattle her grandfather would get up from his armchair by the fire and go out into the front porch where he would shoulder the old door firmly into position and shoot the bolt. Then he would throw a knitted jumper that he had worn for many years during the winter ploughing along the bottom of the door. The heavy old jumper was a patchwork of darns, but it kept out the draught and soaked up the driving rain. He was an old man at that time and the cold chilled him. She had been eight when he died twenty-four years ago, but she could still remember him.

As Kate turned the brass knob with its familiar dents, and the door did not open she knew immediately that Martha had it bolted on the inside. The first time this had happened Kate had felt a sharp stab of rejection, for this had been the front door of her childhood and had always stood open in summer. Every year the ivy had grown down around it and her mother had peeled it back gently so that it had thickened to form a deep fringe above the lintel and two long curtains down the sides. Each time the stations came to Mossgrove it had got a fresh coat of paint. Over the years it had worn many different coloured coats, but when the hot sun of a few summers dried and split the top one, all the others hiding underneath peeped out and gave the old door a rainbow appearance.

Kate had felt some of her childhood carved away when Martha, soon after her arrival in Mossgrove, had stripped it of all its coats and painted it a pristine white. Now it was glossy and perfect, but it no longer smiled in welcome.

As a child Kate had sat on the warm flagstone outside this door doing her lessons. Her schoolbooks would be scattered on the step when she wandered out into the garden to pick some of her mothers Gallica roses. She would bury her nose in their dark velvet petals and breathe in their heavy rich fragrance. Sometimes she had eased the petals apart and laid them between the pages of her schoolbooks. There for a short while they would hold the musky scent, but gradually it would die and the petals crinkle up until all that remained of their former beauty was the faded pink colour. Other evenings she would pick daisies from around the garden and sit on the doorstep making daisy chains while Bran snoozed beside her. Often he would wake up with a start to snap at inquisitive flies who insisted on investigating the inside of his nostrils or the dark channels of his ears.

This doorstep had been her favourite place. From here she could watch the birds around the garden darting in and out under the hedges and bushes. She had discovered all their nests secretly tucked away. The wren had the best nest of all, a ball of feathery fur with her own front door knitted into the centre. When she sat on her eggs her brown beady eye peered out. Kate decided that she was far wiser than the crows who built their nests on the top of the beeches at the bottom of the haggard to be tossed back and forth on windy days.

Standing on the doorstep she could see down along the fields of Mossgrove and over to the farms on the hills across the river. The house faced south into the warmth of the sun and had its back to the cold north where Grandfather had planted sheltering belts of trees. The summer before he died, when she was seven, he used to sit out here in his chair and doze in the sun, his thick black stick against his large bony knees and his long white hair falling sideways like a pale curtain over his face. It was her job then to pick up his pipe when his grip loosened in sleep and it slipped to the ground.

Years later, when she returned on holidays while nursing in England, she had opened this door to feel the house welcome her back. She had loved to creep in quietly and take them by surprise. A flood of joy lit up their faces when they saw her and it washed away the loneliness of the big impersonal hospital in London. Her mother with her strong, kind face. A face that had endured suffering but had not been bowed by it. She would open her arms wide, and as they wrapped around her Kate felt the warm love fuse through her. Then darling Ned, tall and athletic, who to hide the emotion of his delight in her return would swing her around the kitchen to welcome her back. And always with them Jack Tobin, who had been her father figure in the world of Mossgrove and whose eyes glowed with joy to see her.

But now there was no warm feeling, no open door and no welcome. The door was not normally bolted but when Martha saw Kate coming she bolted it. She was deprived of the old freedom of just walking in. The neighbours had never knocked on the front door of Mossgrove or any other house in the townland. They just walked in and announced their arrival by whistling or singing or even talking aloud to themselves. It was one of the local unspoken practices that everyone observed. The only ones who knocked were strangers or people unsure of their welcome. The fact that she now had to knock forced Kate into that category. From Martha there was never a welcoming smile, only a lift of the eyebrows and a cool "Oh it's you" as she would turn on her heel and Kate would have to swallow hard and follow her in.

Martha had started this practice soon after her arrival in Mossgrove. A few years later she had a porch built at the back of the house with a door out into the farmyard so that the farm traffic came in that way. Kate had made the mistake of thinking that she too could use it. Martha had informed her that she would prefer if she used the front door as the back way was only for the family, although sometimes Kate had found herself outside the front door being told from behind the bolted door to go around to the back.

This place where she had grown up had a deep grip on her. The little saplings that her grandfather had planted were now big trees, and she had watched them grow. Even to walk down the fields with the familiar names where she had picked mushrooms and blackberries stirred forgotten memories and made her feel at one with this place. Ned understood how she felt because he shared her feeling. It was an unspoken agreement between them that they never discussed Martha. She was his wife and would have to be accepted gracefully into the fold.

Now as the January east wind whipped up the valley Kate shivered and realised that she had been standing in the cold for too long. Just as she was about to put her hand up to knock at the door, it was whipped open. Martha looked down on her with veiled hostility. Tall and slim, she favoured long dark dresses and wore her glossy black hair caught back in a knot which accentuated her high cheek bones and large dark eyes. She always put Kate in mind of a graceful black swan.

"What are you standing there on the doorstep for?" she demanded now, looking down at Kate.

"Just thinking," Kate told her evenly.

"Fine for those who have the time," Martha said dismissively, sweeping into the kitchen ahead of her. Before every visit Kate had to brace herself not to feel cowed in her presence. Martha never showed the slightest interest in anything that she did or inquired about her work as district nurse.

"I'm going away on a course at the end of next week. "Kate attempted to make conversation.

"Nice for you," Martha said sharply and continued to write on a pad at the table. She's trying to freeze me out,

Kate thought, before Ned and Jack come in. She knew that they had a cup of tea together in the kitchen every morning and she wanted to wait for them.

Kate looked around the spotless kitchen. Martha might not be a loving sister-in-law but she was an efficient housekeeper. The long dresser that stretched the entire length of the wall at the end of the kitchen was loaded with ware and beneath it the kitchen pots were neatly stacked. On one end of the dresser was a white enamel bucket full of fresh spring water that was drawn daily from the well and on the other end another gleaming bucket which was filled each morning with milk from the churn in the yard. To the left of the dresser the stairs curved upwards, and beneath them a door opened out into the back porch which had been rechristened the scullery. In the yard behind the scullery all the farm activity took place and could be viewed through the back window of the kitchen. Kate now sat on a chair beside this window and was glad of the warmth of the fire while Martha sat at the kitchen table beneath the front window that looked out into the garden.

As they heard the clatter of the pony and cart coming into the yard, Kate looked out the window. Across the yard Ned and Jack chatted as they unloaded the churn out of the creamery cart. As it was January and only some of the cows had calved, there was just one churn. The small wiry figure of Jack had an agility that belied his sixty-five years. He eased up the tight-fitting cover and wheeled the heavy churn full of separated milk to the edge of the cart and tilted it towards the big barrel on the ground. Ned reached up to steady the churn, lowered it slowly until a white river of milk poured down into the waiting barrel and then swung the empty churn out of the cart.

Years of physical work on the land had filled Kate's slim brother out into a solid muscular man and turned his blonde mane of hair into a bronze thatch. Easy-going by nature he moved calmly and quietly through life. She was the one with the inclination to be hasty. Jack had said that they took after the two different sides of the family: Ned tall, calm and measured like their mother Nellie, and herself small and dark, with the impetuous nature of their grandfather Edward Phelan.

The back door opened and they came in together. Ned had to stoop to come in clear of the door, but Jack, who was at least six inches shorter, had no such problem.

"Hello," Ned smiled at her. "I saw your bike outside. We seldom see you on a Friday morning."

"I had to make a call back this way, so I thought that I'd hit the tea after the creamery."

"Good," he told her, going to the dresser and taking down some cups."Do you want me to make the tea, Martha?" he asked.

Martha rose silently and catching the teapot off the dresser went to the kettle that was boiling over the fire. Kate caught Jack's eye and understood that normally the tea would have been on the table for them.

"How are you, Jack?" she asked.

"Grand," he told her. "We're not too hard pushed at the moment though we have some of the cows calved."

Most farm workers took the month of January off, but Jack was not the usual run of the mill and even helped out over Christmas.

"Aren't you going away on your course soon?" Ned asked.

"The end of next week," she told him.

"Will it be a bit of a holiday?" Jack smiled.

"I doubt it,"she laughed. "I haven't studied for a good few years so my brain is probably gone rusty."

"By God, Kate, if your brain is rusty I'd hate to see into my old model," Jack declared. "It's probably suffering from dry rot."

"Jack, you're as sharp as a needle," Ned assured him.

"It's well for some people who can have a few weeks off whenever they feel like it," Martha intercepted coolly. "But then again when you haven't husband or children there's nothing to stop you from doing what you like."

"It isn't a holiday," Kate said evenly; "it's part of the job."

"Well, some of us don't have cushy jobs with plenty of time off," Martha told her sharply.

Kate had to constantly remind herself not to rise to the bait. She had inherited the quick temper of her grandfather but so far had kept it in check where Martha was concerned. She could never let anything come between herself and Ned. With her father and mother gone he was the only family she had left, and they had come through a lot together, what with their father's early drinking and sudden death and watching their mother struggle to keep Mossgrove going. Now thankfully times were good in Mossgrove. Ned was an excellent farmer, but of course Jack had trained him well. Kind and faithful Jack who was the backbone of the place. She looked across the table at his brown weather-beaten face and thought that they could never thank him enough for all he had done for them.

He had cushioned her against the reality of her father's drinking. After his death, Jack had assured her that her father had been a good man, and he had related stories of their early days in school together. It had been important to her then to think well of her father. Her mother, like Jack, had never pointed out her father's weaknesses to her, and for that she was grateful to them. Ned had woken up to the reality much earlier, but then he had been a few years older.

"What are you dreaming of, Kate?" Ned asked, smiling at her across the table.

"I was just thinking what a great job yourself and Jack have made of Mossgrove compared to the way it was when our father died," Kate said.

"He wasn't up to much by all accounts," Martha commented.

"Well, I suppose," Jack put in easily, "we're all as good as we can be in one way or another."

Good man, Jack, she thought, always the one to pour oil on troubled waters. She could see Ned's jaw tighten so she rose from the table.

"I'd best be on my way," she said, "but I'll probably see you all again before I go away next week."

"I'll walk up the boreen with you," Ned told her. "I want to check the sheep in the well field anyway."

As they walked up the boreen her brother drew his pipe out of his pocket. When he had checked that there was still some tobacco in it, he lit up, drawing deeply until he was satisfied that it was lighting sufficiently well to keep going.

"You'd want to get a new pipe," Kate told him; "isn't there a crack in that one?"

"There is, and I'll get a new one some time," he smiled.

They walked on together in companionable silence, but she sensed that Ned was thinking out something that he was finding it difficult to say.

"Kate, I would never want you to feel that you aren't welcome here," he began slowly. "When we were growing up, you put in a lot of hard work to keep this place going. You're entitled to be treated well here."

She knew that he was apologising and her heart ached for him. She put a hand on his arm.

"Ned," she told him, "it will never be a problem."

"Thank God for that," he said, his face clearing. "We're the only two Phelans left, so we might as well stick together."

"What about your children?" she smiled. "Nora and Peter are the next generation of Phelans and the future of Mossgrove."

"That's right," he agreed cheerfully. "Peter seems to like school better than Nora, and I hope that when it comes to it that he will like the farming as well. Jack says that he's more like our father than the old man. It makes me smile sometimes the way Jack always refers to our grandfather as the old man."

"I suppose that's because our father was never an old man. When Jack started here as a young fellow our grandfather must have been in his prime, and Jack saw him become an old man," Kate said.

"As far as Jack is concerned, Grandfather was the one who created Mossgrove," Ned smiled, "and he has kept him alive around this place by constantly talking about him."

"He certainly did that," Kate agreed, "but to me it was Nellie who gave the heart to Mossgrove because she was so easy and uncritical of everything that we did."

"She was great," Ned agreed; "she worked hard but she never became hard."

"Strange how we always called her Nellie," Kate mused, "almost as if she was a sister rather than our mother."

"In a way she was a bit like a sister, wasn't she?" Ned said. "And then of course Jack always called her Nellie, so we picked it up off him after our father died."

"Jack and herself were a great team, weren't they?"

"The best."

"He loved her of course."

Ned came to a standstill, his face full of surprise.

"I never thought of it like that," he said slowly. "It never even crossed my mind."

"Somehow I always felt it, and in the end I think that she grew to love him too. It was an unspoken understanding between them."

"That's a revelation to me," Ned said quietly.

"I can never remember being surprised by it, because it was an awareness that grew on me over the years and it made home a warmer place," Kate told him thoughtfully.

"Was I blind or something?" Ned asked.

"Not at all. Maybe because I was away from here I could see things more clearly."

"When you were away they talked about you all the time, but of course when you got the job here they were over the moon. It was new life to them."

"To me too," she confessed. "I love nursing, but doing what I'm doing now is more than nursing. You're going into people's homes and becoming part of families, sharing their joys and their tragedies. You can work as many night hours as day, but I enjoy it."

"It's so good to be doing what you like," Ned said seriously, stopping to relight his pipe. "I don't think that our father liked the land and some day I must ask Jack about that. But if ever I bring it up he kind of shies away from it," Ned finished in a puzzled voice.

"Jack would be very slow to criticise Dad," Kate told him. "But those few years before Dad died must have been a very rough time, with Dad squandering money that was needed for Mossgrove. Jack probably does not want to remember those days," Kate concluded.

"But it would be well to know," Ned said thoughtfully, "and we might learn from past mistakes."

"Why, what makes you say that?" Kate asked curiously.

"I'm thinking of Peter," he answered. "Jack says he's like our father, so I don't want history to repeat itself. I'd like Peter to have more schooling than I had, and there seems to be no way around it only boarding school. But he'd probably hate being away."

"He's finishing in the Glen school this summer, isn't he?" Kate asked.

"He is, and the nearest secondary school is twenty miles away, so we'll have to come to some kind of a decision over the next few months," Ned said.

"Would anybody ever think of starting a secondary school in the village I wonder? The place around here badly needs one."

"That would be too good to be true."

"Well, you've six months to get things sorted out," Kate told him, "and a lot can happen in six months."

CHAPTER TWO

JACK TOBIN SAT on a sagging sugan chair in a shed in the yard of Mossgrove sorting out seed potatoes. He was getting ready for the cutting of the sciollans. It was a cold dry January evening and a north-east wind whirled sops of straw around the yard.

It ruffled the feathers of the scratching hens, hurrying the lighter ones along faster than they had intended. Only the younger hens were out in the centre of the yard, the older and wiser ones having abandoned it in favour of the hedge by the stable. I'm a bit like the old hens, Jack thought, in here taking shelter from the cold.

The cap that he seldom removed was pulled down firmly around his ears, and for extra protection he had wrapped an old jute bag around his shoulders and across his knees. Small and weather-beaten, he moved with agility and precision. Old man Phelan, who had liked things to be well made, had once said to him, "Jack, you're well put together." The comment had pleased him because he too liked a horse with a balanced gait or even a cow with good proportions. They were easy on the eye.

On one side of him was the bag of potatoes and on the other side an old tin bath half full of rejects that would be boiled later for the pigs. At his back a round stone boiler used to boil the potatoes still glowed warm from the morning fire and took the chill out of the air. He dipped into the bag with his left hand and rolled the dry potato around his palm, removing the outer layer of dry earth with his fingers feeling for the dip that denoted the eyes. Later when he would be cutting the sciollans he would run his knife between the eyes. He liked sorting the potatoes and cutting the sciollans.

Old man Phelan had taught him how to cut sciollans during his first spring on the farm. He could still remember the old man holding the potato in one hand and the knife in the other.

"You must go between the eyes, Jack," he had instructed; "that gives you an eye on both sides. That's the seed where the growth will come from. All life starts from a seed, Jack, human and otherwise," the old man had proclaimed. He loved to hear himself talk and Jack had liked listening. When they sat down to sort the seed potatoes he would announce dramatically: "This is the first move in the resurrection of the whole farm from the dead of winter". Jack smiled as he remembered.

That was a long time past. Must be all of fifty years ago and he had been a lad of fifteen then. He had come to work in Mossgrove straight from school where Billy Phelan, the old man's only son, had been his best friend. Mossgrove had been in great shape at that time because the old man was a perfectionist. When he grew older and Billy had taken over, things had slipped, but now with Ned running the place everything was shipshape again.

He had worked here with three generations of Phelans. They were the owners and he never lost sight of that fact, but the soul of this land was his. He had dug drains down into her bowels to run off surplus water and make her rich and fertile.

He had eased the nose of his plough deep into her soft moist earth and had ploughed long straight furrows across her brown belly and deposited seed like semen into her waiting womb and year after year had watched the crops grow. His heart had gone into this land and he knew and loved every sod. It had taken the place of a wife and children in his life. Many of the fine elm and chestnut now straddling the ditches of the farm he had nurtured from spindly young slips. He could not imagine living outside of Mossgrove because it was the core of his being and had given a deep fulfilment to his life. The only time that he had ever even thought of leaving had been many years ago when Nellie had married Billy and come to Mossgrove as the woman of the house.

The three of them had gone to school together, and he had loved her since the day that she had come to his rescue when one of the big Conway boys had him cornered in the schoolyard. She was tall and slim with curly fair hair and a laughing face, but she had a serious side that was kind and sensitive.

He had been in Phelans' for about ten years at the time of her marriage to Billy and had considered leaving then. He had thought that he would find it very difficult to watch her as someone else's wife. But the reality was that there could never have been anything between the two of them. She was a farmer's daughter and would bring a fortune on to Mossgrove while he lived in a labourer's cottage and had nothing much to offer her. He had accepted that there was no way that he could cross that divide. Later there were times when he had thought that maybe it was better that way. Sometimes he doubted that he was husband material at all, and watching the Phelans' marriages he felt that there was a lot to be said for the single state.

The old man had doubts as to the suitability of Nellie for the farm.

"A bit frail for farming, I'd say," was his opinion.

"You're wrong there, boss," Jack had told him. "She may be tall and willowy but she could hold her own in any tussle. Came to my rescue once when one of the Conways was getting the better of me. So I'd say she'd be the right woman for this house."

"You could be right there, Jack lad," the old man had agreed; "anyone that tackled the Conways can only be good."

Over the years it had become a bonus in his life to be near Nellie, and the fact that Billy and himself had always been such good friends had somehow made it easier. Sometimes he thought that Billy guessed how he felt about Nellie but it was never a problem between them. When Ned and Kate came along it had made things easier because it had broadened the circle. He was fond of both children but Ned was his favourite because he was so like Nellie.

Watching Ned grow up combining the shrewdness of the old man and the gentleness of Nellie had been like seeing two roses grafted together on the one stem. Nellie had been good to the old man, and over the years the old man had grown fond of her. When he grew frail and ill Nellie had nursed him, and when he died he was laid out in the big iron bed with the brass knobs in the parlour.

Strange, Jack thought, how sorting the seed potatoes always awakened memories of old Edward Phelan and of his own early days in Mossgrove. The old man had taught him all he knew about farming: how to help a cow with a difficult calving, how to know when a meadow was just ready for cutting and to judge the following day's weather by the evening sky. The old man had tried to teach his own son as well, but Billy did not listen. Billy was more interested in horses and racing, and in later years when the old man was gone it was himself and Nellie who had struggled to manage the finances and succeeded in keeping the farm from going under. Billy had gambled heavily and drunk too much to ease the pain of his loss. He had always wanted more money and even accused them of ganging up on him. Those had been hard times in Mossgrove. He never liked to remember them. When Billy died suddenly it had taken a heavy financial drain off Mossgrove.

He had then taught young Ned all that the old man had taught him, and when Ned had finished school he had pulled in and worked like a man on the farm. In fairness to Kate she had not been afraid of work either. Nellie had been very proud of the two of them. Not that she was ever one to blow her own trumpet, but he could see it in her eyes. Pity that she had not lived longer. She was gone two years now and not a day passed that he did not think of her.

"Jack, you look as if you're a thousand miles away." Ned

stood looking down at him with an amused smile. "You're sitting there looking into space with a far-away look on your face."

"Thinking of old times," Jack smiled; "sorting the seed potatoes always makes me think of the old man."

Ned smiled. "He must have been some man because people around here always talk about him. Much more than they do about my father."

"Your grandfather," Jack told him, "had an opinion on everything and usually a well thought one at that. He lived to be a good age whereas your father died a young man."

"We'd never have managed only for you, Jack," Ned said reflectively. "You really kept this place going against all odds."

"Well, it's all behind us now," Jack said; "we're up and running."

"Well, we're up, whatever about running," Ned smiled, "but I suppose compared to my father's time things are much better."

"There were times then when I thought that we'd go under," Jack said ruefully.

"He drank a lot, didn't he, Jack?" Ned asked.

"All water under the bridge now."

"I'd like to talk about those days, Jack," Ned said, and Jack looked up at him from beneath the peak of his greasy tweed cap.

"Right, lad," he agreed quietly; after all, he thought, the lad had a right to know about his own father.

"Your father never liked farming," he began carefully; "he found it dull. There are men, Ned, who find fulfilment on the land. Your grandfather was one of them and you and I are like that, but your father wanted more excitement in his life. The horses provided that, but he was never lucky with them."

"He gambled heavy?" Ned asked.

"Yea. Couldn't seem to stop. I was very fond of him and it seems a hard thing to say, but if he had not died when he did I don't know what would have happened. As it was we barely kept our heads above water. But then things straightened out because we were ploughing the money back into the land. Your mother worked very hard. She was a great woman, Ned."

"When I was growing up my mother always seemed to have a bucket hanging off each arm drawing feed to pigs or hens or calves."

"She worked day and night after the old man died because your father went to hell altogether then. But the strange thing was that she almost succeeded in keeping it from you and Kate. She said to me once, 'Jack, I don't want them to be ashamed of their father'; so she always put a brave face on things."

"You know, Jack, for years I thought that he was great," Ned said slowly, "but then little things did not quite add up. He in bed in the morning and yourself and my mother out milking. I was about twelve then and was beginning to ask questions. But for some reason Kate thought that the sun shone off him."

"Fathers and daughters, Ned, are a strange combination; they only want to see the best in each other," Jack said reflectively. "Mothers and sons can somehow love each other warts and all."

"You could be right. Jack, can I talk to you about something else that has bothered me over the last two years since my mother died?"

Here it comes, Jack thought, and may God direct me to say the right thing. He had known that one day Ned would need to talk about his mother's last years and now he had come around to it. Strange, Jack thought, how we can't talk about things when the wound is raw. We have to wait until the healing has reached a certain stage. Ned had apparently now reached that stage, but he still began uncertainly.

"You know, when I married Martha I thought my mother would be able to take things easy and end her days in comfort, but it didn't work out like that, did it?" he said regretfully.

"Not quite," Jack said cautiously.

"You know, Jack, I always thought that it was mother-in-laws who caused the problems."

"That's the general idea," Jack agreed.

"But I could see my mother bend over backwards not to cause problems for Martha, but it was no use."

"I watched it too," Jack said evenly. There was no point in telling Ned that it broke his heart to see Nellie become a shadow in her own house, afraid to open her mouth because no matter what she said Martha read it wrong.

"Why didn't it work out, Jack? I tried everything but nothing seemed to work."

"Jealousy is a very powerful emotion," Jack said slowly. "Martha felt threatened by your mother. She knew that there was a very close bond between the two of you and she resented it, and then when the children came along she was afraid that they would become too fond of your mother."

"I found that very hard," Ned admitted, "because I have

such good memories of the old man. I wanted my children to have good memories of their grandmother."

"Ah well, I'd say now that Nora and Peter have good memories of their Nana Nellie," Jack said.

He knew that Ned had had to put up a struggle so that his children could have those memories. In her later years Nellie withdrew to the parlour altogether and Martha would come up with all kind of excuses to keep Nora and Peter away from her and to turn them against her. He remembered Nellie at the end of her time up in the parlour like a visitor in her own house, but still she never complained.

"It doesn't matter, Jack," she had told him, "as long as they are getting on all right themselves. We had trouble enough here when Billy was drinking. All we want now is peace and quiet."

In his estimation she had paid a high price for peace and quiet, but then that was her choice. And she had seemed contented enough in her own way. A good woman to read and to pray, she had an inner strength that could put up with a fair amount without retaliation. He knew that when it all got too much for her she visited Kate. But she never told Kate anything about what went on in Mossgrove because, as she had told him, "it would only cause bother".

He looked up into Ned's troubled face. The last thing that Nellie would have wanted was to have Ned's conscience bothering him about her last years. He had done the best he could in the circumstances. Maybe Ned should have been a bit stronger with Martha, but then that was all right for himself to think because he knew nothing of the emotional intricacies of the marriage bed.

"Listen, Ned," he said, choosing his words with care, "your mother was happy in many ways. Maybe herself and Martha could have got on better, but there is another side to that story. Martha has worked hard in Mossgrove and done a lot to improve the house and the yard and your mother appreciated that. She loved Mossgrove and would have hated if you had married someone who would have let the whole place go to wrack and ruin after all the effort she had put into building it up."

"I never thought of it like that," Ned said, his face clearing.

"Well, that's the way to think of it," Jack said, almost convincing himself. "And another thing, Ned: even though your mother is dead she still walks around here in your daughter Nora."

"She's very like her, isn't she?" Ned agreed with satisfaction.

"That she is!" Jack declared.

And if right was done, he thought, she would have been called after her grandmother like every other child in the neighbourhood.

"Today is her anniversary," Ned said, "but of course you never forget."

"No," Jack agreed," I went over to the grave on Sunday after mass, and the daffodils are just peeping up."

"They're early. They could be buried under snow yet," Ned prophesied.

"Do you remember about five years ago we had snow that lasted for weeks?"Jack said, glad to change the subject. "In all of my years farming I never experienced a winter like it. It will probably be remembered around here as

White '47. Peculiar in a way, when a hundred years ago we had Black '47 with the famine."

"Yea, it was an extraordinary winter," Ned said and then smiled. "Nora and Peter had the time of their lives – it was nothing but skating and snowmen."

Jack was glad that the conversation had veered away from the delicate subject of Martha and Nellie. What had needed to be said was now said. He had always known that the situation had caused Ned a lot of distress. Today was the first time that Ned had been able to bring it out into the open. That was a good thing, but it was as well to shut the door on it now and forget. Thankfully Ned moved on to another subject.

"I think that there is something bothering Nora at the moment. It's something to do with school: she goes off there some mornings as if the weight of the world was on her shoulders."

"Could it be the Conways?" Jack asked.

"Every problem around here seems to begin and end with the Conways," Ned sighed.

"It was the one thing that always worried me when times were bad, that they would get their hands on this place. The possibility of that happening would be enough to send me into an early grave," Jack admitted.

"Well, that danger is past now, but I think that one of them might be getting to Nora," Ned worried.

"Nora would find the Conways hard to handle," Jack said; "she'd be too fine for them."

"Oh, here she comes like a sióg ghaoth," Ned exclaimed as the back door burst open and a little girl came running across to them, long fair hair flying behind her and strong boots clanking off the stone yard, scattering hens and ducks in all directions.

She looks as happy as Larry, Jack thought, but her opening remark explained why.

"I love Saturdays," she announced, her small pointed face alive with excitement; then, seeing what Jack was doing, she demanded, "Jack, do you want help?"

"Who's going to help?" Jack asked, looking up into the rafters of the old house where the cobwebs draped like grey cloths.

"Me!" she said indignantly. "Didn't I help you last year too?"

"So that's why some of the spuds grew upside down," Jack declared.

"Dada," Nora appealed to her father, "make Jack take me seriously."

"When I was your age, Norry, he never took me seriously either," Ned said, smiling down at her.

"Were you here when Dada was my age?" Nora asked in surprise.

"I was indeed, and I knew your grandfather when he was your age. We went to school together, and I remember your great grandfather when he was an old man and I was a young lad," Jack told her.

"Jack," she said in amazement, "you must be as old as the hills!"

"Older, I think sometimes." He laughed and continued, "Do you see that oak tree up at the top of the haggard?" He pointed to a tree that they could see towering over the cow sheds. "Well, my first autumn here I planted an acorn in a tin bucket, and as it grew bigger over the years I transplanted it on and now look at it."

"So you and that big tree grew here together," Nora said with interest, looking from Jack to the tree.

"Well, I suppose that's one way of looking at it," Jack said. "But whereas the tree is growing up I think that from now on I'll be growing down."

"I'll soon be as tall as you," she said, standing on her toes; then, swinging around to Ned she asked, "Dada, have you planted any trees?"

"All over the farm," Ned said smiling down at her. "Jack taught me well."

They're like peas in a pod, Jack thought. He remembered the day that she was born and how it had thrilled Ned to have a daughter.

"Where's Bran?" she asked.

"Probably up in the barn sound asleep. That's the place for a dog to be on a cold day like today," Ned told her.

"Mom says that he gets fleas in the barn and that we bring them into the house then," Nora said.

"She could be right," Ned smiled, "but what's a flea between friends?"

"Is Bran your friend or my friend?"

"A shared friend."

"I'd say he prefers you," she said thoughtfully.

"What makes you say that?" Jack asked.

"Well, if he's with me and Dada calls he runs away. But if I call him when he's with Dada he won't come. So I'd say that he prefers Dada."

"He probably does," Jack agreed, "because I've the same problem with him. But what about all this help that I was going to get with sorting my potatoes?"

"Do you really want help?" she asked, wrinkling up her nose and peering into the bag of potatoes, not so sure now that she wanted to help.

"Well of course I do. Two heads are better than one even if they were only pigs' heads."

"I haven't got a pig's head," she told him indignantly.

"I'll leave the two of you to it," Ned laughed. "I must give hay to the cows." As soon as he went out into the yard a black sheepdog with one white ear and matching front paws emerged to jump around him wagging his tail.

"Hello, old boy," Ned said, patting his head and running his hand down along his broad glossy back.

"See what I mean," Nora said; "when Dad is around he wants no one else."

"Sheepdogs are like that," Jack told her. "They have many friends but only one master. Your father reared him from a pup and fed him every day."

"Why was he called Bran?" Nora asked.

"Every dog that we ever had was called Bran," Jack told her.

"That shows that you had no imagination," she told him.

"Where did you learn a fine big word like that?" Jack wanted to know.

"It was our new word in school last week, and I think that if you don't have it you're fairly dull."

"That describes us pretty well around here, I suppose," he admitted, trying not to smile at her serious face.

She had forgotten about her plans to help him and had seated herself on one of the bags of potatoes.

"How was school this week?" he asked, hoping that he could unravel the problem that was worrying her father.

"All right," she said slowly, "but I prefer Saturday and Sunday best, especially Sunday 'cause I like going to mass."

"Aren't you the holy girl!"

"Ah Jack!" she protested, "you know that it's going to

town that I really like." And then a new thought struck her: "But I like going to mass now too since Fr Brady came."

Jack thought to himself that she was not the only one. What a relief this young priest was compared to the old parish priest who would put you to sleep for half an hour every Sunday.

"Do you know what I'm going to do in town tomorrow after mass?" she asked him.

"Do you want me to guess or will you tell me?" he asked.

"Guess."

"Now, let me think," he said, putting his hand under his cap and scratching his head. "Maybe you're going to stand at the chapel gate and make a political speech after mass."

"What's a political speech? I'd have to know what it was if I wanted to do it."

"Not at all. A lot of people do it and they don't know what it is."

"Jack, you're fooling again. If you're not going to talk serious, I'm going to bring hay to the cows with Dad instead of helping you," she threatened.

"Right," he said, "what are you going to do in town tomorrow?"

"I'm going to buy a new pipe for Dada because you know that the stem of his old one is cracked since he left his coat in the stable and the pony stood down on it, so," she told him in a rush of words, "he needs a new one and you know that Dada never buys anything for himself."

"Where did you get the money?" Jack asked. "Pipes are expensive."

"Aunty Kate," she told him. "I told her about his broken pipe so she priced one in town and gave me the money the last time she was here. But it's a secret and it's a surprise from me."

Martha won't be too pleased about that, he thought, because as far as Martha was concerned the farther away Kate kept from Mossgrove and the children the better.

"By God," Jack said, "but that will take him by surprise all right."

"Isn't it exciting?" she asked. "I can't wait for tomorrow, but now I must go in and polish the shoes for Sunday. Dada's and Mom's and Peter's and mine. That's my Saturday night job."

"You're the shoe-shine boy!" Jack declared.

"I'm not a boy," she protested indignantly.

"Well, the shoe-shine girl, so."

"Are you codding me, Jack?" she demanded.

"Would I do that?" he asked innocently.

"You know you would," she told him, smiling in spite of herself; "but don't forget now, Jack, to keep my big secret."

"I won't even tell Bran!" he assured her.

CHAPTER THREE

When she opened her eyes she saw him. He was running along the top ridge of the blanket right below her chin: a long grey white flea who was obviously in a hurry. Nora wondered if there was such a thing as a lazy flea; they always seemed to be busy about their own business.

This one had a definite target in view and was headed in its direction with great intent. Suddenly he stopped dead in his tracks. Nora felt that if he had ears which she could see, they would be standing erect, listening. She held her breath and watched him without a blink. One false move now and he would be gone, but if she hesitated too long he would make his move before her and then she would not stand a chance. She pounced on him but he was too fast for her. He burrowed down into the deep wool fibre of the blanket, and even though she did a certain amount of excavating in the vicinity of his disappearance, her small probing ten-year-old fingers were no match for his magical ability to become invisible. She wondered if the flea kingdom had a whole maze of underground tunnels running through the wool blankets and heavy quilt.

On Monday mornings her mother laid siege to their underground kingdom with a canister of sickly yellow Keating's Powder. That night when Nora smelt it off the blankets she thought that the strong whiff off the Keating's Powder was worse than the fleas. Her mother drove them into temporary retreat but they were not defeated. Later the following week, with reassembled forces, they came back into the attack. Nora had to admire their determination not to be permanently evicted. Even when her mother made an all-out assault on them with blanket washing in the summer and totally eradicated them, they still found their way back. Their ability to muster extra troops meant that they sometimes outflanked her mother with their sheer numerical strength. Now as Nora lay in bed thinking about her mother's arch-enemies, she felt her scalp that was still tender from the usual Saturday night fine combing.

The previous night, when supper was over after the milking, her mother had backed a sugan chair up against the kitchen table and put Nora kneeling on it with her hair pouring forward over her face like a blonde waterfall on to a newspaper on the table. She then put a firm hand under Nora's forehead and proceeded with determination to plough a fine comb with long pointed teeth through Nora's thick mane. She started at the nape of her neck and pushed forward over the crown of her head and then down the long stretch of hair until she came out at the ends that skirted on to the newspaper. A hapless flea tumbled forward and, before he had time to right himself and scurry to safety, she squashed him beneath a determined thumbnail. Then she inspected her comb and tut-tuted in annoyance when she found in the midst of the ribs of hair and hay-seeds that the flea corpse on the newspaper had a travelling companion.

"Who were you sitting beside in school last week," Martha demanded.

"Kitty Conway," Nora told her.

"Oh, those Conways!" her mother fumed. Her father rattled the newspaper that he was reading beside the fire. Her mother did not elaborate on the subject, but she returned to Nora's head with renewed vigour. When she next inspected the comb Nora expected to see a bit of her scalp amidst the hayseeds and ribs of hair. Martha continued relentlessly until Nora squealed in protest.

Her father came from behind his newspaper and taking the pipe from his mouth asked mildly, "Martha, are you trying to scalp the child?"

"Would you have us walking with lice like the Conways?" her mother demanded.

"Are the Conways walking with lice?" Nora asked in amazement and saw through her hair her father throw a warning look at her mother as she bundled up the newspaper and thrust it behind the pot over the open fire where it blazed yellow and then fell in a grey cobweb of ashes on the red sods of turf. Nora straightened up and swept the hair back off her face. She felt dizzy after all the forward pressure on her head, so she climbed on to her father's knee while her mother filled up a tin pan with warm water and put it back on the table. Her father rubbed his stubbly chin across her face and she screamed in mock horror. It was a game they played every Saturday night before he removed the blond bristle from his strong chin.

"Come on, Nora," her mother said. She resumed her kneeling position on the chair and her mother plunged her head into the pan and started to lather her hair with a bar of white soap. When she had it scrubbed to her satisfaction she changed the pan of water and poured a chilly stream over Nora's head until she was satisfied that all traces of the soap were removed. Nora sighed in relief when a towel was finally wrapped around her head. While she sat drying her hair by the fire her mother was busy filling a big timber tub with warm water out of the black pot over the fire.

"Start taking off your clothes, Nora," her mother instructed as she tested the temperature of the water by swishing her fingers through it.

"I think I'll check the cows." Her father rose to his feet and stretched himself before the fire.

"Better put on your coat, it's cold," her mother advised. "And send Peter in soon. He's next."

As he left the kitchen Nora saw her father raise his eyes to heaven and knew that he sympathised with Peter, who considered himself at twelve to be too big to be washed in the timber tub. But her mother was adamant about the Saturday night routine. While Nora dreaded the hair combing and washing, she enjoyed the bath. As she lay soaking in the warm sudsy water, she never wanted to come out of it. When the water started to cool her mother made her stand up and poured lukewarm water all over her out of a white enamel jug. The feel of the water running down her back was so nice that she wished that it could go on for ever. Her mother's long pale face was flushed from the hot steamy water and strands of her dark hair had come loose from the knot at the back of her head. Nora laughed with delight as the water ran down her back and a smile lit up her mother's normally serious face.

"You're nice when you smile, Mom," Nora told her.

Then they heard Peter dragging his feet reluctantly in along the yard, so Nora was lifted easily out of the bath and dried quickly. A fresh clean nightdress was pulled down over her head and her mother put her on the bottom step of the stairs. Later as she dozed off she could hear her mother and Peter battling it out below in the kitchen.

Now in the cold morning light Nora snuggled down in her warm and comfortable bed. She should really get up and lay the table for the breakfast before they came in from the cows, but the thought of the cold kept her under the blankets. The two windows of her small room were both clouded up with grey frost and she could see her breath sailing up towards the ceiling like the steam from the boiling kettle over the fire. She wished that her room was not so cold. It had three items of furniture: her black iron bed with the brass knobs, the dressing table with the wobbly leg and an orange crate standing upright in the corner under the sloping roof. One deep-set window between the orange box and the dressing table looked out over the farmyard and the other window beside the bed looked out over her mother's garden.

Her room was at the top of the stairs just over the kitchen so it was the warmest bedroom in the house and Peter's identical room at the end of the narrow corridor was the coldest because it was over the parlour which they seldom used. Her parents' room in between was twice the size, with a dark wardrobe and a wide timber bed which Nora got to sleep in whenever she was sick.

She put her foot out to test the temperature and swiftly drew it back in under the warm blankets. She wished that she was downstairs all dressed and the table laid for the breakfast. She would get up now in a few minutes. She envied the flea who could stay in bed all day. She wondered if fleas knew just how lucky they were and what life would be like as a flea.

"Nora, get out of that bed or you'll have us all late for mass." Her mother's voice coming up from the kitchen brought her wide awake. She looked at the grey frost on the window pane and knew that as soon as she slipped out from under the warm blankets the cold would wrap itself around her like a sheet of ice.

"Is Peter up?" she called down to her mother as a delaying tactic.

"You know well that Peter is up with an hour, helping your father and Jack. Get yourself up out of there now and no more dilly dallying out of you."

Nora could imagine Peter and her father out in the stalls sitting on their milking stools with their heads resting against the warm flanks of the cows and chatting companionably together. She knew that as soon as her mother had left the stalls that Peter and her father slowed their pace. Peter was probably telling his father and Jack the story of the film that had come to the local hall on Friday night. Her mother was not very keen on those kind of conversations and was only interested in "getting on with things". Now her voice came loudly from the foot of the stairs.

"I can't hear any sound from up there. Will you get out of it or do you want me to come up?"

Nora's answer was to jump out on to the floor with a loud thud which brought a welcome silence from the kitchen.

She shivered as the cold wrapped itself around her. Earlier she had dragged her clothes in under the blankets to warm them and now she pulled them out and poked around in the bundle for her stockings. Sitting on the edge of the bed she eased the long black knitted stockings up over her pale thin legs and secured them in position with two black garters. Then she jumped into her navy blue knickers, pulling it up over her bottom and stretching the legs down over the tops of her stockings. The next step was the toughest, when she had to whip the warm flanelette nightdress off over her head. Her teeth chattering as the cold hit her bare skin, she quickly located her long sleeved wool vest and dragged it on over her head, tucking the tail of it inside her knickers. After that the soft bodice and then her grey-skirted petticoat with the white sleeveless top. Now she began to feel a bit better. When she had eased a light jumper and then a heavy knitted jumper over her head, her top half began to warm up, and the warmth started to extend downwards when she put on the thick tweed pinafore frock that her mother had made out of a remnant. Nora wished that remnants were not always such dull colours. She sat on the window sill to lace on her black shoes.

Weekdays she wore heavy high-laced boots with studs and iron tips, but on Sundays it was shoes. Light, patent, shining shoes! She danced across the floor to feel how light they were on her feet. She twirled to a halt in front of her dressing table with its tip-over mirror and peered in at herself. A long pale face looked out at her from a tangle of fair curly hair. She wished that she had red hair like Kitty Conway and was small and pretty. At the thought of Kitty Conway she felt the usual lump of fear forming in her stomach. But today was Sunday and she was not going to think about her, and besides today she was going to buy Dada's pipe. Wasn't he going to be surprised?

As she ran down the stairs she heard her father and Peter come in from the milking and felt guilty when she saw that her mother had the table laid and was dishing out the porridge.

"Sit down now before this gets cold," she told them. Catching sight of Peter's boots, she frowned: "Could you not have left those out in the scullery?"

"For God's sake," he protested, "what's wrong with a bit of cow dung."

"Nothing," she told him sharply, "as long as it's where it should be."

"Oh, all right," he said in disgust, heading for the scullery door. Putting his toe to the heel of one boot he eased his foot out of it and then kicked it across the scullery and followed up with the other.

The scullery, the small room behind the kitchen, her mother used as a filter to try to prevent the dirt and mud of the farmyard from reaching the kitchen and the rest of the house. Her father sympathised with her efforts but Peter clashed with her, and on a few occasions it was only her father's intervention that prevented a row. Nora felt that she could see both sides: her mother wanted everything done properly and the house kept nice and clean, but Peter was getting big and wanted to do things his way and she could understand that as well.

Sometimes in school he sorted things out for her and she regarded him as a second guardian angel. It was good to have a big brother in the older classes. But she had never told him about Kitty Conway because she found it very difficult to admit that she could be made so miserable by one so much smaller than herself, even though they were the same age. Kitty Conway made her feel big and awkward and stupid. She never hurt her physically but she could cut her to pieces with her acid tongue until in spite of herself Nora would feel her eyes fill up with tears, and then Kitty would smirk and call her a softie. Once when Nora was gardening with her mother they had come on a plant that had died; her mother had dug it up, and in the earth, clinging to its roots, was a little white worm.

"That's the cause of the trouble," her mother had said, and a picture of Kitty Conway had sailed into Nora's mind. She is like that little white worm, she thought, eating me away, and some day I will die and nobody will ever know what happened to me.

"What's wrong with you, Norry?" her father smiled at her from across the table. "You look as if you have the troubles of the whole world on your shoulders."

"Was anybody ever at you in school, Dada?" she asked unthinkingly.

"Who's at you in school?" her mother demanded.

"Nobody," Nora lied. Her mother was the last person she could tell. She would be across the fields to the school to sort it out and that would only make the whole thing worse because Kitty Conway would sneer even more and say that she was a real baby having to get her mother to fight her battles. Her father always understood things better than her mother.

"Norry," her father told her, "people were often nasty to me, but the secret is to take no notice and they soon get tired of it."

Just like Dada, she thought. But it was hard to take no notice when you were sitting beside the white worm. Ever since that day in the garden she thought of Kitty Conway as the white worm and she saw no way of getting rid of her. She wished that she could hit her with the shovel like Mom did to the worm and cut her up into tiny pieces.

"Sometimes you have to fight back," Peter declared. "If people think that they can walk all over you, they will do just that."

Nora wondered if he guessed that there was something wrong in school, because sometimes she was sick just before they reached the school, but she did not want to tell him about it because he was usually friendly with the Conways boys, and anyway it would be hard to explain. To change the subject she asked, "Is Jack gone home?"

"Yea," her father said, "he had things to do before mass so he went up to the cottage."

"What are you and Jack going to do about Conways' cows?" her mother demanded of her father.

"Very little we can do, I suppose," he said calmly, "only fence before them again."

"You know well that they break down the fences to let the cattle through."

"I know, but we can't prove anything, and it's easier to re-fence than to be drawing them on us," her father answered.

"Dear God, but it drives me mad to think of their hungry cows eating our good grass!" her mother said with disgust. "And they probably laughing at us behind our backs."

Nora felt a fellow feeling with her mother. Was there no end to the treachery of the Conways?

"Let's forget about the Conways – it's Sunday," her father suggested. "I'd say the road will be icy this morning. Hope that it won't be too slippery for Paddy."

"Won't the frost nails hold him?" Nora asked fearfully.

"They will of course," her father assured her. "I put new chisel frost nails on him last week, so that should hold."

"Is he tackled?" her mother asked.

"No," Peter answered, "but Jack tied him up in the barn and I'll tackle him in a minute."

After breakfast they went upstairs to get ready for mass. Nora's Sunday coat was hanging on the back of her bedroom door. Her mother had hung an old bageen sheet over it to keep it free from dust and her cap was in a paper bag in the bottom of the orange crate. The money for Dada's pipe was screwed up in a bit of newspaper under her cap.

She reached on tiptoe and took down her coat: it was bright green and the collar and pockets were trimmed with navy. Her mother had made the cap out of material left over after the coat. The first Sunday she had put them on she had felt like a princess, but the following day in school Kitty Conway had sniggered, "You looked like St Patrick yesterday."

Since then she had not been so happy with the outfit, but there was no question of not wearing it as her mother had given weeks to its creation. First she had laid the material out on the kitchen table and then placed the pattern carefully on top. Then after a lot of thinking and repositioning of the pattern she had started to cut with the long shinning scissors. To cut had taken courage, Nora had decided. If her mother had got it wrong it would have been terrible because weeks of her egg money had gone into that material. It was the first piece of material about which her mother had asked her opinion, and it was she herself who had decided on the green. At first she had wondered how all the odd pieces of material with the long white tacking stitches would ever become a coat, but gradually it began to take shape. The night that it was finished Nora knew that her mother was very pleased and so was she.

She tried to angle the small mirror of her dressing table to get a better look at herself. She knew that it fitted perfectly but she wished now that she had chosen a different colour. She put the pipe money deep into her pocket.

"Come on, Norry, we'll be late for mass." Her mother came in to inspect her and to see that she had no threads trailing below her coat and that her cap was at the right angle. Norry was her father's name for her but her mother used it when she was in good humour. In her navy hat and coat her mother looked splendid, and as she walked out into the backyard after her Nora thought that her mother walked as if nothing could stop her. Peter had tied Paddy to the water barrel, and Nora patted the horse's soft nostrils with her fingers before following the others. Her mother settled them all into the trap and wrapped a rug around Nora, but when she attempted to include Peter he tossed it aside.

"Ah Mom, for goodness sake!"

"Well, aren't you the man for us," his mother chided, but Nora could see that she was more amused than annoyed.

Her mother sat behind her father at one side of the trap and she sat behind Peter at the opposite side. Her father took the reins and guided Paddy out of the yard, which Nora always thought looked different when viewed from the trap. She was high enough to be able to see all over it, and she decided that it looked lovely with all its dark red doors and stone walls. Peter sheltered her from some of the cold, but even at that she could feel it biting into her face and she was glad of the warm rug around her legs. She put her hand into her pocket to check on the pipe money. She could see that her father was giving all his concentration to guiding the pony over the steep slippery road. His strong fingers were curled around the reins and he guided the pony with firmness and skill. Paddy was older than herself so he knew the road well, but the ice could be dangerous. Her mother and Peter were talking, but Nora was not listening. She was watching her father's face and she could see that he was worried about Paddy.

"I think I'll get out and lead him by the head," he said, and just as he stood up it happened with terrifying suddenness. Paddy's back legs went from under him and he crashed down between the shafts. There was a tearing sound of splintering wood and the trap shuddered, then lurched forward and hit the road with a jolting thud, and Nora found herself flung forward with great force. Then she was swimming through darkness.

CHAPTER FOUR

ALL HER BODY was hurting. She tried to struggle out of the darkness that was stifling her, but it was too strong and kept sucking her down. From far away she could hear Paddy grunting in distress.

Then the grey fog cleared and she saw him lying on the side of the road tangled up in harness and broken shafts and from a long way off she heard Peter's voice trying to soothe him and straighten him up. Did Peter think that she was under the trap? Where was Dad that he was not helping Paddy? She crawled on her hands and knees around the back of the trap. She tried to stand but her legs had turned into wobbling jelly and she kept falling. Then she saw her mother through the mist that was swirling before her eyes. Her mother was kneeling in the middle of the road and was bending over something. Her long black hair had come loose and had fallen forward forming a curtain between them.

"Mom." Nora said the word in her mind but it never reached her tongue. Something had gone wrong with her voice.

The grey fog engulfed her again and when it cleared her mother had raised her head and was looking at her. Her eyes were like two black holes in grey shrivelled paper. Then she saw what her mother was holding. Mom's lap seemed to be full of blood, and it was when she saw the blonde hair that she realised that it was her father head. Then she felt Peter's arms around her.

"Norry, Norry, don't look, don't look. Oh God, don't look, don't look."

"Dada, Dada!" she screamed, struggling to get to him, but Peter held her firmly. "Peter! Oh, Peter, Dada, Dada," she cried, looking beseechingly up into his face.

"Paddy's hooves got him. He fell the wrong way. He was standing." Peter's voice came in gasps as if he had to tear the words out of the back of his throat.

The blackness came back in a swirling cloud and this time she went with it.

When she woke up she was back in her own bed and she was so cold that she felt frozen on to the sheets. It was almost dark and at first she thought that there was nobody in the room, but then she saw a movement by the window.

"Peter," she whispered.

He moved slowly across the room. It was almost as if he had lost the ability to walk properly. She could not see his face in the darkness, but everything about him had slowed down.

"Dada?" she asked.

"Norry," he told her, "Dada is dead."

He sat on the edge of the bed and looked out the window into the gathering darkness.

"What are we going to do?" she whispered.

"I don't know," he sobbed. "I wish that we were all dead."

"Oh, Peter," she gasped. "I'm so frightened."

"So am I," he said, and when she put up her hand to his face she could feel the tears.

"Where's Mom?" she asked tearfully.

"Downstairs," he answered, and then she became aware of the sound of voices coming from below.

"Who's below in the kitchen?" she asked.

"Nana Lehane is here, and Jack and Aunty Kate and the Master is here, and Miss Buckley and the Nolans and smelly old Mrs Conway and a lot of others." Peter listed out names in a monotonous tone and then added with a sob, "I wish that half of them would go home. They're down there talking stupid talk. That old lump of a Mrs Conway told Mom that it could be worse. Imagine, that it could be worse! And then she kissed me and said that now I'm the man of the house. I don't want to be the man of the house."

He put his face down on the pillow beside her and sobbed into it. "At least we can cry up here," his muffled voice came out of the pillow.

Nora cried with him. She had not seen Peter cry for a long time. Grown-ups did not cry as much as children and Peter was almost grown up. When the sobbing eased she put her arms around him and asked, "Is that a wake downstairs?"

"Yes," he said bitterly, "where they all come and tell you that they are sorry for your troubles and they are thinking, 'Thanks be to Jesus that's not me.'"

"It's like when Nana Nellie died," Nora said.

She remembered the "Sorry for your trouble" from when Nana Nellie had died and people saying it to Mom. She remembered thinking that it was no trouble to Mom because Mom had never liked Nana Nellie anyway.

"I think that I'd like to go down," Nora said. "I want Mom."

"Are you able?" Peter asked, turning back the bedclothes to help her out.

"God! Norry, you're frozen stiff," he said when he felt her cold legs. "Will I rub you like Dad does the greyhounds? He says that it's good for the circulation and warms them up."

"Try anyway, but go easy 'cause I'm awful sore." But she felt that no amount of rubbing would warm her because she was frozen inside too. Peter rubbed her legs firmly, but when he touched her arms she winced with pain.

"I must be all scratched," Nora said.

"Aunty Kate and Doctor Twomey spent half an hour picking thorns out of you and cleaning you up, but he said that you had nothing broken and that the worst thing was the bump in your head."

"So that's why I'm sorest up there," Nora said, feeling the lump at the side of her head. "And what about you, Peter, are you hurt anywhere? And what about Mom?" she asked anxiously.

"We're all right," he said, and added, "If they knew downstairs that you were awake there'd be somebody up like a bullet."

"Why are we all all right and Dada is not?" she wanted to know.

"Do you remember, Norry, he was standing up to go out to lead Paddy by the head, so he fell down by Paddy's legs.

I wish that I had been watching the road like he was," he added desperately.

"Pete, will you help me to get dressed?" She did not want to remember that scene on the road.

She clambered painfully out of the bed; it felt as if the hinges where her bones connected were refusing to turn. Peter helped her to put on her stockings and, slowly, the rest of her clothes. He moved very quietly on the floor.

"I don't want them to know down below that you are awake or they'd be up like a swarm of ants. Aunty Kate or Nana would be all right. They were here all evening but are gone down for a cup of tea," he told her.

"Why are the rest of them annoying you so much?" she wanted to know.

"Wait till you go down and see."

After half an hour downstairs she found out what Peter meant. All the talk made the pain in her head worse, and people talked about her and above her as if she was not there, and her mother sat in the middle of them like a statue as if in some way she was not there at all. Nana Lehane and Jack were the only two who were more like themselves. Nana took her by the hand and, sitting on Dad's chair by the fire, put her on her knee.

Close up, Nana's face was as white as her hair that was caught up in a knot on the top of her head. Even though she tied her hair up firmly little curly bits escaped and Nora usually enjoyed running her finger through them. But now she clung to Nana, feeling that of all the people in the kitchen she alone was the nearest to having Dada here. Though Nana was Mom's mother Nora often felt that she was more like Dada. Mom and Nana did not even look like each other. Mom and Uncle Mark were tall and quiet whereas Nana was small and dainty and was always telling stories. Now she wrapped her arms around Nora as if she could breathe some warmth into her.

"You're like a lump of ice, child," she said.

"There is only one cure for that," Jack told her. "Can she come with me for five minutes?"

Nana and Jack exchanged glances.

"All right," Nana conceded, and Nora thought that Nana sounded doubtful, but Nana and Jack agreed about most things. Nana always said that she considered Jack to be "sound".

"Give me a few minutes' head start," he said to Nora, "and then slip out the back door after me and come over to the calf house.

"Why?" she asked in a puzzled voice.

"Just do as he says," Nana said quietly.

They watched him edge his way unobtrusively across the kitchen, a small-boned, wiry little man with tufts of white hair curling up around his grey tweed cap.

"Now, Nora," Nana instructed, rising from her chair and leading her across the kitchen. They were intercepted several times by neighbours wanting to talk to Nana and to pat Nora on top of her sore head. Old Mrs Conway loomed in front of them, so large and wide that there was no getting past her. Nora shrank back against Nana.

"Ah, he's the heavy loss to ye," she boomed. "Herself won't be able to manage at all without him." Nana agreed quietly but kept going. The scullery was full of women, but Nana being small was able to slip out behind them, and as she closed the door she somehow managed to have procured a coat off one of the hooks on the back of it and wrapped it around Nora.

“Run over to Jack now, child, “she said and stepped back into the scullery.

Nora looked around the yard. This was Dada’s yard and she almost expected to see him come out of the stalls or Paddy’s stable or the calf house. But it was Jack who called across the yard.

“Over here, Nora.” She walked across slowly. A cold white moon glittered off the frosty stones. Her legs were stiff and she felt numb inside and outside and the bitter night air pierced the scratches on her face. Jack was standing in the shadow of the house and he had a mug of hot steaming water in his hand.

What on earth is Jack doing? she wondered, but next to Dada Jack was the man she knew best, so she felt sure that whatever he was doing must be right.

“Up you go, girlie,” he said, lifting her on to the wall that divided the calves. She heard them snuffling in the house behind her.

Then she saw Jack’s outline move across the house and heard something being dragged and a clink of glass against stone. He came back with a bottle, and when he wiped the cobwebs off it with the sleeve of his coat, its contents glinted in the moonlight. He uncorked it carefully and poured a precise amount into the steaming mug and followed it with a pour of sugar from a crumpled brown bag.

“Now, girlie, drink that very slowly,” he instructed, and Nora felt that she was being allowed into a secret department in Jack’s life that would never have been opened to her but for the terrible thing that had happened. Slowly she raised the warm mug to her lips with Jack’s eyes fastened on her face. She took a sip and spluttered.

“Jack,” she protested, “I never tasted anything like it!”

"That you didn't, girlie," he said, "but desperate situations need desperate remedies, and if anyone told me last night that I would be giving you the cure tonight, I would have thought that they were off their head. But then today was enough to send us all off our heads."

"Is that what it's called?" she asked. "The cure?"

"That's right," Jack told her; "it will warm you and heal you and make you feel better."

She had to agree with Jack because as she continued to sip she began to heat up slowly. A warm thaw started at her big toes and seeped up her legs and the stiffness eased out of them, and by the time it had reached the lump at the side of her head, she did not feel so frozen.

"Jack," she declared, "that's a magic cure: why don't you give it to everybody?"

"Listen, Nora," Jack said urgently, "this is best kept between ourselves."

"But doesn't Nana Lehane know?" Nora said.

"Your Nana is a rare woman," Jack told her; "other people might not be as understanding." Nora felt that her mother might be included in the other people.

"Jack, would it help Peter?" she asked.

"Don't think so," Jack said slowly. "Peter is hurt and angry; the cure would be no good there, only maybe make things worse, but you are battered and frozen with shock. The cure gets the blood flowing again."

Nora wondered was there any end to Jack's knowledge and decided to ask him the awful question.

"Is Dada up in the parlour the way Nana Nellie was when she died?"

"That's where he is, Nora," he said; "that's where the corpse is."

"I'd be afraid to see him."

"But you want to, too "he said.

"Would you come with me?" she asked.

"What about your mother?"

"I'd rather you," she said. Jack looked the same as he always had but Mom looked like a different person.

"We'll see," he said doubtfully.

"Promise, Jack, promise," she demanded, standing in front of him and tugging the sleeve of his coat.

"Right, right," he agreed hurriedly.

"We'll go around to the front door and up into the parlour without going into the kitchen," she said, taking him by the hand. "There are a lot of the people in the kitchen and I don't want to go in there. Are there many in the parlour?"

"Not many."

As they walked around the corner of the house a dark form slunk out from under the hedge and jumped up on them.

"Jesus Christ!" Jack gasped.

"Jack, it's only Bran," Nora told him, bending down and wrapping her arms around the sheepdog. "My poor, poor Bran," she crooned as she kissed and cuddled the dog who had loved Dada too.

"Do you think that he knows?" she asked Jack.

"Hard to tell," he said. "Animals have a sixth sense about these things."

"When I feed him soon will you give him some of the cure?" she asked.

"We'll do that," he said, "but keep it under your hat."

They arrived at the front door and Nora felt fear tightening in her stomach. Would she be afraid of Dada?

Would he look like Dada? Jack edged open the front door and they went into the small front porch. Two men were sitting on their haunches chatting quietly. She recognised Con Nolan from down the road and young Davy Shine from back by the cross. They were Dada's friends. Davy Shine was crying. Nora and Jack stepped by them into the parlour.

The table was gone from the centre of the room and the big iron bed that had been Nana Nellie's was back; it stood in a pool of yellow candlelight leaving the rest of the room in shadow. Everything was white except the brass bed knobs and the shining brass candlesticks and the black rosary beads in Dada's hands.

Nana Nellie had brought him the rosary beads from Knock a long time ago, and when it had broken after a few years he had fixed it with a bit of brown thread. She could see the bit of brown thread that he had cut too long. Her eyes travelled from the rosary beads up along the white bed spread. Why had Dada that strange brown thing on him? His face looked grey but it was Dada's face with his eyes closed and a white cloth across his forehead. She stood looking at him while she held Jack's hand firmly.

You are not really in there, Dada, she thought, you're gone away. She gave Jack's hand a jerk and they moved towards the door.

A figure rose out of one of the chairs at the foot of the bed. Tall, thin and angular with foxy hair, it was Miss Buckley, her teacher. Nora did not like her: she slapped with a hard black stick and never listened, and Nora was sure that she liked the white worm and let her torment her.

"Nora," she said, "I'm sorry about your Daddy."

Nora looked at her and thought, why would you be sorry

about Dada? Dada was kind and fond of everyone, but you're not like that.

"Dada was very fond of me," Nora told her.

"I'm sure he was," Miss Buckley agreed.

"But you're not fond of me," Nora told her quietly. Jack moved her quickly toward the door.

"Nora, girlie," he told her when they reached the sanctuary of the porch, "you could have burned your boats behind you in there."

"I didn't mean to say it," she said; "it just came out."

"Well, never mind," Jack said philosophically, "maybe it was time that someone told the old bat the truth."

"Don't you like her either?" Nora asked with interest.

"Never had much to do with her," Jack said, "but it takes a lot of bad temper to give someone a big bold face like hers."

The men were still in the porch. Con Nolan knelt down and put his arms around Nora.

"Rosie said to tell you that she is sad for you," he told her. Nora could not imagine her best friend, bouncing happy Rosie, being sad. Davy Shine was no longer crying but looking bleakly into space.

"Jack, I'm awful sleepy," Nora said suddenly.

"That's to be expected. Come on in to your Nana," he told her, opening the kitchen door.

"What about Bran?" she asked.

"Let Bran to me," Davy Shine said, coming to life, "and you get your Nana to put you to bed."

That night she dreamt of Dada and Paddy and Bran, and then she was falling, falling into darkness with no one to hold her. She woke up screaming but Nana was there with her arms around her.

"Easy, Nora, easy, you're all right," Nana comforted.

She was afraid to go to sleep after that, but in spite of herself she drifted off.

When she awoke in the morning the terror of the previous day jumped into her mind. But, could it be possible that it had never happened? That it was all a bad dream? But she knew that it had and that nothing could take it away.

The day dragged on in a haze of people calling and crying and making fresh pots of tea and it going cold and throwing it away and starting again and changing the candles around Dada. Mom sat unmoving, talking to nobody; Aunty Kate moved around the house, a grey shadow. For the first time Nora thought that Nana looked old and frail. She wondered where was Uncle Mark. Mom always said that Uncle Mark was never where he should be. Betty Nolan, Rosie's mother, from down the road and Sarah Jones, who lived near Jack, looked after everybody, giving some women strong tea and others weak tea and encouraging some men to take a drink and trying to hold it back from those who did not know when they had had enough. Nora knew that Sarah Jones had laid out Nana Nellie when she died and wondered if she had done that to Dada. It must have been hard on Sarah Jones to do those two things, because she had been Nana Nellie's best friend and she had often heard her tell Dada that she had brought him into the world. All that day Jack was the one to whom they all turned to for help. How was Jack so calm and brave, Nora wondered.

Then late in the evening the house packed up with people so there was hardly room to stand and Nana Lehane gave out the rosary and Peter and Mom and herself knelt beside the bed. She knew that Peter didn't feel comfortable so near the bed and Mom looked as if she did not know where she was, but Nana looked calm and tired. Then all the people poured out of the parlour and there was only Mom, Peter, Nana, Aunty Kate and Jack left in the parlour. Then Mr Browne, who buried people, brought in the coffin. It looked huge.

"I'll leave you for a few minutes," he said.

When he left the room you could hear a pin drop as they all looked at Dada, and then Jack made a move. He bent over the bed and put his hand on top of Dada's.

"Goodbye, lad," he said, "you were a good one." He went to the window and stood looking out with his back to the room.

Jack, please don't cry, Nora begged silently. Please, please, don't cry. I can't bear it if you cry.

Everyone else was crying, Aunty Kate in loud sobs, and Mom had suddenly come alive and was thrown on the bed moaning; Nana had her arms around Peter and they were crying together. Nora went over to the window and slipped her hand into Jack's.

"Jack," she whispered, "I'm here."

"That you are, girlie," he said, and when he looked down at her his eyes were bright with unshed tears, but he dashed them away with the sleeve of his coat and shook his shoulders and said, "Better gather ourselves together," and then he was her Jack again.

"Best say the goodbyes," he said, gently turning back into the room.

Nora, like Jack, put her hand on her father's and was shocked that it was so cold and rigid. She went over to the window and turned her back on the room because she did not want to watch the others, and then Peter stood beside her sobbing, and gradually they all gathered around the window and Mr Browne and his helper came in and quietly transferred Dada into the coffin.

Nana had their coats piled high on a chair beside the door. Nora was surprised when she handed her a black coat that she had never seen before. She put it on, wondering where it had come from, and was surprised that it fitted perfectly. She followed the others out of the parlour. Outside the door four men stood with the coffin on their shoulders. Jack, Con Nolan and Davy Shine. She stretched her neck around to see the other man. It was Uncle Mark. There was no mistaking the long black hair, the same as Mom's when she let it down. The hard knot in her tummy eased a little just to see him. They shouldered the coffin slowly through the silent people and eased it gently into the hearse.

Horse and traps were tied up around the yard but there was also a big black car beside the hearse and Nora found herself steered in its direction by Nana. Peter and Jack fitted easily in the front with the driver and Mom and Nana and herself in the back. The seats were brown like chestnuts and had small wrinkles that sighed when you sat on them. It smelled like her new leather school sack, and if Dada had been with them it would have been great fun to bounce up and down on the seat. But there was no bouncing up and down, and she watched out over Jack's shoulder as the low black hearse went slowly up the boreen. She looked out the back window and saw that Dr Twomey's car was behind them and knew that Aunty Kate and Uncle Mark would be with him.

In the church it was all prayers and holy water and shaking hands, and she was glad when they came home. She opened the parlour door and peeped up. There was no trace of the bed or the candles, the table was back in the middle of the room and laid for tea and the fire was lighting in the grate.

"The neighbours are very good," Nana, who had come in behind her, said gratefully.

"Some of them," Jack confirmed as he put turf on the fire.

Everything about the funeral the following day was black. Fr Brady was dressed in black and so were Mom and Nana, Aunty Kate and herself. Peter had a black diamond cloth stitched on the sleeve of his jacket. Nora was surprised when Jack did not have one.

"Jack, why don't you have a black diamond like Peter?" she whispered to him in the church before the mass.

"I'm not family," he told her.

"But you are!" she insisted.

"Not blood related," he said, "and there are people here today who would say that I should be down by the back door like I am every other Sunday, and the Lord knows but I'd feel more at home back there."

"But it would be worse up here without you."

"That's why I'm here," he told her.

The mass droned on, and her headache got worse, and she looked at the shiny brown coffin and tried to imagine Dada inside in it. Bits of the sermon came from the altar – "great husband and father, good worker . . . helpful neighbour". She wished that he would just shut up and say "the best man in the world", because that was the truth. She walked down the aisle with Mom and Peter, all the people standing. She supposed that Mom and Nana and Aunty Kate and even Peter, because he was tall, could see their sad faces but she could only see their hands and she was glad.

The graveyard was worse than the chapel because it was cold and wet and the rain danced off the shiny coffin making it more shiny. Big blobs of raindrops shone like small glass marbles on the varnished wood. It was horrible when the coffin thudded down into the deep hole, and she could hear the water slushing beneath it, and then the earth thumped down on top of it and she thought: Dada, the real you is not down there. But if he was not, where was he because he was gone? All the talk about heaven was all right, but where was it and was he there?

"Jack," she said, tugging his hand, "where is Dada really?"

"That's the big question," Jack told her.

When they came back home the grown-ups had tea and talked, and cried between the talking and the tea. She wandered out into the calf house and found Bran asleep in the straw. When he heard her he opened one eye and wagged his tail as if to say come and sit here with me. She sat down beside him and put an arm around him.

"Bran," she asked him, "will we be crying for ever after Dada?"

CHAPTER FIVE

IT WAS MONDAY morning and she was going back to school. Nora had never thought that she would look forward to going to school, but home was so strange that she wanted to be where things might be the same as they had been before the accident. Everybody called it "the accident" or "the terrible accident", and it was easier to say that than to say "the day Dada died". But no matter what they called it Nora felt that home was a different place since then.

Mom and Peter and herself were like strangers to each other because they were all changed. Mom was gone silent. Instead of being busy and keeping things moving as she always had, she sat looking into space, with no interest in what went on around her. It frightened Nora to see her like that. Peter was grumpy and sullen and Nora knew that he cried in bed at night. One night when she woke up terrified after dreaming that she was back on the road behind the trap, she had crept along to his room. Just as she put her hand on the knob of the door she heard him sobbing. Something had stopped her from turning the knob. She tip-toed slowly by her mother's door and listened, but there was no sound though she was almost sure that her mother was not asleep. She had heard Mom tell Nana the day before Nana went home that she was awake all night. Nora wished that Nana had not gone home, but after a few weeks Nana was not feeling well and had wanted to get back to her own house and to Uncle Mark.

Sometimes Uncle Mark did not come out of the house for long periods because he was working out tunes on his fiddle or painting pictures. Nora knew that people thought he was odd but when she looked at his pictures she felt that he had magic inside in him. She wanted go home with Nana to be with her and Uncle Mark, but Nana had told her gently, "Your mother needs you."

"But Mom is gone all queer," Nora complained.

"Give her a chance, child," Nana told her. "It's early days yet."

Later she had heard Nana tell Mom to make some effort for the children, but Mom did not seem to be listening.

It was Jack who had decided that they should go back to school.

Peter objected sullenly. "I'm not going to school," he said; "I'm going to stay here and run this place like my father did."

"Peter," Jack said firmly, "you'll be finished in the Glen this summer and then will be time enough to make decisions."

"I should be running Mossgrove, not you," Peter said mutinously.

"That's Conway talk," Jack told him sharply, and Nora knew that he had hit home when Peter's face went red.

"Listen, Peter," Jack said kindly, "this is a quiet time of year, and if you milk the cows with me morning and evening we'll manage until it gets busy, and then you'll have holidays and we'll take it from there."

"All right," Peter agreed reluctantly, but Nora felt sure that he was secretly relieved to be going back to school.

They arranged that Jack would call Peter when he came down from his cottage early in the morning, and then, when the two of them had the most of the cows milked that Peter would come in to call Nora and she would get the breakfast for the three of them while Jack and Peter finished off the milking. Nora felt strange that they were making all these arrangements as if Mom were dead as well, but when she voiced her thoughts Peter said bitterly, "She might as well be."

"Don't be too hard on her," Jack said. "She's had a mighty shock but there's too much fire in her to stay down long; she'll rise again." Nora hoped that he was right, but then Jack was usually right, so maybe things would get better.

Before they left for school they tidied up the kitchen.

"Will I take up a cup of tea to Mom before we go?" Nora asked Peter.

"Suit yourself, but hurry on or we'll be late," he told her.

Nora quickly buttered a cut of bread and poured what was left in the teapot into a cup and, balancing a plate on top of it, ran upstairs.

Her mother was lying in bed staring up at the ceiling, her black hair in lank strands on the pillow. The bones stuck out in her long face and she had black patches under her eyes. Nora had heard her mother described as "the best-looking woman in the parish". It frightened her now that she was so changed. A light seemed to have gone out inside in her and she looked like a corpse. It would be terrible if she died too.

"Mom, here's a cup of tea for you," she said quietly. "Peter and I are going to school."

"Oh," her mother said blankly.

"We are, Mom. Do you remember we told you last night?" Nora said.

"I forgot," her mother said vaguely.

"The kitchen is tidy and Jack is out in the yard if you want anything," Nora told her.

"Oh, is he . . . ?" her mother said as if she had forgotten Jack.

It was almost as if they had changed places. Maybe Nana was right and it would be better for Mom if there were things that she had to do.

As they put on their coats it felt odd that Mom was not there checking that they were well wrapped up and warm before leaving the house. Nora was glad to be back in the old familiar school boots. As she looked down on their leather toe caps, she stamped on the floor to warm her toes and the iron studs gave a metallic clank.

"It's very cold this morning," Peter told her. "We were nearly frozen out in the stalls doing the cows. Be sure that you have plenty of clothes on, Norry, because the school will be freezing."

Nora thought that Peter was a bit more like his old self this morning, and it made her feel better.

As they walked out through the yard Jack put his head out of Paddy's stable. "Don't worry about your mother now. I'll keep an eye on her."

"How's Paddy this morning?" Nora asked.

"Almost as good as new," Jack told her.

Paddy had been cut and bruised in the fall and Jack had been doctoring him with his own remedies. The accident had not been Paddy's fault, but somehow seeing him brought it all back, so she had not called to see him very often.

They walked along quickly in order to keep warm. The high ditches at each side of the boreen were draped with faded brown ferns and tiered moist moss. It was a short, steep boreen that led up to the road and Jack's cottage was just beside their farm gate.

"Hello, Toby." Nora leant over the stone wall that divided their boreen from the cottage yard and a small brown terrier put his front paws on his side of the wall and shook his tail in welcome. They were old friends, but if a stranger called when Jack was out Toby attacked with great ferocity. In the yard behind him hens and ducks wandered around scratching and picking. They could see Jack's cat sitting on the back window of the cottage washing her face and tidying herself up for the day.

"I love Jack's cottage," Nora said.

"Oh, every time we pass Jack's cottage you say that!" Peter protested.

"I know," Nora said agreeably, "but it's grand the way it's all huddled into the trees so that you can't see it from the road, and when you look out the front windows you can see down over Nolans' fields away down to the village.

"Well, I never heard such a palaver about an old house," Peter said. "Our house, because it's lower down, is more sheltered."

"That's what Dada says," Nora remarked.

"Norry, you'll have to get used to saying 'Dada said', because Dad isn't here anymore," Peter said, biting his lip.

"But Pete," she protested, "sometimes I forget and I expect him to come out the stable door or to be sitting on his chair by the fire. Part of me knows that he is gone, but another part of me keeps forgetting because he was always here," she said.

"We better not start talking about Dad because we can't cry today," Peter decided.

He bolted the farm gate behind them and they walked back the road away from the cottage, both silently preparing themselves for the day ahead. When they came to Sarah Jones's gate they saw the small neat woman with grey cropped hair out in the acre feeding the hens. She put down her bucket and, wiping her hands on her apron, she came towards them smiling.

"I'd rather she'd let us pass and not be delaying us," Peter muttered under his breath.

"Shush," Nora whispered.

"Good to see you on the road again," Sarah smiled, putting her hand into her pocket and drawing out two sticks of barley sugar. Peter's face broke into a smile of appreciation and Nora, standing on tiptoe, kissed her gratefully.

As they walked away from her gate Nora grinned at Peter. "Now are you sorry that she stopped us?"

"She's not a bad old sort," he admitted.

"Jack told me that she laid Dada out."

"Nora, we're not going to talk about Dad this morning."

Then they rounded the first bend of the road and saw two figures trudging just ahead of them.

"The Nolans," Nora said with relief. It would be good to have Rosie beside her facing back into school.

“Yoo-hoo,” Peter shouted after them as they ran to catch up. The two Nolans waited with smiles of welcome on their faces. Rosie was solid and serene with heavy blonde hair down to her waist, while her brother Jeremy was gangling with a short unruly thatch over a cheery, freckled face. Rosie was Nora's best friend and the only one to whom she had confided about the horror of the white worm. In the play yard her ample presence had often shielded Nora from further threats. If only she was sitting beside Rosie in school, life would be so much easier.

“We missed the two of you,” Rosie said simply, and Nora smiled in gratitude because she wanted to feel that her school world was waiting for her. But even that world was darkened by the threat of the white worm. She did not like Miss Buckley either, but then nobody liked Miss Buckley. She knew that she had said something to Miss Buckley the night of the accident, but she could not remember exactly what it was because those days were all mixed up in her mind like bits of a broken jug that would not fit together.

The two boys forged ahead and Nora cracked her stick of barley sugar in half and gave it to Rosie, who looked at her with concern.

“Your face is as white as whitewash,” she said, but added comfortingly, “You'll get better. My mother says that when things are bad they can only get better.”

“Hope so,” Nora said a bit forlornly.

“They will,” Rosie told her reassuringly, sucking her stick of barley sugar. That was one of the nice things about Rosie, she could always see the good side of things, and she was full of all kinds of exciting news.

“Wait until I tell you about the big fight Jeremy had with Rory Conway while you were missing,” she began.

Rosie chatted on non-stop and Nora was happy just to listen. The last couple of weeks had been a time of subdued whispering, so now just to listen to Rosie's happy voice was a welcome change.

When they arrived at the long low school the door of the front porch was closed and there was nobody in sight.

"We must be late," Nora said in alarm.

"Don't worry," Rosie assured her, "the foxy greyhound can't say anything to you on your first day back."

Rosie had christened the red-haired Miss Buckley "the foxy greyhound" because, as Rosie explained, she was long, lean and mean and always barking.

Rosie put her shoulder to the heavy old porch door and pushed it in before her, and the familiar smell of sour milk bottles and damp coats came out to meet them. They hung up their coats and Rosie lifted the latch of the door into the schoolroom. Every eye in the room swung towards them. Rosie sailed serenely up to her place at the end of the front seat and Nora slunk on to the edge of the back seat beside the white worm. Miss Buckley after a glance over her shoulder in their direction continued to write on the blackboard.

"So you came back at last," Kitty Conway greeted her. Nora thought that she looked like a cat waiting to pounce on a mouse.

"Silence," Miss Buckley demanded without turning around, and there was instant silence. "Take out your sum copies and take down these sums off the board."

Nora found it very difficult to concentrate and had to rub out the wrong numbers several times while Kitty Conway watched her with a smirk on her face.

"You stupid lump," Kitty whispered, but because Miss

Buckley was so cross there was no chance of further exchanges, and for that Nora was grateful.

As the morning wore on she felt tired and found it difficult to keep her eyes open. It was a relief to hear the Master's bell for lunch hour. She moved quickly from the desk and was out the door before Kitty had time to say anything.

Out in the play yard the other children looked at her curiously, almost as if they expected her to have changed in some way. She knew that they had all heard about her father. They gathered around her in a silent cluster. Nora felt threatened by their unspoken expectations. She felt Kitty Conway moving in near her to mock, to some way blame her for her father's death so that they would all think that she was a freak. Their faces swam before her eyes, waiting and watching. Then Rosie was beside her, large, solid and assured.

"What are ye all gaping at?" she demanded. "How would ye like if your father was dead and ye had no Dada at home?"

Eyes opened in dismay and then sympathy washed over their faces.

"It would be just awful," one little girl said, biting her lip at the thought of it.

"Well, then, play with Nora and stop acting like mugs 'cause it could be you next week," Rosie threatened. "So come on and we'll all play the cat and the mouse."

They looked at Rosie as if she was wise beyond her years and started to form a long line, and once the game got going they laughed and screamed with excitement. Nora found herself joining in and for a while forgot everything only the fun of being one of them again.

But as they trooped back into the school after lunch she saw Kitty Conway watching her. Later that evening they would have the sewing class, when they were allowed to talk quietly. That would give the white worm a chance to attack. Nora liked sewing, but she dreaded this class, when Kitty Conway would have her cornered in the desk and at her mercy. All of a sudden Nora wished that she was at home. School would be all right if she did not have to sit next to Kitty Conway, but now it all washed back over her and she felt trapped.

Catechism class was the first after lunch. Miss Buckley barked out questions at them and then pointed a finger at somebody for an instant answer. Everybody was on tenterhooks in case they were next and would not know the answer, and if you hesitated or stuttered she demanded that you come up to the top of the room where she wielded her little black stick with vigour.

Suddenly there was a loud knock on the door and silence descended. They seldom had callers at the school except the inspector, who terrified them mainly because they sensed that he terrified Miss Buckley, and anyone who frightened her had to be pretty bad.

"Tar isteach," Miss Buckley instructed.

When the door was whipped open and young Fr Brady walked in, there was a simultaneous outbreak of smiles all over the room. Miss Buckley's stick disappeared from view and a false smile appeared on her face. They all rose to their feet as she had trained them.

"Sit down, children," he smiled, "I'm only the curate. Now what are we at?"

"The Sixth Commandment," Miss Buckley told him primly.

"Oh boys," he said, "that's heavy stuff for a cold day. Will we have a song instead? Who would like to sing a song for me?"

Several hands shot up but Rosie's was first. All the Nolans had fine singing voices and Rosie was forever learning new songs out of *Ireland's Own* and trying to teach them to Nora.

"Good girl, Rosie! Off you go," instructed Fr Brady.

Miss Buckley's face was a picture of suppressed rage, and Rosie, well aware of it, was enjoying it to the full. With Fr Brady in the room Miss Buckley had to take a back seat. Rosie was at the end of the front desk and she stepped out to the side of the room where everybody could see her. There was nothing that she liked better than an audience. She put her shoulders back, and her clear young voice filled the room with "Danny Boy". Nora closed her eyes and followed every word with her. When she came to the line "and I shall hear though soft you tread above me", Nora felt a knot in her throat, but she swallowed hard and forced it down. As Rosie finished on the last low note there was silence for a moment and then thunderous applause.

"Rosie, you've a wonderful voice," Fr Brady told her; "you should thank God for it, and all of you should thank God for everything he has given to us."

"Would you like to examine them in their catechism, Father?" Miss Buckley asked.

"Yerra, I'm sure they're full of knowledge after your good teaching," he said, bringing a thin smile to her face. Then he walked over to where Nora sat and, going down on one knee, he smiled at her.

"I'm glad you're back, Nora," he told her.

Then he was gone, banging the door behind him, and they were all sorry to see him go.

As soon as the door banged behind him Miss Buckley announced: "That's the catechism class over. Get out your sewing boxes now."

There was a clatter of boxes along the desks as the girl nearest to the cupboard lifted them down and they were passed along, mostly tin boxes with crinoline ladies and faded roses on the covers.

When each girl had a box in front of her Miss Buckley said, "Open your boxes now and I'll be around to each one of you in turn."

It was the one time of the day that she relaxed a little, and for most of the girls it was their favourite class of the week.

"I bet you think that you are great with everyone feeling sorry for you," Kitty started straight away, but Nora was determined to say nothing, remembering what her father had said about taking no notice.

"Well, I'm not one bit sorry for you," she continued, sticking her face up close to Nora's, "because I know that you really killed him, and do you know what's going to happen now?" She stopped to let her words soak in. "My father says that your old mother will sell Mossgrove and ye'll be all out in the road like the tinkers."

Suddenly Nora felt that she could take no more. This was beyond endurance. All the scenes of suffering at the hands of Kitty Conway floated in front of her, and all the hurt of the past weeks, and she felt a white fog of fury uncurling in her brain. She jumped up and, grasping Kitty by the shoulders, she shook her till she heard her teeth chattering and then thumped her head down on the desk where her nose collided with the edge of the tin sewing box and blood squirted all over the place. It happened so fast that some of the girls missed it, and those who saw it could hardly believe their eyes. Those far away from the action jumped up on the desks for a better view.

"Good God, Nora Phelan, what do you think you are doing?" Miss Buckley shouted at her from across the room before racing over and dragging her out of the desk by the hair of her head. "Stand there," she said, "until I see to this child."

Kitty was yelling – "like a beagle" as Rosie later described it – but when a towel was produced and the blood wiped away, the extent of the damage was a slightly swollen nose and a bad nosebleed.

"Get out to the Master's room, you brazen huzzy," Miss Buckley screamed at Nora.

It was the biggest punishment that could be meted out, to be sent to the Master's room to be slapped.

Nora walked slowly up to the Master's door. The Master was judge and jury. How was she going to explain what she had done? She stood at the door trying to think up an explanation but nothing came to mind.

"Nora Phelan," Miss Buckley shouted, "will you get out to the Master and explain yourself." And because Nora still made no move she ran over and wrenched the door open and, catching Nora by the back of her jumper, threw her headlong into the room.

It was a big room with a row of desks up both sides and the Master's rostrum at the front of the centre aisle. As Nora made her crashing entrance at the back of the room, there was a general turning of heads in her direction and a stunned silence descended. Nora regained her balance but kept her head down. Then all of a sudden she felt perfectly calm. There was no going back now. She would not make up any explanation; she would tell it as it happened. Peter always said that the Master was strict but fair. She saw all the faces turned in her direction and she caught Peter's look of embarrassed amazement. She swallowed deeply and looked across the room to where the Master stood on the rostrum and then walked slowly with her head held high in his direction. As soon as she faced him she sensed that he was more surprised to see her than anything else.

"Why are you here, Nora?" he asked.

"I hit Kitty Conway," she said quietly.

"Why did you do that?" he asked.

"She said nasty things about my mother," Nora said in an anguished voice.

"She shouldn't have done that," he said, "but you should not have hit her either. Run away back to your class now and forget about it."

She gave him a look of sheer gratitude and walked slowly back through the room. She caught Peter's eye and he winked encouragement at her. She felt she had won this battle, but she had no intention of letting on that she had not got slapped. That would bring further fury from Miss Buckley who was waiting for her at the top of the classroom.

"Now, Nora Phelan," she said, "that will teach you a lesson, and to make sure that you behave yourself properly in future you sit up here in the front desk by Rosie Nolan where I can keep an eye on you."

Nora could hardly believe her ears. She was free from the white worm and sitting with Rosie. It had all been worth it! She kept the look of joy off her face and slipped into the front desk beside Rosie with her head down.

"Thank you, Dada," she breathed.

Aunty Kate had told her to pray to him for help, and though Nora was doubtful if he could hear she still had prayed every night since the funeral to be delivered from the white worm. Now Dada had done it. She had wondered where he had gone when he died. Even Jack was not sure, but Aunty Kate had no doubts about it and now neither did she. He was up in heaven and he was listening and he could work miracles. She closed her eyes again and prayed: "Thank you, Dada, thank you for saving me from the white worm. Thank you, thank you. But now I want something else. Will you straighten out Mom and don't let Kitty Conway be right about Mossgrove?"

"Thank you, Juda," she [illegible].

Juda [illegible] had told her [illegible] to [illegible] the baby, and [illegible] Nora was [illegible] that she had [illegible] remembered [illegible] the white worm. Now Juda had [illegible] it. She had [illegible] face was [illegible] had [illegible] and [illegible] he could [illegible] and she closed her eyes again and prayed: "Thank you, Juda, thank you for saving me from the white worm. Thank you, thank you. But now I want something else. Will you [illegible] and [illegible] about [illegible]?"

CHAPTER SIX

JACK RAN HIS hand along the back of the young cow as he walked in beside her to close the stall of her companion.

"You won't be long more, Daisy," he assured her as he eased his fingers down over her belly and felt for the cleft between her back flank and udder that would tell him how much time she had before the arrival of her calf.

Since Ned had gone he had taken to talking to himself and the animals, to break the silence of the farmyard. Of all his years in Mossgrove this was the most gruelling time. After Billy's death it had not been this bad. There had been huge financial worries then, but he and Nellie had been in it together.

"I thought that those were dark days," he said to Daisy, "but they were a holiday compared to now."

The financial problem seemed a major issue then, but it was a reason to keep going, and Nellie and himself had carried the burden together. Money had solved that problem. True for the old man.

"Jack," he used to say, "money can solve money problems, but there are other problems that nothing can solve."

The old man was right, as he had been about so many things. It was only as he grew older himself that he had fully come to appreciate the sayings of Edward Phelan. Jack sometimes wondered how any one person could have had such wisdom.

Daisy looked back at him out of large liquid eyes as she chewed the cud contentedly. Cows were gentle creatures, big, placid, undemanding animals, and he always found that they had a calming effect on him, especially when he was worried about something and had no solution to the problem. He had no solution to Martha's problem. She had just simply come to a standstill. If it continued like this, things would come apart at the seams on the farm.

In Mossgrove, the woman of the house had always managed the yard, which produced a big part of the farm income. She fed the hens, geese, ducks, pigs and calves, and helped with the milking. Martha had been good at it and her farmyard had been run like clockwork. She reared fine healthy calves and fattened pigs to the right balance so that they sold well at the pig market or graded high if sent to the new factory. She had baskets of eggs for the egg lorry every Wednesday and a flock of geese fattened for the Christmas market. When things were quiet out the fields he helped her with the yard jobs and had always been impressed by her efficiency. She had her faults but she knew her stuff regarding livestock, and if Ned and himself were busy out on the land she could manage single-handed and always had the cows in and the milking started when they came in from the fields. She was a determined woman with endless energy and had she kept them all on their toes. It was hard to think that she was thrown inside in the bed now at two o'clock in the day.

When, after their father's death he had told Nora and Peter that he thought their mother had too much spirit to stay down and that she would be on her feet soon again, he had meant it. He had been wrong. The poor little divils, he thought, it's very hard on them trying to battle on the best way they can and coming home every evening to a cold house and a makeshift dinner. He wished that he had more time to make decent meals, but he was stretched as far as he could go, with Ned's and Martha's work to do as well as his own. Martha had closed up and shut everyone out including the children. She had never been a good one to talk things out or to encourage the neighbours to call, though that did not stop them now, but they were met with a cold, set face and few words. Most of them had stopped coming, except good-hearted Betty Nolan who would not be discouraged.

"I'd come oftener and do more," she told Jack, "but I'd be afraid I'd get the door and then I'd have burned my boats altogether and I'd be no help at all."

The Nolans had always been close neighbours of the Phelans and there had been a lot of toing and froing between the houses in the past, but that had dried up a bit with the coming of Martha, who liked to keep the neighbours at a distance. She was a bit too stiff for her own good, Jack thought, but then the father had been like that as well. He thought of the old man again and what he used to say: "Bad to be too rigid; better to yield a little. Rigid people don't bend, they break." By God, he thought, but the old fella had it all worked out. How would he solve this one, he wondered.

"Hurry on there now, Daisy," he told the cow, "and produce that calf before night so that I can go home to bed and not have to stay here with you."

She was a young cow and it was her first calf, so he could take no chances with her and would have to be there to see that everything went right.

Ned had always covered the night deliveries, so it was a long time since Jack had to stay up with a cow, but he was back now doing a lot of things that he had not done with years. Keeping his fingers crossed that he would be able to cope with everything, he was glad that it was a quiet time of year with not much to be done in the fields, although there were things that he should be doing out there even now. The spring ploughing should be started, but the way things were at the moment he just could not get around to it. He decided that he had better go into the kitchen and put on the spuds for the dinner and while they were boiling he would feed the pigs and collect the eggs.

In the scullery he had to step over muddy boots on the floor; some coats were hanging off the back of the door but most were down on the floor and across the little table where Martha had kept a pan of water for washing before they got as far as the kitchen. There was not much point in washing before you went into the kitchen now because it was worse than the scullery. The breakfast ware was still on the table and the fire had gone out. He had lit it this morning but he had not had a chance to come back in to put on more turf and logs, so it had burnt itself out. The ashes of previous days were piled high to the side because no one had got around to taking them out, and probably the ash hole underneath was at explosion point. But it would have to wait for another day. He screwed up pieces of newspaper and put a few bits of soft dry turf and some sticks around it, but when he turned the bellows to fan the flame it had no effect because, as he had suspected, the ash hole beneath was choked. But the fire lit up anyway as the turf was dry and reddened quickly. He put the pot of potatoes over the fire and then went to light the primus to boil a saucepan of water to wash up the breakfast ware.

The primus was handy as a back-up because otherwise he would have to wait for the potatoes to boil before he could warm water for the washing up. After a long search he finally unearthed the primus from under a pile of dirty clothes in the corner of the kitchen. He was relieved that when he shook it he could hear oil gurgling; but when he looked for the methylated spirits to light up he discovered an empty bottle up on the top shelf of the scullery. He sighed in frustration and decided that while he was waiting for the potatoes to boil he would do a bit of a tidy-up. Nora was doing the best she could, but a ten year old was no match for the work of a farm kitchen. She had spent all yesterday evening cleaning the eggs for the egg lorry tomorrow. Thanks be to God, he thought to himself, that Betty Nolan is doing the washing, as he piled it all into a jute bag. She whisked it away quietly every few days and brought it back neatly stacked and ironed, and a few cakes of brown bread with it. She'd clean up the place for them, too, he knew, but she was afraid that Martha would walk in on her and give her her marching orders. There was no doubt but that Martha had got herself fenced into a corner, and us with her, he concluded.

When the potatoes came to the boil he moved them sideways and hung the kettle over the fire. While he waited for it to boil he brushed the floor and looked down ruefully at the crusted mud and bits of dried cow dung along the floor. You could track us, he thought, from the scullery door to the table and from the table to the fire. It was a big change, no doubt, from lining their dirty boots up carefully under the table in the scullery. Ned and himself had often laughed and compared the order of it to army living, but by God it was a lot better than this carry-on. The kettle started to steam so he poured the hot water into the tin pan and washed up all the ware and dried them with a not-too-clean tea towel, the best he could find. There seemed to be a wet tea towel on the back of every chair and the dry ones looked as if they needed a wash, so he collected them all and pushed them into Betty's bag.

Martha always had a stack of clean tea towels in the little press beside the fire, and he had heard her say that you could judge a housekeeper by her tea towels. As he collected the dirty ones he decided that they told their own story. When he opened the big kitchen cupboard to put away the ware, a mouse scuttled out of the sugar bowl. That meant there were about twenty more in hiding. The word must have gone round, he thought, that Phelans' was now a safe house.

He was straining the potatoes when he heard footsteps in the yard. He put down the pot and looked out the back window, but it was clouded up from smoke so that he had to rub it with his fingers to be able to see Nora and Peter trudging across the yard.

"Oh, Jack," Nora smiled in relief to see the fire lighting, "you tidied up: aren't you great?"

"A bit of a cat's lick," he told her.

"Is she still in bed again today?" Peter demanded with a face like thunder.

"That's right," Jack said lightly, trying to make as little fuss as possible, but Peter was not going to be sidetracked.

"It's not fair," he said angrily, "she should be helping us. If she was dead there is no way that Dad would carry on like that. I wish to God that it was the other way around."

"She'll come around," Jack said easily.

"You've been saying that with weeks," Peter accused, getting angrier.

"It's not Jack's fault," Nora protested. "It's very hard on Jack too with all the extra jobs."

"Well, I'm going to get her out of it," Peter growled, heading for the stairs.

Jack was pouring milk into mugs but he quickly put the jug on the table and took two long strides to the foot of the stairs.

"Easy, Peter," Jack said as he stood on the bottom step of the stairs with his back to the door that closed it off from the kitchen. "We can't solve the problem this way."

"Well, how're we going to solve it?" Peter shouted, red-faced with eyes full of angry frustrated tears. "She'll have to get out of that bloody bed. Nora is tired every morning going to school; she fell asleep today and was sent out to the Master by that bitch of a Miss Buckley. And you're shagged from trying to do everything, and we should be starting the ploughing because it's the time and they're all at it but us, and I'm fed up with the whole bloody cursed mess," Peter finished in a rush of words and a sob.

Jack stepped down and put his arm around Peter's

shoulder, half expecting it to be tossed aside, but instead Peter put his face down on his shoulder and cried. The poor lad, Jack thought. Because he's so tall we think that he's older than his years.

Nora came over and took Jack's hand and put an arm around Peter's waist. "We'll be all right, Peter," she comforted. "I'm praying to Dada and he'll look after us."

"He'd want to hurry on then," Peter declared angrily.

"But Dada never rushed anything," Nora protested, which caused Peter all of a sudden to start laughing, and then Nora and Jack joined in because they all remembered Ned's easy-going ways.

"That's better," Jack announced. "Laughing is better than crying any day."

Suddenly the door behind them was whipped open. Three faces swung upwards in astonishment. An unwashed Martha stood there in a long, stained nightdress, her black hair in limp strings down over her shoulders. She looked down on them with disdain.

"You should be ashamed of yourselves and your father hardly cold in his grave." Her voice cut like a whiplash through their laughter with icy coldness. There was a stunned silence. Peter was the first to recover.

"It's bloody better than staying in bed all day like a shagging sick calf," he asserted angrily.

She turned on her heel and disappeared up the stairs; they heard the bedroom door bang behind her.

"Oh," Nora whispered, "that was awful."

"Maybe no harm though," Jack decided. "It might be the beginning of the turn. Now we'd better get these eggs in the pan."

He cracked half a dozen eggs into the small black

bastable and hung it over the fire. The fat spluttered and spat around them as he turned them over with a fork.

"Fried eggs again today, Jack," Nora smiled.

"My menu is a bit limited, I suppose," he admitted.

"I like fried eggs," she said loyally, "and we have plenty of them."

They sat around the table and ate the fried eggs and mashed potatoes yellow with butter. Then he made tea and buttered thick slices of Betty Nolan's nutty brown bread. They might not have variety but at least it was solid fare, he decided.

"We'll stack up the ware now," he told them when they were finished, "and I'll wash everything together tomorrow. It's handier that way."

"I'll finish cleaning the eggs for the lorry tomorrow," Nora said. "And did today's eggs come in?" she asked.

"Never got a chance," Jack explained.

"That's all right, Jack," she told him, "I'll do it and then I'll clean them all. Oh, I forgot Mom's tea – I'd better do that first." She went to the press and took out a large mug and then went to the fire where the teapot still sat.

That tea is probably pretty chilly at this stage, Jack thought, and he knew that Martha hated to drink out of a mug, but he would not upset Nora by interfering. Peter had already voiced an opinion that his mother should be starved out of it.

"Are the pigs fed?" Peter asked.

"No, not yet," he said.

"I'll do them so, and then we'll do the milking together," Peter told him. He was glad to see that Peter was a bit brighter. He was probably in the better of that outburst of temper and crying, and the fact that they had been able to laugh at themselves afterwards was good for the three of them.

He went out to check on Daisy, but there was no need for supervision as she was at ease, hay dribbling from her jaw.

"Your mother was a slow starter before you," Jack told her. "Looks as if I'll be burning the midnight oil with you tonight, my girl."

He fed the calves and gave hay to the horses in the stables next door. Paddy, looking small between the two farm horses, Jerry and James, who had a manger at either side of him, was back in his old form. There was timber railing between them because you could never be sure when horses might get a contrary notion. Paddy was a placid animal and James was easygoing, but Jerry could give you a lash of a kick if you were not careful with him. But to compensate for that mean streak he was a great worker out in the fields and more often than not pulled James along. Animals, he often thought, were no different to people; they all had their own peculiarities, but if he had a choice he preferred dealing with the animals.

As he came out of the stables he saw Nora with Bran on her heels going in the back door with her gallon of eggs. She walked with a tired drag to her feet and the clothes seemed to hang off her. A picture of the little girl who had bounced across the yard to Ned and himself a short while ago came into his mind. She's having to grow up too fast, he thought; she needs her mother. Thank God that Kate would be back this week. She had worried about going away so soon after the funeral, but this special course that she was going on had been arranged with a long time and a substitute nurse booked to stand in for her and do her rounds. Ned's death had hit her hard and maybe it was good for her to go away on this course. She had been very fond of Ned and had come often to Mossgrove because she had a deep attachment to the place. Jack knew that when Ned was in town he called to her house next door to the dispensary and they had long chats. Ned had been delighted when she had got the job as district nurse and it had suited Kate to come back to her own stomping ground. With just the two of them in the family they were very close, and he could see the same thing happening between Nora and Peter. As Ned used to joke, the Phelans seemed to come in pairs.

As Peter and himself milked the cows he could see that Daisy was restless and moving around. Maybe with a bit of luck she would get down to business fairly soon and produce the calf before he went home. But when he checked her after the supper she seemed to have quietened down again, so he decided to go home to feed Toby and the cat and to lock up the hens and ducks for the night and to come back later. He went into the kitchen to collect the storm lantern and to tell Peter that he would be back and not to worry about Daisy. They were both at the table doing their lessons. Nora was having difficulty with long division and Peter was trying to sort her out.

"If you're gone to bed when I come back and if Daisy goes on too long, I might come in and make tea, so don't take any notice if you hear noises," Jack told them.

As he passed the kitchen window he stopped and looked in at them. They needed more than he was providing. He remembered when Billy died how anxious Nellie had been about Ned and Kate – especially Kate, who had been so attached to him. Now Nora was trying to battle through this ordeal on her own, and he was more worried about her than Peter, because Peter was lashing out and complaining while Nora was trying to help him and to look after Martha as well. It was a heavy load for young shoulders.

When he got back down to the stall Daisy was prancing around, so he knew that things were starting to move. He lit the storm lantern and hung it carefully off a hook in the ceiling. The rest of the cows, who were placidly chewing the cud, looked around curiously but were in no way disturbed. They were accustomed to the yellow rays of the lamp roaming nightly over their heads when they were checked before the farmyard settled down for the night. He collected a big bundle of hay from the barn and made a comfortable seat for himself against the wall behind her. The lantern only partially lit the stall but thankfully there was a good moon which poured bright pools of light through the narrow windows. He could see the grey cobwebs hanging off the low ceiling and sometimes a slight breeze disturbed them which cast floating shadows along the stone walls. In the silence he could hear the occasional rustling of mice who had colonised the thick walls over the years.

Daisy scrope her two front legs off the stone floor and danced her hindquarters back and forth in an agony of protestation, and then a violent contraction forced her back legs to skid forward and she moaned in pain as two small hooves appeared beneath her arching tail, only to disappear again when the contraction subsided. Jack nestled down into the hay as the cold of the night settled in around him. This is a right good place to get a fine belter of a cold, he thought, so he pulled an old bran bag around his shoulders. Daisy moaned mournfully and, swinging her neck around, she looked back at Jack and rolled large reproachful eyes in his direction. He swung his legs off the hay and went over to rub his hand knowingly into the cleft between her flank and udder.

"Not long more now, old girl," he told her, massaging her back, but Daisy decided that maybe lying down might be an easier way to handle this new painful experience. She threw her enlarged body awkwardly on to the floor, grunting and trying to make herself comfortable, but her swollen belly threw her off balance and her legs stuck out rigidly like the legs of a corpse.

"Well, Daisy," he told her, "if you're going to lie down on the job I might as well do the same." He returned to his hay bed and pulled the bags up around him.

It was a long time since he had done this night vigil and he had almost forgotten the sounds of the farmyard at night. The occasional grunt came from the piggery across the yard and now and then the horses' hooves clanked off the cobbled floor as they moved their weight from one leg to the other. The ducks gave an odd quack as they jockeyed for a more comfortable space in their communal bed. The cows around him chewed contentedly, and he felt himself dozing off to the crunching rhythm of their jaws.

Daisy woke him as she made a convulsive movement to swing her giant belly into a better position so that she could stand upright, but she failed and tilted backwards again. Then with a mighty effort she rocked herself sideways and with a great heave scrambled into a kneeling position on her two front legs, and as she straightened them beneath her she hoisted her hindquarters upwards. When she was on all fours she swished her tail in preparation for the oncoming contraction, and Jack knew that his night vigil was drawing to a close.

He was stiff with the cold and he thought longingly of a hot glass of the cure. Always during night calvings Nellie would arrive at some stage with a hot steaming mug with cloves floating on top like black imps. That was the boy to heat you up on a frosty night! Daisy brought him back to reality with a bellow of anguish and with a convulsive heaving motion forced her hind quarters to eject a small brown head that rested on two white hooves that had appeared and disappeared earlier. Now Jack grasped the hooves and pulled steadily until the clinging calf slithered on to the sodden straw behind her. He rolled the calf over and was pleased to see that it was a sturdy heifer. He helped it to its feet. It wobbled drunkenly against its mother's belly and he lifted it firmly and placed it beneath her head; her long, grating tongue licked away its slimy coat and yellow beastings dripped from her overflowing udder on to the stone floor. He straightened himself up and walked out into the quiet farmyard.

The dark sky was shot with light behind the bare branches of his oak tree at the top of the haggard and the birds were gently waking each other up for the start of a new day. It was times like this, Jack thought, that made all the hardship worthwhile. A new birth, a new day and a feeling that all was well with the world. But the problem was that at the moment all was far from well in the world of Mossgrove.

He looked across the shadowy farmyard and down over the fields where the grey morning mists were rising and swirling along the hedges. You could pray on a morning like this, he thought, because you could feel God in your bones.

"Ned, old friend," he said, "wherever you are, keep an eye over us because we're in a right mess since you left."

CHAPTER SEVEN

KATE TURNED THE key in the lock and pushed open the door of her house. Before turning on the light she stood with her back against the door and savoured the essence of her own home. The warm whiff of polish permeated the air, and she knew that Julia Deasy had given everything an overhaul to greet her return. The smell brought the sense of Mark's gentle spirit into the house. He made his own furniture polish from his beeswax, which fed the wood and gave it a deep rich glow. The streetlight shone through the fan slash over the door, bathed the stairway in green light and threw shadows along the corridor that led back to the kitchen. At the foot of the stairs the door into the front room was ajar. She pushed it open and stood there looking at the familiar room partly lit by the streetlight outside the window. She knew by the warm fresh air in the room that Julia had lit the fires and looked after the house well in her absence.

Along the back wall, the mantelpiece was cluttered with much-loved objects from her childhood in Mossgrove. On winter nights when she sat by the fire it was good to run her eye over them and to look up at the large photograph of Grandfather Phelan. She went over now and studied it above the fireplace. The face was in shadow, but she knew every familiar curve: the broad forehead beneath the thick thatch of white hair, the strong aquiline nose and shrewd eyes that seemed to see through to the back of your head. His presence was almost real because Jack had kept him alive with his constant reference to him. She was so glad that she had brought his picture from Mossgrove. There had been a reluctance on her part to take it at the time, feeling that it belonged in the family home. But Jack had counselled, "Take it. You can always bring it back afterwards, but you could never take it away."

How wise he had been. She had often thought of his advice in later years as she had watched in silence old familiar photographs disappear from the walls of Mossgrove. She would have so loved to have had them, but she had not taken them when she could have, before Ned got married, because she had felt that they belonged in Mossgrove. How stupid she had been. Jack had been far wiser. She had never mentioned it to Ned because she did not want to cause any trouble. He had always been so good to her. When she had got the job here as district nurse and this house had come on the market, he had helped her to buy it. When she had protested and said that she could go to the bank, he had told her, "You worked hard in Mossgrove when times were tough. Mossgrove owes you this."

When he put it like that she did not feel under a compliment, and it meant that she could afford to spend more on the restoration of the house.

She walked into the kitchen where the fire still glowed behind the bars of the old black range, glinting off its heavy brass door knobs. The range had been in the house when she bought it and it still served her well by keeping the place warm and providing a plentiful supply of hot water as well as doing all the cooking. She had made very few changes in the kitchen because she liked the old dresser and the heavy-beamed ceiling. She had just thrown a large rug in the centre of the quarry-tiled floor and put a comfortable armchair by the range. The chair had been her grandfather's, and she remembered him sitting in it beside the parlour window in Mossgrove. The springs had collapsed, but she had got them resprung and covered it in the same old rose velvet. Sometimes coming home on cold nights it was a relief to fall into its deep warm cushions and put her feet up on the range. She had enjoyed working on the house and maybe when she was younger she would have seen a house like this as part of a package with husband and children, but they had not become part of the scene. Only once had there been somebody with whom this might have been possible, but that was in the past. Now at thirty-two she had almost decided that the single state was her chosen path.

As she put on the kettle to make a cup of tea she thought about Mossgrove and wondered how things were going on out there. It was hard to imagine it without Ned. The dull pain that was now her constant companion welled up inside. She had cried long into the nights in this old chair during those first heart-breaking days. The course had partly occupied her mind but the crying had gone on inside. She sat into the chair now and ran her hand over the soft, warm arms. Grandfather and Nellie had sat for many hours in this chair. Neither of them had had easy lives, but they had both possessed the spirit of survival and neither had bowed down under calamity. She was the product of strong, resilient people, so she too would straighten up and keep going. It would be bleak in Mossgrove without Ned's sunny, calming presence. She had always looked forward to the times when he had called in here for a chat. She was going to miss those visits. Thank God that they still had Jack on the farm. He had brought it through tricky times before. She had thought, from the letter that she had got in answer to hers, that he was worried about something, but Jack was not one to spell out problems when you were too far away to be able to help. The little note that Nora had sent had somehow worried her as well. She knew that they were devastated, but somehow she felt that something else was wrong. If she only had a car she would run back there now, but she was dependent on her bike. A two-mile cycle after a long day travelling was too much. She decided that a good night's rest was a better option before she faced Mossgrove.

The following day when she stood in the cold of the grey morning light in the yard of Mossgrove and surveyed the condition of the place, she was glad that she had a good night's rest behind her. Bran, who was chewing a bone on the step of the back door, was the only sign of life and he welcomed her with a joyous wagging tail and a few high jumps to lick her face.

"Bran," she questioned, "where is everybody?"

The yard showed signs of neglect. Martha had never

allowed dirty buckets at the back door, but now there were several scattered in disarray. Some were turned sideways with hens' tails protruding and others had cackling hens perched on their rims. These are hungry hens, Kate thought, so she picked up one of the buckets and went to the feed house where she filled it with oats. The hens followed, squawking in anticipation, as she swished the oats around the far corner of the yard, and with heads down and tails bobbing they gobbled it up in sharp pecks.

Dog bones were strewn around the scullery. It was unheard of previously that Bran would be allowed to put his nose inside the back door. It was obvious from the smell that it had become a second home to him. She opened the door into the kitchen and stood transfixed.

"Good God!" she gasped.

It was incredible that Martha, who was so house-proud, could tolerate these conditions. It was difficult to know where to begin.

She decided that she would make a start with the ashes that were piled high. She went out to get the ash bucket, but even that was missing from its usual place. She found it eventually outside the duck's house where it had obviously been used to carry their feed. It took two fills of the bucket to clear the ashes around the fire before she could clear out the ash hole that was packed to capacity. Soon a blazing fire roared up the chimney. She hung the large black pot off the crane and filled it with water from the timber barrel outside the back door.

When Jack come in an hour later there was a stream of sudsy water rushing out the back door against him. He had seen Kate's bike at the gable end and a weight had lifted off his shoulders.

"Kate," he said with fervour, his face alight with welcome, "thank God you're back."

"Jack," she said, "oh, it's so good to see you again." At a glance she saw that the weeks had taken their toll.

Jack had always looked the same to Kate: neither old nor young, just hardy and ageless. Now he looked old and worn. He had loved Ned deeply, much more than he had herself. She had known it but had never resented it, just as she had known that his love of her mother had gone above and beyond the call of duty and she had loved him for that. He had said often that Ned was like Nellie but that she herself had a lot of their grandfather in her. It was one of the reasons that he had wanted her to have the picture. All these thoughts ran through her mind as they looked at each other across the kitchen and she felt her eyes fill with tears. This great little man who had always put her family before himself. She ran across the wet floor and put her arms around him and she knew that he understood that she was wordlessly thanking him for many things.

"We've let ourselves get into a bit of a rí-rá," Jack said gruffly, clearing his throat to cover his emotion.

"Where is Martha?" she asked, although she had already guessed, and in reply Jack pointed a finger towards the ceiling.

"All day, every day?" she asked.

"Almost," he answered, and then in desperation: "Can you sort her out, Kate, because we can't go on like this. It's very hard on the two young ones."

And on you, too, she thought.

"We'll get it sorted out, Ned," she assured him, though she had no idea how, because she had never really understood Martha. But she felt that Jack needed reassurance. "Are you going to the creamery?" she asked.

"In a few minutes," he told her.

"Call in to Danny the butcher and get a good big lump of boiling beef."

"That's the job," he said smiling; "that will put hair on our chest and pep in our step."

When she had the table and chairs scrubbed and the floor washed, she cleaned the smoky windows. When the glass was sparkling she opened them top and bottom to air out the kitchen while she tackled the ware in the dresser. To her disgust she saw mouse droppings when she opened the small press where Martha kept the bread and butter. She poked around in the drawer of the dresser and found two mouse traps and, having cleared the press, she put them into action.

The kitchen finished, she went up into the parlour. It smelt of stale musty air. She opened the windows wide and threw the mats out on to the hedge in the garden. When she had the floor brushed and the furniture polished, she closed the windows and lit the fire. The garden outside was full of daffodils, so she picked a big bunch when she went out to bring in the mats. She left half of them on the kitchen table to be arranged later and put the rest into an old glass jug of Nellie's and stood it in the centre of the parlour table. Daffodils, she thought, belong in a glass jug where you can see their vivid green stems glistening in the clear water. She stood back to admire the effect. They were vibrant and brought new life into the room. There was something encouraging about daffodils, she thought; they spoke of a new beginning and the resurrection. They hung out over the sides of the jug, admiring their reflections in the polished table top. She had always liked this room and had spent a lot of time here in her mother's last years.

On the morning of her First Holy Communion they had had a special breakfast around this big table. Grandfather had been alive then and he sat at the head of the table while she sat at the other end. She had laughed up at him, saying that she was actually at the head and he was at the bottom. Her father and mother had been to the left and right of the old man and Ned and Jack on her left and right. She must have been about seven then, so Ned would have been twelve. She had always been proud of Ned's good looks, and that morning with his new dark suit and blond hair he had looked very handsome. She had felt pretty herself in her all-white outfit, though nobody had ever described her as pretty because she had the strong, dark features of the Phelans. She had once heard old Molly Conway remark, "You couldn't say that one was good looking but she is attractive in a strange dark way." The statement had occupied her teenage mind for weeks trying to figure out if it was a compliment or an insult.

"Memories, memories," she sighed aloud; "that's the problem with old houses, they're full of memories. But I suppose that's what makes them interesting."

Tongues of fire were licking around the sods of turf and warming up the room, so the time had come to face upstairs and see Martha. She was very nervous of the reception that awaited her. The kettle over the fire in the kitchen was boiling, so she made a fresh pot of tea and sat it on some hot coals to draw. Martha liked her tea strong and hot. She dressed a tray with a clean cloth that she poked out of the back of a press and set it with fine china from the parlour and then toasted bread to the glowing fire. Then, with nothing further to be done, she opened the door at the foot of the stairs and climbed upwards.

The stairs were covered in dust. When she reached the top step she could see at a glance that the narrow landing had not been brushed with weeks and that Peter en route to his room past Martha's door had dropped clothes along the way. There was a time, Kate thought, when he would not have got away with that. The door to Nora's room was open and she saw that Nora had kept it as tidy as possible, but from where she stood Kate's nurse's eye judged the sheets to be grey rather than white. Probably not changed since the funeral, Kate thought. She went past Nora's door on to Martha's room and knocked gently. There was no sound from inside. She waited for a few minutes and tried again. When there was still no response she decided that her best approach was to adopt her professional attitude and treat the situation as if she was the district nurse and that Martha was just another patient.

She opened the door quietly and was taken aback by the disorder inside; she had to pick her steps across the litter on the floor and when she reached the bed all she could see was the top of Martha's head. The rest of her was buried in the clothes strewn around the bed.

"Martha," she said gently, and when there was no response she repeated herself more firmly. The clothes stirred and a hand that had not been washed for a long time came out to pull down the clothes. Kate needed all her professionalism to keep her face expressionless. Martha was dirty and her hair was stiff with grease, but it was the smell of foul breath that almost forced Kate to take a step backwards. Oh my Jesus, Kate thought, she's on the bottle.

"It's not what you think," Martha said dully. "I couldn't sleep last night so I made a hot whiskey. I'm not going to turn out like your old fella."

"Sit up now and have your tea," Kate said briskly. Martha complied wordlessly.

Having seen the condition of Martha, she decided that she needed a plan of action. She went quickly downstairs, brought the big tin bath from its hook on the wall of the scullery, put it before the fire in the parlour and drew buckets of hot water from the pot beside the kitchen fire until the bath was half full. Betty Nolan's bundle of washing produced two large clean towels. She draped one over a chair in front of the fire and, before her courage deserted her, she marched up to Martha's room with the other across her arm.

"Come on now," she said firmly, removing the tray. Before Martha could object she turned back the clothes and, putting her arm under her shoulder, brought her upright. Then she swung Martha's legs out over the side of the bed. Martha opened her mouth to protest, but Kate wrapped the towel around her and propelled her towards the door. Martha was about four inches taller than her, so if she decided not to co-operate there was very little Kate could do, but Martha, taken by surprise, came along. When they reached the kitchen Kate guided her towards the parlour door.

"Why are we going up there?" Martha objected, but Kate kept moving her along. The element of surprise was working in her favour. When they had closed the parlour door behind them and she saw the bath of steaming water, Martha balked.

"Not having a bath," she asserted.

"Oh yes, you are," Kate told her with determination.

She stooped down and, catching the tail of Martha's dirty nightdress, she whipped it off over her head before Martha realised what was happening.

"You bitch!" Martha spat.

That's a good sign, Kate thought. If she was gone into a deep depression there would be no reaction, just meek acceptance.

"Now, into the bath," Kate instructed in her firmest voice, and she held out her hand to steady Martha. But Martha caught the back of the chair and got in wordlessly.

She's got a beautiful body, Kate thought; tall and slim and long-limbed, and not a spare pound on her.

"Now wash your hair as well and there's a spare bucket of water there to rinse it," Kate told her, "and I'll be back with clean clothes."

She whipped up the dirty nightdress and took it with her down to the kitchen.

"Oh God," she gasped as she collapsed into a chair by the window, "I brought that off by the skin of my teeth."

The piece of beef was on the table. Jack must have come in while they were in the parlour and like the wise man that he was he had left it and disappeared. She put it on to boil and took the stairs two at a time to get going on all that needed to be done up there. Just as well that I'm a nurse, she thought, as she stripped beds and remade them as fast as possible. A breeze whipped around her from the windows she had opened. She packed the dirty bedclothes into a bag and decided that when Jack was going to the creamery in the morning he could drop it off to Julia Deasy, who took in washing and ironing. It would not be fair to expect Betty to take on this lot. She would call to

Julia tonight and arrange it with her. Julia provided an excellent service and Kate had found her a great help when she came across awkward situations on her rounds and she needed clothes to be washed and dried fast.

When she had the beds made she brushed the rooms and stairs and closed the windows. At least things smell better, she thought, looking around her in satisfaction. She went to Martha's room and found some clean clothes and underwear and a brush and comb.

When she returned to the parlour Martha was sitting by the fire wrapped in the towels, and the bath with a grey scum on top was pulled sideways. Kate put her clothes on a chair beside her.

"Feeling better now?" she asked quietly.

"You're the real Florence Nightingale, aren't you," Martha said grimly, "washing the destitute."

"When you're dressed I'll brush your hair," Kate said matter-of-factly, dragging the bath along the floor into the front porch and then out the door where she tilted it sideways on the step and it poured out under the rose bushes. When she returned to the parlour Martha was busy brushing her hair.

"Do you want any help?" Kate asked.

"No," she was told abruptly.

Kate returned to the kitchen and started on the dinner. When she had everything simmering over the fire, she arranged the rest of the daffodils in a two-pound jam pot on the table where they hung over the sides like old women exchanging the news. Then she made a small arrangement for the Sacred Heart. As she placed the fresh bunch beneath the picture she smiled to see that Nora, despite all the trauma, had continued the house tradition of keeping seasonal flowers beside the Sacred Heart lamp. Nora was so like Nellie it was uncanny. She was grateful to Ned that he had not let Martha turn the children against Nellie and herself, and of course Jack, wise old Jack, who understood people so well, was always there to put in the good word. She often wondered if Martha could see the resemblance between Nellie and Nora. Martha, who could not bring herself to accept Nellie, and here she was now with a duplicate of her on the floor. Life played strange tricks, Kate thought. Peter was more of a mixture, with a bit of Martha and his grandfather Billy and, hopefully she thought, a bit of Ned or else there are stormy times ahead.

When she heard the latch of the back door being lifted she knew that they were home from school. She was glad to have achieved her target of having the dinner on the table. The door into the kitchen burst open and they stood there with beaming smiles of welcome. For the second time that day she had to control her reaction to appearances. Both of them looked wretched. Nora's small face seemed to have shrunk and her hair that had always been a glow of curls was now a dull, tangled mess. She was painfully thin and her clothes seemed to hang off her. Peter was gaunt, with dark smudges under his eyes. They were children who had lost the carefree look of childhood.

"Perfect timing," she told them, smiling.

"Aunty Kate!" Nora shrieked and hurled herself across the kitchen into Kate's arms.

She looked at Peter over her head and could see that he, too, was relieved to see her. The poor misfortunates, she thought, they must have gone through hell with the last few weeks, judging by the state of the house and their mother. Peter lifted his nose and sniffed appreciatively.

"Oh, that smells good," he smiled.

"Well, sit yourselves down now and we'll tuck in," she told them, and then asked, "Jack is coming, I suppose?"

"Yea," Nora laughed, "he'll be right in 'cause we could smell the dinner out in the yard."

They threw the school sacks on to the chair by the fire and made eagerly for the table.

"Well, how have you been?" Kate asked.

"Terrible," Peter said, his face darkening. "Is she still in bed?"

"No," Kate told him, smiling, "your mother is up in the parlour by the fire."

"Aunty Kate," Nora gasped in delight, "you're magic. When did you come home?"

"Last night," Kate told her, "so I was here early this morning."

"You've done a lot of work," Nora said slowly, looking around the house taking it all in. "How did you get so much done in one day?"

"By half killing herself," Jack answered, coming in the door. "And by God but that dinner smells good."

"Well, sit yourself down, Jack, and we'll see if it puts hair on your chest," Kate told him.

"I don't want it to put hair on my chest," Nora protested, much to Peter's amusement.

It was a pleasure to watch them scoff the big bowls of soup.

"There's eating and drinking in this," Jack said and added, winking at Nora, "better than fried eggs any day."

"Ah, Jack, the fried eggs were all right too," Nora told him loyally.

"Well, we were getting a bit tired of them," Peter

admitted, "but they were the best we could manage with her in bed and Kate away."

"Aunty Kate," Nora wanted to know, "what were you doing away for so long?"

"A course about people with mental problems," Kate told her.

"That would be most of us," Jack decided.

"Not you, Jack," Kate smiled, "you're the sanest person that I know. How are things out in the yard – are many of the cows calved?"

"Most of them," Peter answered for him, "and we manage the milking between us morning and evening."

"It's no joke having to milk that many before school every morning, Peter," Kate told him admiringly.

"We manage," he said proudly. "Dada told me once that he did it after his father died."

And before he died, Jack thought, remembering Billy's mornings in bed after late night drinking sessions. He caught Kate's eye across the table and knew that she was thinking the same thing.

"Well, how were things in school today?" he queried, to change the subject.

"We had Fr Brady," Nora smiled. "He's just lovely and drives Miss Buckley mad because he won't ask catechism questions. We had a concert today and he sang himself, a funny song only I can't remember the name of it."

"That went down well with old sour puss, I'd say," Jack commented, remembering her since the night of the funeral.

As if the same thought ran through Nora's mind and brought back that day, she asked, earnestly gazing at Kate across the table, "Do you remember, Aunty Kate, the money that you gave me for Dada's pipe?"

"I do indeed," Kate told her, feeling the dull pain tighten in her chest. It seemed like a hundred years ago.

"Well, do you think that he knew afterwards that I was going to buy it for him."

"I'm sure that he did, Norry," she said gently.

"I'm glad of that," Nora told her. "I thought he would but I wanted to make sure. You know that you told me to pray to him if I wanted anything and that he would hear me in heaven?"

"Yes," Kate said quietly.

"Well, you were right, because he sorted out a problem that I had in school after I asking him."

So that problem is solved, Jack thought; he had wondered a few times about it.

Nora continued seriously, "I'm praying for something else now, that he'll look after us and won't let Mossgrove be sold."

"Mossgrove be sold!" Peter gasped in horror. "What the hell put that into your head, Norry?"

"Kitty Conway said that Mom will sell Mossgrove and that we'll be all out in the road like tinkers," Nora told them.

"That's rubbish," Peter told her scornfully, "and don't you mind the Conways."

"It would take that crowd to think of a thing like that," Jack said furiously.

Then quietly the door of the kitchen opened slowly and all their eyes swung in that direction. Martha stood there looking at them with a strange smile on her face.

CHAPTER EIGHT

"You'll have to get help into Mossgrove," Betty Nolan declared firmly.

Kate and herself were sitting in Nolans' bright airy kitchen having tea. She was a large, fair-haired woman with a sunny disposition who said exactly what she thought, and she and Kate had been friends since childhood.

"You're right there," Kate agreed. "There is just too much work for Peter and Jack."

"And Peter is only an overgrown lad anyway," Betty asserted.

"He wouldn't like to hear you say that," Kate told her.

"I know," Betty agreed, "but you know what I mean. His father had to become a man before his time, and now Peter is caught in the same trap. But this time it's worse because Ned had Nellie as a back-up, whereas Martha is a different kettle of fish altogether. You wouldn't know what way that one would jump."

"Well, you know," Kate told her, "that I could never really figure Martha out.

"Well, I never had that problem," Betty said firmly. "She's a fine, tough, selfish woman, and you'd do well not to forget that. I know now that she's been through hell, but I doubt if that is going to change the nature of the woman. You could finish up killing yourself struggling to keep that place going as well as trying to do your own job, and what you'll get from Martha in the heel of the hunt is a fine good kick in the arse. You'd do well to remember that now!"

"You could be right," Kate agreed, "but then there is Jack to be thought of and the children."

"Of course, that's her whip hand isn't it?" Betty declared. "She knows that where Jack and the children are concerned she has you by the scruff of the neck, as she had Nellie before you."

"It's a bit like the fox, the goose and the sheaf of oats isn't it?" Kate said ruefully.

"Yes, but the first thing for this goose to do," Betty told her, "is to get help into Mossgrove. Young Davy Shine back the road is home from England and his mother told me that he would stay if he got a job."

"Is Davy home from England?" Kate asked.

"Sure, he was at the funeral – didn't you meet him then?" Betty told her in a surprised voice.

"I think that I went blind and deaf for those days," Kate said; "it's all a blur in my mind."

"Maybe it's better that way," Betty said comfortingly, putting her hand over Kate's on the table. "Nature has its own way of dealing with hurts."

Kate felt a lump in her throat but she swallowed hard. This was no morning for crying: there was too much to be done.

"You're right about Davy," she agreed; "he would be ideal for Mossgrove."

"Didn't he work there as a young fellow with Ned and Jack?" Betty asked.

"He did indeed, and we were very fond of him. The Shines were always honest and hard-working, and Peter and himself got on well, so we'd have no problem there. But what about Martha?"

"Kate, will you stop pussyfooting around," Betty said impatiently. "Just get that young fellow into Mossgrove and worry about Martha afterwards. You'll be the cause of killing Jack. He's overworked and, worse still, he's worried sick about the work that he just can't get around to."

"You're right, of course. Sometimes I can't see things clearly where Mossgrove is concerned."

"Well, anytime you get dim vision, call to me and I'll clear the fog."

"Betty," Kate said gratefully, "you make everything seem so straightforward. I'll call to Mossgrove now when I'm passing and tell Jack, and then I'll call to Shines on my way to Conways."

"What the hell is taking you to Conways?" Betty demanded in alarm.

"Old Molly Conway must have cut her leg badly, and Doc Twomey sent the girl who replaced me to dress it twice a week, so it was on my list this morning."

"Well, aren't they going to get a surprise to see you arriving!"

"There wasn't a Phelan inside that gate for three generations, I'd say," Kate said slowly. "My grandfather was the last one."

"And it cost him dearly."

"Well, that's all in the past now."

"People around here have long memories," Betty told her.

"Well, I'd better get moving anyway," Kate decided, rising from the table. "I've a good few calls to make. Thanks for the tea and the chat: it did me good."

As she cycled away from Nolans', Kate thought that Betty as usual had the situation sized up pretty well. Getting Davy Shine was a brilliant idea. It would take a lot of pressure off Jack.

When she met Jack, going down the boreen to Mossgrove, he thought so as well.

"I'll call to Shines now when I'm passing. When will I tell him to come?" she asked.

"Oh, the sooner the better," Jack said in a relieved voice; "tomorrow morning if possible."

"What about Martha?" Kate asked.

"Leave that to me," Jack decided. " 'Twill be all my idea."

"How is she today?"

"Up, thanks be to God!" Jack said fervently. "You did the trick over the weekend. There is no way that you are going to get the run of her house."

"I don't care for what reason," Kate declared. "Once she's out of the bed at all, she'll keep moving and gradually things will work out."

"Hopefully," Jack said.

"I won't call in at all now," Kate told him, turning her bike around; "she wouldn't want to see me anyway so I'll keep going."

"God bless you, Kate." Jack smiled with understanding and headed off down towards the house.

Toby barked inside the wall as she bolted the farm gate beside the cottage.

"Hello, Toby," she said, "you're minding the house for Jack?"

He wagged his tail when he recognised the voice and she put her hand in through the bars of Jack's gate to pat his head. He danced with delight and licked her hand in appreciation.

As she cycled along she was so intent on her thoughts that she had sped past Sarah Jones' cottage before she realised that Sarah was standing at the gate and looking after her in surprise. Kate braked and swung around, coming to a stop with a scatter of gravel.

"Sorry, Sarah," she said, "I almost didn't see you. I was away in a world of my own."

"Not surprising," Sarah said sympathetically, putting an arm around her shoulders and giving her a soft kiss on the cheek.

"It's so good to see you, Sarah," Kate told her, smiling into the caring face of the little woman who had been her mother's best friend.

"How are they below?" Sarah asked, nodding in the direction of the farm.

"Not bad, I suppose," Kate answered slowly, "but it's going to take a long time."

"It's such a relief to Jack to have you back," Sarah said; "he's nearly gone demented and poor Agnes Lehane is at her wits' end over Martha taking to the bed and leaving the children to their own devices."

"Well, at least she's out of the bed now anyway," Kate told her.

"And how are you yourself?" Sarah asked kindly.

"Oh, Sarah, it's such a relief to be back. I miss him around every corner here, but at least it's real. Away I felt as if I was living in an artificial bubble."

"It's easier to grieve in you own place," Sarah said; "it's more natural somehow. How was the course?"

"You'd have enjoyed it," Kate told her; "you could probably have taught them a thing or two with all your experience."

"Well, I suppose you learn something about people in thirty years of delivering their babies and laying out their dead," Sarah admitted.

"Probably a lot more than I'll ever know."

"Over the years it will come to you too," Sarah assured her. "In our job you see people stripped of pretence. I've seen family funerals where all the hidden cracks opened up and deep-rooted emotions buried for years floated to the surface."

"Death and grief throw normal life off the tracks, don't they," Kate said thoughtfully. "You're sort of swimming in uncharted emotional waters and the people around you are doing the same thing."

"Something like that," Sarah agreed, "but I best not be delaying you, you probably have calls to make."

"Yes," Kate said, "I'm going back to Conways' now."

"That should be interesting," Sarah said evenly.

"I've never been there before," Kate told her, "but you must have often been called."

"Only when they had no other choice," Sarah told her. "The Conways like to sort out their own problems. That Matt Conway is a strange man."

"It's his mother that I'm calling to see – she cut her leg."

"Old Molly is getting on a bit," Sarah mused, "and she's

not the worst of them. My guess is that they didn't call the doctor until blood poisoning was threatening."

"That's exactly what Doc Twomey said."

"Some things never change. But I won't delay you any more now, and Kate – it's such a lovely spring day – try to look around you as you cycle along. No good in having your head down, it will only give you backache."

"Right, Sarah," Kate agreed.

As she cycled along she took Sarah's advice. Sarah had been such a staunch friend of Nellie's. She probably knows more about my family than myself, Kate thought, but unlike Betty Nolan, Sarah was one to keep her opinions to herself.

She cycled slowly, taking in her surroundings, and her mood lightened a little. She noticed the soft green shoots ready to uncurl on the beech trees that Ned had planted along the boundary ditch. He would never see them fully grown now, but they would reach their full height in Peter's lifetime. Ned had always said that you planted trees for future generations.

She came off her bike and stood looking up at the tall young trees and felt that the spirit of Ned was in them. She climbed up on to the ditch and ran her fingers over the cool, smooth bark. From this vantage point she could see along the entire valley. She remembered Mark once telling her that they lived in a horseshoe-shaped valley. He was right. The road curved left above at the school and it ran parallel at the opposite side of the valley, so the houses at both sides looked across at each other with the river in between. He had pointed out that there were seven nails in a horseshoe and there were seven houses in the valley. Starting at the end of the hill there was Nolans', Jack's,

Mossgrove, and Sarah Jones' at one side. Then above at the turn stood the school, to match the clip of the horseshoe, and across the river was Shines', Lehanes' and Conways'. The full horseshoe! Mark had got his perspective when he was painting a picture of the valley. Since he had told her that she now saw it through his eyes.

"Kate," a voice behind her said, "I'm glad you're back."

"Jesus Christ!" Kate gasped, swinging around to look down into the smiling face of Mark, who was clambering up on to the ditch beside her. "Mark, you frightened the living daylights out of me!"

"Sorry, Kate," he said, putting his arm around her shoulder and giving her a quick hug. "I didn't mean to frighten you."

"Oh, I know that," Kate assured him, "and the strange thing is that I was just thinking of you and your horseshoe theory about the valley."

She had to take a step sideways to look up at Mark. Incredibly thin and well over six foot tall, he wore his black hair down around his shoulders, which earned him the title of the Apostle in the locality. Kate often wondered at the mystery that he and Martha were brother and sister. Martha was dark, deep and driven, whereas Mark was gentle and almost childlike in his simplicity. Some of the locals regarded him as a "duine le Dia", one of "God's people", but Kate felt that through some strange mixture of genes he was an artistic genius. He had no interest in farming, so the small family farm was rented out in conacre.

He was lucky to have been christened Mark because it had changed his life. His maternal grandmother had had two distant relatives living in the village. They were known to everybody as the Miss Jacksons. Kate could remember them as two tall, dignified old ladies dressed in black satin and furs who walked grandly to the front seat of the church every Sunday. They filled the air around them with the smell of faded lavender and mothballs. Jack had always said that the Jacksons had "old money". They had an older brother in America and a much-loved younger brother who had been lost at sea. This brother had been called Mark, and his death had grieved them deeply. When they became aware that there was another Mark in the family, even though not a close relative, they had taken him under their wing. The name Mark meant a lot to them. They had arranged with an artist friend of theirs to give young Mark special tutoring. They had lived in refined comfort in the largest house in the village and had little to do with the locals. They went away occasionally on foreign trips, often taking Mark with them, which made him the envy of every child in the parish but also set him apart from them. Mark spent his time painting and writing music. Old Tady Mikey, a travelling fiddle player, had taught him to play as a child and it seemed to have awoken a hidden world in Mark's soul, which had led him on to sketching. It was his sketching that fascinated Kate.

"Mark, have you been doing any drawing lately?" she asked him now.

"Yea," he admitted shyly. "I was actually finishing something that I started a good few years ago."

"Will we have a look at it?" she asked.

Mark pulled the canvas bag on his back around to the front, poked into it and produced a large sketching pad.

"Ned bought me this," he told Kate as he turned back the cover.

The drawing was of Ned planting the trees just beside

them. Kate drew in her breath sharply and there was a tightening in her stomach. She felt that Ned could almost step off the page.

"Mark," she said, looking at him with awe-filled eyes, "you really captured him."

"Ned was a good friend," he said simply.

"It shows," said Kate.

"Would you like to have it?" he asked quietly.

"Oh Mark," she said, "I would love it but . . . but maybe Martha would like it."

"You know that Martha doesn't like my drawings," he told her, a shadow coming over his face.

"Mark, I would be so happy to have it," she said gratefully. "I will have it framed and hang it on my wall. Thank you."

"There is nobody that I would prefer to have it than you," he told her. "You can't take it now on your bike, but I will drop it in to you some night."

She knew that Mark had a habit of walking around by night because, he had told her, he found it easier to think things out in the quietness of the night and sometimes he got inspiration at night.

"How have you been, Mark?" she asked.

"A bit bothered," he admitted.

"That makes two of us," she said ruefully.

"With Ned gone I have no one to talk to," he told her.

She knew that Ned and himself used to spend hours walking the fields together talking. Ned would never listen to a word of criticism of Mark, and none of the neighbours would criticise him in Ned's presence.

"I can understand that," she told him. "I feel as if some part of me has died with Ned."

"I always envied you and Ned," he told her.

"Why?"

"Because growing up you always had such fun together. Martha and I were poles apart by comparison."

"Maybe Ned and I were too close," she said; "maybe it would be easier now if I had not loved him so much."

"Oh, don't regret it, Kate," he told her. "It was a great blessing. I wish Martha and I had it. She was always critical of me and I felt threatened by her."

"Families are strange things."

"They could destroy you."

"I've seen it happen," Kate agreed.

"Joining the Phelans was the best thing that ever happened to us, though I'm not so sure that it worked both ways."

"Well, I'd better be going," Kate told him. "I've a good few calls to make."

"I'm so glad that we ran into each other, and it's great to have you back."

"We'll have to keep each other going," Kate said. "Ned would not have wanted us to fall asunder."

"That's for sure," he agreed, "so I think that I'll walk down to the river. I find the sound of the water comforting."

She watched him saunter down the fields with his satchel hanging off his shoulder like a fishing bag and his long black hair flowing behind him.

When she knocked on Shines' door it was whipped open by Ellen Shine, a dour-faced, sharp-voiced little woman with a cigarette in the corner of her mouth and a skimpy head scarf knotted under a hairy chin.

"Davy," she screeched over her shoulder when Kate asked for him.

Davy appeared with a matching cigarette, but there the resemblance ended because he towered over his mother, was twice her width and had the round moon face of his father and generations of Shines before him.

"Yerra, Kate, how're 'ou?" A broad smile lit up his fine, honest face like a semi-circle, and when she asked him about coming to work in Mossgrove the smile became a circle.

"Grand job," he told her, which meant that he would be there in the morning bright and early. Ellen Shine did not believe in having any son of hers lying in bed when there was work to be done.

As she cycled past Mark's home she decided on impulse that she would call in for a few minutes to see his mother. Nana Lehane, as the children called her, was a small, fine-boned woman with a serene face. It was easy to see where Martha's beauty had come from, but in personality they were two different types of people. For some reason, Agnes always put Kate in mind of the Virgin Mary. Mark and herself were ideal occupants of the same house.

"Kate, how nice to see you," she smiled. "I heard that you were back and that you were straightening things out."

"News travels fast."

"Jack came and told me the good news because he knew that I was worried. I gave up and came home early in the time because I could make no hand of Martha," she confessed, "and it was beginning to get me down."

"You did right to come home, Agnes," Kate told her, "and with your asthma you could finish up laid low yourself."

"That's what I was afraid of," the older woman confessed, "and I don't like leaving Mark too long on his own because at times he simply forgets to eat."

"I just met him over the road now and he has done the most wonderful drawing of Ned. He really has a great talent."

"He has, I suppose," his mother sighed, "but it's not much good to him here. But that's enough about Mark. Will you come in for a cup of tea?"

"I won't just now because I must go over to dress Molly Conway's leg."

"Be careful of their dogs," Agnes warned her. "I always think that they're dangerous because they're half-starved."

"Thanks for warning me," Kate said, "and don't worry about Martha – I think that she'll be all right now."

"Thank God," her mother said.

Now, down to business, Kate thought, as she cycled on towards Conways'. She was not looking forward to facing into a house where she knew she would be far from welcome. All her life, standing where it did on the hill across the river valley from Mossgrove, surrounded by sheds and rusty-roofed outhouses, Conways' had spelt trouble in Mossgrove. She had backed Jack into a corner years ago and demanded the whole story.

Her grandfather Edward Phelan and Rory Conway had gone to school together and had been close friends. Both farms were doing well, but Rory Conway for some reason hit a bad patch. The Conways had never been great farmers. Grandfather came to his rescue and secured him in the bank for five hundred pounds, which was a lot of money back then. But in farming things always turn around and Grandfather knew that it was only a matter of time before Rory Conway would get straightened out and he would be able to pay off the bank. But when Rory

Conway got on his feet he got greedy and did not pay back the bank, and grandfather had to cover the debt.

A few years afterwards Conway bought two fields from a farmer who bounded them at the far side of the hill away from Mossgrove, and he bought it with the money that should have cleared the debt in the bank. Grandfather had a great heart, but he had a temper to match. There was no one going to treat him like that and get away with it. He went and he measured the two fields that Rory Conway had bought, which were at the other side of the hill and too far away to be any addition to Mossgrove. But he solved that problem by measuring the same amount of Conway land along the riverbank beside his own farm and fencing it off. He decided that it was a fair return for his money. Conway did not take that lying down. Grandfather took Conway to court and won his case, and the land became Mossgrove land, but it had caused trouble ever since.

Now, as she turned in Conways' laneway, she told herself to forget past history and just remember that she was the district nurse here to see a patient. As she opened the gate of the farmyard, dogs came bounding in all directions, but she held her ground, and having parked her bike against the wall she walked across the yard with barking dogs all around her. She liked dogs and was never afraid of them, and apart from that there was no way that she was going to give the Conways the satisfaction of calling for help. She guessed that Matt Conway was probably watching her from one of the sheds.

Then he appeared and lumbered across the yard towards her. He had the gait of a bear because his back sloped forward and a stumpy butt of a neck stuck out. He had a large red face beneath strings of ginger hair combed across a bald head.

"What do you want?" he growled contemptuously.

"Nothing," Kate told him sharply. "I'm here to dress your mother's leg."

"Where's that other nurse?" he demanded, coming up so close to her that she had to step back to avoid physical contact.

"She's finished now," Kate said icily, drawing herself up to her full height and looking him straight in the eye.

"Well, we don't want the likes of you here."

"That's all right," Kate said, turning to go; "when your mother gets gangrene from the blood poisoning and has to have her leg amputated, you can tell her that."

"You'd better go in so," he snarled, "but no poking around into things that don't concern you."

"I'm here to dress a wound, that's all," she told him, and he turned on his heel and, calling the dogs, disappeared back into the shed. Kate knew that he would wait there until she had gone.

When she knocked on the door it was opened by his wife Biddy, a wizened, nervous little woman who would not look her straight in the face. Does he beat her? Kate wondered. The kitchen was dark, smoky and smelly, and she decided that it was a long time since they had opened the windows. Biddy pointed to a door at the end of the kitchen.

"She's down there," she said.

When she opened the door her nostrils were assailed with an assortment of stale smells, predominantly of stagnant urine. In the bed old Molly Conway sat like an enormous beached whale.

"Well, if it isn't the small dark Phelan one," she boomed; "how well Matt left you in."

"Would you rather get gangrene and have your leg amputated?" Kate asked sharply.

"Oh, saucy like all the Phelans," the old lady laughed scornfully, and her huge body shook like a giant jelly. "Come on, my girl, and do what you came for."

Kate unrolled the dressing and found the wound to be healing well. As she put on a fresh dressing she remarked, "That was a bad gash. What happened?"

"Mind your own business," was the answer.

"You're a tough old bird," Kate told her.

"Ah! I'd want to be tough to spend my life living across the river from your crowd. But maybe with young Ned gone now 'twill be easier to talk to ye." There was a veiled threat in the old woman's voice.

CHAPTER NINE

KATE DREW THE comfortable armchair closer to the fire. She watched the flames lick up through the logs and sods of turf, and then, without warning, a wave of utter desolation swept over her. The pain of Ned was like a dark stagnant pool in the middle of her stomach. It had been there since the day of the accident and occasionally it erupted and a black lava of depression flooded through her. She dreaded these times. Her hands started to shake and she thought that her heart was going to pound up her throat and choke her. A cold sweat broke out on her forehead. She sat paralysed in the chair.

"Easy now, Kate," she told herself, "this will pass. It has passed before."

Should she have some of Jack's cure? But she was afraid to open the bottle. Once started, she might not be able to stop. The memory of her father's drinking, and what it had done to all of them, haunted her. She could not forget lying in the bed over the kitchen in Mossgrove and listening as he demanded money off her mother, and Nellie's voice full of anguish trying to reason with him. Then, hearing the knob of her bedroom door turning and seeing the shadow of Ned standing there in the darkness listening as well.

Ned had been part of her life. Every decision she had ever made she had discussed with him. Since he died she felt like a house with no gable end wall, all her securities washed away and all her vulnerabilities exposed. She worried about Mossgrove, Jack, Martha and the children. Jack was getting old and Mossgrove was his whole life. Martha did not share his feeling for the place. Hard to expect that, really, when she had not been brought up there, but then neither had Nellie and she had loved the place and made it her own. Could Mossgrove be kept going now? If Martha wanted to do it she could run Mossgrove as well as Nellie had, but maybe she did not want to? Maybe Betty Nolan was right and she should not think that it was her responsibility. But Ned would have expected her to do it for the memory of the old man and Nellie, but most of all for Jack, who had given his whole life to Mossgrove. Thoughts chased each other around her head.

She looked up at the picture of the old man. You didn't have it easy either, she told him; the betrayal by Rory Conway over the money must have hurt. It was a lot of money at that time and you wouldn't have secured him in the bank if you had not trusted him. But you settled that score and moved forward. Jack says that I'm like you. Well, she thought, during the coming months we will find out one way or the other.

She sat for a while and slowly the panic subsided. When she felt a bit easier in herself she went back to the kitchen to collect her tray to place it on a low table beside her.

When she got home at night the first thing she did was to light the fire, and then when she had her dinner eaten in the kitchen, the front room had warmed up and she liked to bring a pot of tea in here and to sit in the comforting glow and unwind after the day.

She was glad that it was Friday, because now she had the *Kilmeen Eagle* to distract her from her thoughts. It was the local weekly paper, and while the national papers came daily and were partly read by most people, page after page of the *Kilmeen Eagle* was absorbed by everybody. It was a window into the activities of the locality. If you made it into the *Kilmeen Eagle* you became the topic of conversation around the village and parish of Kilmeen and surrounding parishes. She threw an extra log on the fire and, easing off her shoes, placed her tired feet on an old brocade footstool. When Nellie had moved into the parlour in Mossgrove she had used it with her rocking chair. The fact that her mother had used it for so many years made it special.

"Always put your feet up, Kate," she used to say; "helps your circulation, and as well as that it's good to have your whole body off the ground."

Just as Kate settled herself more comfortably back into the chair and opened the paper, there was a knock on the door. Who could that be, she thought wearily, rising reluctantly out of the chair and at the same time doing some mental arithmetic on the babies due and the old people who could have fallen ill.

When she opened the door and saw Dr Twomey on the doorstep she smiled with relief. "Oh, I'm so glad it's you, Robert, I was just thinking what baby was ready to arrive or if somebody had taken a bad turn."

"I knew that's what you'd be thinking," he smiled.

They had worked together for about seven years. Though in his sixties, he looked far younger with his slight build and pale complexion under an unruly mop of thick black hair that was only slightly flecked with grey. He had been their family doctor in Mossgrove since Kate was a child.

"To what do I owe this pleasure," she smiled, pleased that he had called. "You're not given to making house calls after hours unless it's a special case."

"Ah, you're special, Kate."

"Were you not worried that you'd spoil my good name, calling in the dead of night and me living alone?" she teased.

"I'd say now that Julia across the road has me under surveillance all right," he told her, "because the usual curtain flicked as I knocked."

"Julia is my chaperone, watches my comings and my goings, and as well as that she has a detailed record in her head of all the patients coming to the dispensary next door."

"Such service," he smiled, "and all for free – you could only get it in Kilmeen."

"Make yourself comfortable there now and I'll get another cup," she told him, going to a china-filled cabinet behind her. It was good to have his comforting presence in the room.

"The best of china," he smiled when he saw the rose-patterned cup and saucer.

"Only the best for the boss," she told him.

"I think that you do more bossing than I do," he smiled, and continued seriously: "These are tough times for you,

Kate, and I know it's an old cliché, but it will get easier, and with the spring here now you'll be able to get out into your garden. There's healing in the earth. I know that when Joan died the garden preserved my sanity."

"How long is she dead now?" she asked quietly.

"Five years," he said.

"You know, Robert," Kate mused, "you sympathise with someone when they have a bereavement and you do feel sorry for them, but it's only when it's your own case that you can really understand. I think that I'll never again say 'sorry for your trouble' so casually to anybody. I always thought that it was a pretty stupid phrase, but no longer."

"You won't always stay as tuned in to bereavement, Kate, as you are now," he cautioned. "In a few years time you'll have lost this sensitivity. Strange thing about grief, it's almost as if it removes our hard protective layer and makes us very vulnerable, but it also brings about a more open view and awareness of other things.

"We could discuss it for ever," she told him, "but there is no understanding the mystery of death. I told Nora to pray to Ned and he has solved some problem for her so she is convinced now that she has a man in heaven simply waiting to do her bidding."

"Well, if it helps her through this time that's a good thing, and who knows but she's right!" he smiled and continued, "But Kate, I'm here for a totally selfish reason."

"I don't believe that. There isn't a selfish bone in your body."

"Well, thank you," he said in surprise, "but I need to discuss an idea with somebody, though it's not my idea, it's David's. You know he'd love to get out of Dublin and back to Kilmeen."

"And what's the idea?" Kate asked, thinking that she too would be interested in having him back.

"What would you think of the idea of starting a secondary school in Kilmeen?" he asked, watching her closely.

Kate's mouth opened in amazement and then a look of delight washed over her face. She sat up straight in her chair and the *Kilmeen Eagle* slid to the floor forgotten.

"I think that it would be simply wonderful," she told him with conviction. "Think of the opportunities it would open up for the children around here. Not everybody can afford boarding school and the nuns over in Ross, where I cycled for two years, can only provide a commercial course and teach music."

"So you think that it might work?" he asked.

"I don't see why not," she declared with enthusiasm. "Oh, I know there will be all the usual oppositions and complaints that go with everything new, but this school can only do good."

"You think so?"

"Of course," she said emphatically; "even from my own point of view it would mean that Peter and Nora could have a secondary school education and Peter could still help on the farm at the weekends. I know that Ned was toying with the idea of sending him to boarding school but hated the thought of him being away. As well as that he was worried that he might grow away from the farm in boarding school, but going in and out to Kilmeen every day he would still be in touch with things."

"That makes sense," he agreed.

"When is he thinking of starting?" Kate asked.

"Take it easy, Kate," he smiled, "he's only thinking about it."

"This will bring new life into Kilmeen," Kate declared enthusiastically. "If he got moving now he could open in September. Has he thought of a suitable place?"

"Well, I don't think that he has thought that far, but I've been doing a bit of thinking since I got his letter," he told her. "What would you say to that old house of the Miss Jacksons up at the cross. It's a real barracks of a place and it's been empty since the last one died."

"Oh, that's in perfect condition," she assured him, "because there was money left in the will to maintain it. Julia gives it the once over every couple of weeks. It's a fine house. As far as I can remember there are four big rooms downstairs and an outside toilet, and upstairs there are three huge rooms and a bathroom."

"By God, Kate," he smiled, "but you have the measure of it."

"You know that I'm interested in old houses," she told him, "and that's a particularly grand one. I had it half in mind when I was looking for a house, but it was a bit big, and as well as that the solicitor said that they were not interested in selling, only in renting."

"You have the homework done on it."

"Well," she said, "all I know is that it's owned by a grandnephew of the Miss Jacksons in America and he thinks that one day he might come to Ireland, but in the meanwhile he would rent it. I wanted to buy, so it was no good to me."

"How would he feel about a school, though, and a herd of young people charging through his ancestral home?" he mused.

"He might well be horrified," Kate decided, "but then again it might appeal to his Irish-American sense of nostalgia to have his house educating the young of Ireland. It could work in David's favour."

"It might," he agreed.

"That nephew should be a nice man," Kate continued, "because his aunts were two wonderful old ladies. They were very interested in art and had a lot of paintings that were shipped to that grandnephew in America when they died. They were so kind to Mark Lehane when he was young and arranged special art classes for him and took him on trips with them to visit galleries. They thought that he had wonderful talent. So if this grandnephew is anything like them, he should be very easy to deal with."

"I suppose David's first step would be to go to old Hobbs the solicitor over in Ross," he said slowly, "and ask him to get in contact with this nephew."

"He'd want to put the pressure on old Hobbs," Kate warned, "because he never heard of hurry and it could take him six months to write to America." A look of relieved satisfaction came over her face: "Do you know something, Robert, I think that I've that nephew's address upstairs somewhere, because he wrote to me at the time that I was interested in the house."

"God, that would be great."

"You sit there now and you can be reading the local scandals in the *Kilmeen Eagle* and I'll have a search," she said, picking the paper up off the floor and handing it to him.

"Local scandals is right," he smiled; "stolen calves and pub fights won't do much to raise my blood pressure."

"Sometimes it can have surprise items," she told him as she left the room.

Upstairs in her spare back bedroom where she kept all

her old correspondence, she opened the deep press that was full of neatly stacked boxes. Now, she thought, an American letter about that house would have come four years ago, so it would be behind all her mother's things that were stored away in boxes waiting for the wet day when she would have the courage and the stamina to sort through them. She had kept putting it on the long finger, and now with Ned gone it would be put on a longer finger still. But at least they were safe in the press and one day she would get around to them. She lifted out some of the boxes and moved others around until she found what she was looking for, a tartan tin box with a pipe-smoking man on the hinged cover. It had been her grandfather's tobacco box and in it he had kept his pipes, tobacco, matches and pipe cleaners; it had sat while he was alive on the shelf over the fireplace in Mossgrove, and as a child she had loved to look into it and to sniff the sweet wild smell of his Garryowen tobacco. Because she was so fond of it, Nellie had given it to her and she had used it for storing old letters. Now as she flicked through the envelopes she could still smell the subdued whiff of aromatic Garryowen. She found the long American envelope with the blue and red edgings. She put it in her pocket, replaced everything as it had been and came downstairs to find Robert deeply immersed in the *Kilmeen Eagle.*

"Any success?" he asked, folding down the paper.

"Here you are," she told him, holding the envelope aloft.

"God, but you're one organised woman to be able to put your hands on it so fast," he declared.

"Not sure that I like the sound of that," she told him. "Over-tidy people can become a bit of a pain, and I've to watch myself, living alone as I do, that I don't become paranoid about it."

He grinned at her and sang:

"Tidy womaneen,
Tidy womaneen,
Tidy womaneen sasta."

"That's exactly what I mean," she said ruefully.

"Well, in this case it worked in our favour," he told her. "I'd hate to be looking for a letter that I got four years ago."

She looked at him appreciatively as he sat across from her in the deep armchair. He had eased off his shoes and his stockinged feet rested on Nellie's footstool. She thought what a kind man he was and how good it would be for him if David came back to Kilmeen. He and Hannah, his housekeeper, would have company in his rambling old house at the end of the village street. Busy at his practice and devoted to several hobbies, he would never be dependent on his children for company, but still he would relish having his son at home. His six children were scattered throughout different countries, but David with his easy-going temperament was the one who was most like himself. He resembled him closely, and in his father's face one could see what David would look like at sixty.

"What are you hatching up now?" he asked. "You look as if you're staring into your crystal ball."

"Thinking how nice for you it would be to have David home."

"And for you too hopefully," he smiled.

"Well, we'll wait and see on that one," she hedged.

"Yea," he agreed, "the school is the first step, so I'd better not start counting my chickens before they're hatched."

"Ah well, no harm in gathering the eggs anyway," she smiled. "When is David coming down next?"

"He'll be down for the Easter holidays, and then I suppose he'll check out the home ground. I think he's been making enquiries with the department in Dublin about the nuts and bolts of putting the whole thing together."

"So he kind of has things moving in some ways?" Kate asked.

"Well, yes and no," the Doc said. "He's been making tentative enquiries through Mick Bradley, the Master's son – he's working in the department, you know, and they went to school together. So that could be a help."

"I can see no problem," Kate told him, "but you seem doubtful enough. Is there something else bothering you?"

"There is something, and it's like a thorn at the back of my mind," he said scratching his dark head. "I've this vague notion that I heard a rumour years ago that the old P.P. here guaranteed the nuns when they came to Ross that no school would be started here to take away their pupils."

"But they only teach girls and they only teach secretarial work," Kate protested.

"Well, I suppose at the time it was better than nothing," he said.

"I doubt that agreement would stand now," Kate asserted; "sure, the Ross nuns are there with years."

"I don't know, Kate, but old agreements are strange things," he said slowly, "and old Fr Burke is as stubborn as a mule and as odd as two left shoes. If this was his idea we'd stand a better chance. He thinks that any idea that isn't his idea is a bad idea."

"Amen to that," she agreed; "he's a real megalomaniac.

But we have Fr Brady and I'd say that he'd be all for the new school because he's a real live wire," she said.

"But you know," he sighed regretfully, "it's the old fellow who has the power."

"And what about us: have we no power or no say?" Kate demanded, her colour rising in annoyance. "It's our parish and it's our children."

"Aha! the old Grandfather Phelan isn't dead yet," Robert laughed, looking up at the picture over the mantelpiece. "You know, I always admired him that he didn't leave the Conways get away with that stroke they pulled on him."

"Some day they are watching to get even," Kate told him, "and now could be the time."

"How is Martha?" he asked.

"I think that she is getting better," Kate said. "I know that I should feel sorry for her, but I think that I'll never be able to forget the way she treated Nellie and the anguish that it caused Ned."

"It's hard to see your mother wronged," he agreed.

"But I could say nothing because if I did she took it out on Ned, and that kept my mouth shut."

"Well, it's all over now," he said, "and Martha's mourning could be painful because in bereavement the strangest things come back to haunt us."

"You know, I would like to be inside in Martha's head for one day because I feel that if I could understand her it would be a big help," Kate said.

"Might not be any great help to you, as some people are not always sure themselves why they behave the way they do," he told her.

"You sound like the lecturer on our course," she smiled.

"Well, on that note I had better be going," he told her, rising from the chair, "and let your chaperone from across the road go to bed, because she can't go until she sees me out first."

"Your company did me good," she told him, rising and putting her hand on his arm. "It was a bad night until you came."

"I thought that when I came in," he said, looking down at her and covering her hand with his, "so I'm glad that I called, even if the purpose was primarily selfish."

"I wouldn't call it selfish," she said, "because if this works out it will benefit the entire district."

"Well," he said, moving towards the door, "hopefully it will all work out, so I'll take this letter with me and that will be the first step in the right direction."

"Thanks for calling, Robert," she said. "As well as passing away a bit of the night you've given me food for thought. It's good to have something fresh to think about."

"We might have a bit of a struggle on our hands. . ."

"Once we get the bit between our teeth, it won't be easy to stop us."

"I've always admired that in you, Kate," he smiled; "you've great spunk."

"Often got me into hot water," she told him, "but I'm a great believer that if you want something badly enough you've got to be prepared to go for it. This house, for example, was a bit of a struggle, even with help from Ned, but now it's mine and I'm delighted with it."

"You made a great job of it," he said, looking around in admiration. "I remember coming in here to old Tom, and it was dark and gloomy. It's very different even though you made no enormous changes."

"There was no need to really, because as you know he had some lovely old pieces of furniture that came with the house. When they were cleaned up and polished I was simply delighted with them," she said, running her hand lovingly over a large oak sideboard that stretched the full length of the wall behind the door.

"It's a different house," he said, opening the door into the hall and standing at the foot of the stairs to admire the warm yellow wood off which Kate had stripped layers of paint. "The entire atmosphere of a house can be changed with a bit of know-how." They had reached the front door and he stood looking down at her with a concerned look on his face. "Kate, try not to worry too much about Mossgrove," he advised. "You need time to heal." He put his arms around her and hugged her before he opened the door and disappeared into the night.

Kate went back into the front room and sat thinking by the dying fire. So David might be coming back to Kilmeen. There was a time when the news would have put her on cloud nine. That was when she had thought that nothing could ever come between them. They had been such friends growing up, more than friends. He was easy to talk to and they had spent so much time together chatting about everything and laughing at nothing. She smiled to remember the evening that they had walked across the bog and got lost. A mist had come down and darkness had fallen, and Jack had found them in the small hours in a sheltered corner trying to keep each other warm. They had come home to a distracted Nellie and Robert, who had joined forces to trace their whereabouts. They were both seventeen at the time and Ned had lectured her severely about "tearing around the countryside like a

March hare". But not even Ned's disapproval could dim the glow of their wonderful night. They had spent a lot of time together that summer.

The following year she had left Kilmeen and slowly got caught up in her new life in London, but she met nobody to compare with David, who had gone to university and made new friends as well. The letters dwindled between them. Nevertheless, she had thought that David would always be in Kilmeen for her when she came back. But on one visit home she ran into him at a local dance with a pretty girl in tow and she was shattered. She had gone home and cried herself to sleep.

"I was young and foolish," she advised the photograph of Edward Phelan as she rose from the chair. "I hope that I've toughened up a bit since then."

[illegible] the glow of their wonderful night. [illegible] time together that summer.

[illegible] many new friends as well. [illegible]

[illegible] of Edward Purnell [illegible]

CHAPTER TEN

JACK STOOD OUTSIDE the back door of Mossgrove and surveyed the farmyard with satisfaction. Things were beginning to look better! Davy Shine was a blessing, a great big, strong lad who worked willingly and did not measure his giving. Having him for the morning and evening milking was a relief, but as well as that he drew hay to the cows and horses and cleaned out the stalls, stables and pigs' houses. He was a good-natured lad and Peter and himself got on well. If he been inclined to throw his weight around, Peter would have felt threatened by him and probably have been a bit awkward. Peter was particularly sensitive at the moment, but Davy seemed to have a sixth sense where he was concerned and discussed all the goings on of the farm with him. Davy, however, found Martha a bit of a puzzle.

"There's very little talk out of her," he remarked to Jack. "When I was here last she did not say very much but she laid down the law when it suited her. Now she's like a statue!"

"A lot has happened since you were here last, lad," Jack told him, "and she's going through her own torment."

"I know that," Davy said, "but she's not talking to the two young ones and that's not good for them."

"Time will solve all that," Jack told him, trying to convince himself as much as Davy.

Now Davy appeared out of the potato shed with a bucket swinging off each arm.

"I'm just finishing off feeding the pigs," he called across the yard, and asked, "Are you going ploughing the well field today?"

"I surely am, and isn't it a grand day for it," Jack told him, surveying the scene in front of him.

In the early morning sunshine the hens, ducks and geese were busy around the yard, all emitting their own sound of appreciation. Above them the newly arrived swallows swished in and out of the stables and piggery. Every year the swallows came back to the outhouses around the yard in Mossgrove. He always watched out for the first arrivals, feeling that on the day they arrived the harshness of winter was behind them and that the best of the year stretched ahead. It was good to see the swallows come back. They were sound judges of comfortable corners for nesting, and the outhouses in Mossgrove were fine drystone buildings. The old man had built a lot and built well. Jack remembered when they had built the new henhouse at the end of the yard.

"We'll put it over there, Jack," he had said, "with its back to the east and facing south-west, and that way they'll get the best of the day. They'll be next to the ducks and the geese and the pigs over there. That way we'll have all the dirty crowd together. Then we have the horses, calves and the cows with the barn opposite. That's good planning, Jack: if you don't plan your farmyard well, you'll spend the rest of your life going around in circles."

Jack had to agree that it was a well-laid-out yard, but when they started on the henhouse he thought that it was a bit bigger and better than necessary. He said so to the boss, but was told, "Jack, lad, we can't afford to do it cheaply; that's the most expensive way to do anything. This will be here when I'm growing daisies and my grandchildren after me. That's the way to build."

As he looked around the farmyard now Jack thought that the whole place was evidence of this philosophy. Every year the old man had painted all the farmyard doors a dark red, and when he had grown too stiff to bend, Nellie had carried on the practice, and then Ned, and now I suppose, Jack thought, it will be Peter or maybe even Nora until she leaves the place, but that was a long time down the road yet.

"Jack, are you going to stand there all day looking into space?" Davy emerged from the piggery swinging his empty buckets.

"I suppose," Jack said, "there isn't much future in that, or to quote the old man: 'This will never keep white stockings on the missus.'"

"Never heard that one before," Davy smiled.

"Yea, old Edward Phelan would say that if we were sitting around doing nothing," Jack told him. "I suppose in his time well-dressed women with well-to-do husbands wore white stockings, and if the income dropped so did the stockings."

"Well, whatever about the white stockings," Davy laughed, "I had better clean out the stalls, or do you want me to get the horses ready for you?"

"No, you belt away," Jack told him, "and I'll look after the horses."

Just then the back door opened and Martha came out. Jack could see that she was dressed for going further than Mossgrove and her words confirmed it. "Jack, tackle Paddy to the trap," she told him, and then went quickly back into the house.

"Where's she off to?" Davy questioned in surprise. Jack wondered the same thing himself. She had only gone to mass since the funeral and then he had driven the pony for her, and when they came to that part of the road where the accident had happened he could feel her tension and distress. But it looked as if she was heading off on her own now. Probably something to do with tidying up the affairs of the farm, he thought, and indeed that was a good thing and not before time.

"I'm off to the cows, so," Davy told him, deciding that there was no more to be discussed.

Jack went over to the stables and backed a reluctant Paddy out of his stall. "Come on, old boy, you're getting a bit of an airing. That'll be good for you."

James and Jerry turned their heads around in curiosity to know where was Paddy off to. "'Twill be our turn in a minute," he told them, "although I'd say that this boy here is going to have a better day than the two of ye."

He lifted Paddy's harness down off the high hooks on the wall, slipped it on to his brown back and then led him out into the yard. The cart-house was beside the stables and there the brown shining trap sat back on its heel with its slender shafts arching up into the air. He was very proud of his repair work on the trap; he had always loved woodwork, and concentrating on it after the accident had been good for him. Catching Paddy with one hand and the high shaft with the other, he brought down the shafts and backed Paddy in between them, then hitched the harness on to the trap and tied the belly-band under Paddy's broad belly. He led Paddy by the head over to the back door and tied the reins loosely to a rusty hook on the water barrel. Then he went into the kitchen and up into the parlour, where the cushions for the trap were kept against the kitchen wall to keep them aired. He brought them down and put them into the trap, returning to get the rug out of the bottom of the press beside the fire.

"All ready for you now, Martha," he called from the bottom of the stairs.

She came down the stairs dressed in a dark coat and hat, and he thought that he detected a new vitality about her. The lethargy of the last few months seemed to have lifted a little and her dark eyes had a spark of life in them. There was no doubt, he thought, but she was a fine-looking woman with her high cheekbones and long narrow face, and she carried herself as if she owned the ground that she walked on. She swept past him into the trap. He untied Paddy's reins and handed them to her. She took them wordlessly and swung Paddy around the yard. Going out the gate she called back over her shoulder, "I'll be back before the cows."

You're giving yourself plenty of time, Jack thought, not that it mattered as she no longer helped with the milking. He wondered if she had left anything ready for the two young ones. A quick look around the kitchen told him that she had not, but he decided that maybe she intended to be back earlier than she had said.

In the stable he untied Jerry and James and put on their winkers and tackling. As he led them out of the stable, Jerry danced around a little in protest but Jack rubbed his neck and soothed him down with calming words. Then, standing between their heads, he led them up the boreen into the well field, where an old well lay hidden under bushes in the corner. Every field on the farm had its own name, some in English and others in Irish. The name he liked best was "Mear na hAbhann" – the finger of the river – which was one of the inches along by the river that the old man had wrestled back from the Conways. Jack always believed that those two fields, because they were at the Phelan side of the river, had probably originally been Phelans' anyway. His father used to say that they had been moonlighted off the Phelans by the Conways back in an earlier generation.

The plough was lying on its side just inside the gap, where he had pulled it into position on his way down that morning. He hitched the two horses on to it and guided them along the headland until he came to the place that he had already decided was to be the starting point. It took a few minutes to manoeuvre the sock of the plough into the right position and get the first cut going. But soon Jerry and James had their stride in harmony and a thick slice of rich brown earth turned over behind them up the long high field.

As they went steadily up and down the field the overlapping folds of upturned earth spread out on either side of the plough. Behind them, crows and seagulls squabbled over uprooted snails that were thrust unceremoniously from the safety of the dark earth's belly into the glaring light of a bright spring day and the merciless beaks of the probing birds. The soil was perfect for ploughing – not too dry and not too damp – and a soft breeze ruffled the manes of the two horses.

It delighted Jack's ploughman's heart to look down the long field and to view the perfectly turned unbroken sod. Ploughing out here in the big quiet field soothed his mind, and as the hours passed he relaxed into complete harmony with himself and his surroundings. He had ploughed this field for many years and always it brought him this feeling of calmness and peace, which he could never have quite put into words. The smell of the red earth took him into a realm beyond his everyday living, and as he ploughed the field he sensed that his mind, too, was being gently ploughed and old strifes and stresses turned up and wiped away as a new ease soaked through his being.

He had tried once to explain the experience to Ned, who had smiled knowingly. "Me too, Jack," Ned had said simply, and so he knew that Ned as well had found in the quietness of the fields a whole, untroubled world. If you were not afraid of silence you could come face to face with yourself out here, Jack thought, and maybe out here is the real God.

"Yoo-hoo, Jack!" Davy called from the gap as he came along the bottom headland swinging a thick grey knitted sock, which Jack knew held a bottle of warm tea. He brought the horses down into the headland where they could have a few mouthfuls of grass while he had his tea.

He rolled the hand-knitted sock down around the neck of the bottle and took a long satisfying drink. "Davy, that's fine, hot, sweet tea: just the job for a ploughman's thirst," he said appreciatively, sitting on the end of a rusty harrow in the dyke and unwrapping the newspaper from around the thick cuts of brown bread.

"I was thinking that you'd be getting hungry," Davy said, joining him on the harrow which sank a little beneath his weight. "And there's no trace of herself."

"Oh, didn't she come back yet?" Jack asked in surprise.

"Wouldn't you have seen her passing down the boreen," Davy protested.

"Davy, when I'm ploughing, the world and his wife could go down that boreen and I wouldn't see them," Jack told him.

"I never thought that ploughing was that interesting," Davy laughed. Looking at his fine honest face, Jack realised that Davy would never understand the feeling for the land that Ned and himself had shared. But Davy's next question surprised him. "Do you think that I'll be kept on here?" he asked.

"I can't see why not," Jack told him. "We need help and you're a good worker and you like it here, don't you?"

"Yerra, 'tis grand here," Davy declared. "I never settled down in England, couldn't get used to it: the money was good, but that was all."

"Well, that settles it then," Jack told him.

"What about herself?" Davy asked.

"What about her?"

"I'd say that she could give anyone the road awful fast."

"She can't afford to do that," Jack told him; "we need you here."

"What's going to happen about Peter in the summer when he finishes?" Davy asked.

"I know that Ned had it in his head to send him to school," Jack told him, "but I don't know what will happen now."

"You mean away to boarding school?" Davy asked in dismay.

"Yea."

"God, that would be awful hard on Peter," Davy decided. "I nearly died with the lonesome in England; that's one of the reasons that I'd hate to have to go back."

"That worried Ned too," Jack admitted, "but he set great store by learning; he himself didn't get that chance, and he wanted Peter to have it."

"Yerra, I don't know," Davy said. "I hated school and was happy to get free of it."

"Well, that's the way of it," Jack said, "but don't say anything to Peter because the poor little devil has enough on his mind right now."

"Oh God, Jack," Davy protested with a distressed face, "I wouldn't say anything to upset Peter. I'm awful fond of him."

"I know you are," Jack smiled into his troubled face, "and he's much better since you came." That indeed was the truth. Even though there was about eight years age difference between them, the gap was much closer in reality because Peter was older than his years and Davy much younger than his. Peter was quick-thinking and alert, whereas Davy was easy-going and lighthearted, so they were a good balance for each other.

"Oh, I'm glad that he's better since I came," Davy smiled in appreciation, "because I remember after my father died that the lonesome nearly ate the heart out of me, so I kind of understand how Peter feels, and my mother was a bit like herself inside and she wouldn't talk about it, and that nearly killed me altogether."

So that's it, Jack thought. He had wondered why Peter, who was not a great mixer by nature, was getting on so well with Davy. Davy just now was the right man in the right place. Davy would have been about Peter's age when his father had been killed by Nolans' bull, so in one sense he had once stood where Peter was right now.

"Well, I suppose we'd better get moving again," Jack said, rising stiffly from the side of the plough. "I'm getting stiff in my old bones, Davy lad."

"You're as fit as a fiddle, Jack," Davy told him. "You trot up and down that field faster than I could ever do it."

That's not saying much for me, Jack thought, because speed was not one of Davy's strong points.

Just then there was a shout from the gap and Nora and Peter came running along the headland with school sacks bumping off their backs.

"Lord, are ye home from school?" Jack said to them in surprise. "The day is nearly gone."

"You've a lot done, Jack," Peter declared admiringly, looking up the long brown furrows.

"Not bad for an old fella," Jack said smiling.

"You're not an old fella," Nora protested.

"I'm no spring chicken either," Jack laughed.

"Are Jerry and James tired?" she wanted to know.

"Not at all," Jack told her. "Those two big fat lumps need some of the lard taken off them. No better job than ploughing to do that. What have they been doing all winter only inside in the stable getting big roundy bums on them."

But something else had caught her attention and she stood looking up along the field. She walked back and forth at the end of the furrows and then she stooped down and peered up along the row of upturned sods.

"What's wrong with you, Norry, have you got something wrong with your head?" Peter teased, winking at Davy, but she ignored him.

"Did you ever notice, Jack," she asked slowly, "that when you look up along a ploughed field it has a sort of a silvery look to it."

"That's right," Jack told her; "whatever it is about the newly turned sod, it has a silvery or metallic sheen." He joined her to look up along the field.

"Come on," she said to the other two, "and see what I mean."

Peter and Davy, with broad smiles on their faces, stood looking up the field.

"Can't see a thing only mud," Davy declared, "but if anybody looked in over the ditch they'd say that Phelans had four new scarecrows at the bottom of the field."

"Go away home, let ye," Jack laughed. "Ye're only come-in-the-way boys here."

"What are come-in-the-way boys?" Nora wanted to know.

"Fellows," Jack told her, "who do nothing themselves and come in the way of other people who have work to do."

"That's us all right," Davy said, sticking the tea bottle into his pocket and taking Nora's hand. "Come on, lads, we'd better not come in the way of this busy man," and the three of them headed for the gap with Nora still pointing up the field trying to make the others see what she found so fascinating.

Suddenly the three of them came to a standstill as Martha in the pony and trap turned in the gate from the road and came down the boreen beside the field. Jack could see from the stance of Nora and Peter that they were stunned to see her actually driving the pony and trap. Then their surprise turned to delight and they ran along the headland pulling Davy with them. They were at the gap to join her in the trap for a drive down to the house. Jack smiled to himself as he thought of Davy's muddy boots inside in Martha's clean trap.

But it was good to see her out and about again. He knew that if she put her mind to it she could do a great job in running Mossgrove. As he ploughed up and down the field he thought about her and decided that though he had never found her likable he had often found her admirable. But as the day wore on and the lengthening shadows stretched across the field, all thoughts of Martha and other problems disappeared and he became totally absorbed in the fulfilment of turning the soft brown sod. There is no doubt, he thought, but there is healing in this earth and a calming in the stillness of the fields.

When darkness came he unhitched the horses from the plough, left it on the headland ready for the morning and then headed down for the house with the horses. He hoped that Davy and Peter were well into the milking, or even had it finished, as he felt that he could do with a bit of a sit-down right now.

There was nobody around the cow stalls, so he concluded that they were all finished and was glad of it. He eased the tackling off the two tired horses and rubbed them down with a scrap of dry hay. After they drank deeply from the water trough outside the stable door, he led them into their stalls where Davy had their mangers full of softly piled hay. Paddy neighed in welcome, and as Jack left the stable he could hear the satisfying sound of hay between crunching jaws. Bran followed him across the yard jumping up to tell him how delighted he was to have him home.

"Good boy, Bran," he praised, rubbing him down and patting him. "Did you get fed yet?" A half-empty bowl outside the back door answered the question and Bran went back to finish it off. Jack lifted the latch of the back door and then sat on a low stool to ease off his muddy boots and the wellington tops that he wore when ploughing to keep the mud off his trousers. Martha's pan of water was back on the table, so he washed his hands and dashed some of the cold water over his face.

When he went into the kitchen the rest of them were gathered around the table and he felt at once that the atmosphere was lighter than in previous days.

"Mom milked with us tonight," Peter said proudly.

"That's good," Jack said cautiously. Martha was not one to expect appreciation, so you had to tread carefully with her or you could get your nose snapped off.

"We're having a fry for our supper," Nora told him with a smile on her face, "'cause we didn't have a proper dinner."

"I could polish off a fry now right enough," Jack declared, looking in appreciation at the bacon, sausages and black pudding surrounding the fried eggs on the plates on the table. Martha knew how to feed a hungry man. As they ate, the children chatted freely and Davy joined in their conversation. Martha as usual was quiet but Jack felt that tonight there was something different about her. He sensed a suppressed excitement and he wondered what had caused it. Maybe, he thought, she was just relieved to have today over her and to have things straightened out.

Jack slept well that night and every night that week as the ploughing continued. It was great to be catching up and getting things done at last. For a while back he had been worried that they might not have been able to keep the show on the road but thankfully they were putting all that behind them now. There was nothing, he decided, to beat the feeling that you were winning though the odds were stacked against you. He felt that he owed it to the old man, Nellie and Ned to keep the place going for Peter, and then once Peter was up and running he could take things easy, but not too easy. He wanted to die in harness, not rust out like an old plough in the dyke.

On Friday the ploughing was finished, and that evening as he walked home after his supper he stood at the gap of the well field and looked across the folded furrows of brown earth. They stretched across the entire field and he could see through the gap in the blackthorn hedge the furrows continue across the adjoining field. These are fields full of promise, he thought, waiting like dark brown wombs to receive the seeds of wheat, oats and barley and even the humble spud. The miracle of growth never failed to delight him, and he knew that one morning in a few weeks time after the planting was done he would stand in this gap and see a fine green sheen along the top of the brown earth. A very delicate ferny growth like a baby's hair. A new beginning, and despite all the hardship what a wonderful thing that was. Ned, he thought, you understood all these thoughts that are running through my mind and I miss having you to share it with me, but somehow when I walk around these fields you are never far away from me. This was your place and your spirit lives on here.

When he reached the cottage Toby went wild with

delight. He lit the fire and then went out to lock up the hens and to check for eggs in the darkening fowl house. I'm like a cat, he thought, I can find my way around in the dark. When he got back in he lit the lamp and was glad to see the *Kilmeen Eagle* on the table. Sarah Jones dropped it in every Friday on her way home from the village. He put a bowl of fresh food outside for Toby, where Maggie the cat soon joined him and they ate peaceably out of the one bowl. That's all the jobs done, he thought thankfully and sat into his low armchair by the fire and eased off his boots to warm his toes.

He put up his hand and swung the lamp in its hinged bowl right over his head so that he could see the print more clearly. It was difficult sometimes to see in the lamplight, though he was fine in daylight. A new pair of glasses would probably help things along, but so far he had got by with an old pair of Nellie's. He eased open the paper in anticipation. The *Eagle* was always full of interesting bits and pieces. As was his habit he glanced through it all quickly before settling down to go through each section in greater detail. When he opened the middle page the word Mossgrove in large letters jumped out at him. He couldn't quite take it in: what the hell was Mossgrove doing in the *Kilmeen Eagle*? Then the large notice hit him between the two eyes like a hard stone.

For Sale. By Public Auction.

The rest of the words ran into each other and danced before his eyes. He could not make sense out of them. Blood pounded into his head. Shock like a bullet hit him in the gut. His hands started to tremble.

"What in the name of Christ is happening to me?" he wondered, taking off his glasses and shaking his head. "I'll put down the paper now and I'll steady up and calm myself. Maybe I'm imagining things."

But when he put on his glasses and picked up the paper again it was still there. Mossgrove, on the instructions of Martha Phelan, was for sale.

"Holy Jesus," Jack swore, "we're going to be sold out."

The possibility had never even crossed his mind. Mossgrove had been Phelan land for as far back as anyone could remember. But since he was fifteen it had been his too. He had worked and nurtured it and the love of this land was ingrained deep into the very fibre of his being. He would rather die than see it sold.

CHAPTER ELEVEN

KATE DID NOT sleep that night. Every time she closed her eyes, the "For Sale" notice in the *Kilmeen Eagle* danced into her mind. The possibility of such a thing happening had never entered her head. Mossgrove in her life had been indestructible. Generations of Phelans might come and go, but the land of Mossgrove remained in the family for ever. She ran the insoluble problem around her head for hours.

At three o'clock she finally gave up all hope of sleep. She came down to the kitchen and made a hot drink with Jack's cure. Poor Jack, she thought, he must surely know by now because Sarah would have brought him the *Eagle* as usual. She knew that he had no inkling beforehand because if he had he would have got a message to her. It was a dreadful way for him to find out. Martha probably had not told anybody. Her style would be to do her own thing and keep her thoughts to herself. The chances were that the children did not know either. It would be terrible if they were told by an outsider. Thoughts and possibilities chased each other around her mind until she was so confused that she did not know what to think. She sat by the warm range in the kitchen and swirled the hot drink around in the mug. When she had it finished she felt fuzzy-headed and more confused.

She went into the sitting room and stoked up the fire; there were still some red embers so she put on more turf and soon it blazed up. She would sit by the fire here and maybe she might doze a little. She looked up at the picture of her grandfather. "Now where do we go from here?" she asked him. He looked down at her with his penetrating eyes and she wondered how he would have handled the situation.

"Your problem," she told him, "came from outside the family, but this one is inside, which is far worse. I can see no solution to it."

She wrapped an old knitted shawl belonging to her mother around her shoulders and sat looking into the fire, but there was no comfort to be found gazing into the glowing turf. Her mother's face and Ned's face swam in front of her.

She must have dozed off because from a distance she became aware that someone was tapping on the window. It did not alarm her unduly because people came to her house at all times of the night. She was startled, however, when she drew back the curtain and saw Mark's pale face peering in at her. She went into the hallway and opened the door quickly.

"Come in," she said. "Are you all right?"

He slipped past her soundlessly like a tall, thin shadow.

"I saw your light, Kate," he said, looking down at her anxiously, "and I hope you don't mind me knocking at this hour."

"No, not at all," she told him, taking his hand and leading him towards the fire. There was something about Mark that always made her feel protective towards him. "You're a real night owl."

"I know that people find it strange, but I like the night. I can play music after being out walking at night and sometimes I draw what I see at night. You see strange things at night, Kate."

"You sit there by the fire and warm yourself and I'll make us a pot of tea," she said.

As she made the tea she wondered if he knew about Mossgrove. She decided that he probably did because Agnes would have got the *Eagle* and probably discussed it with him. When she returned with the tray he confirmed her thoughts.

"I knew that you'd be upset about Mossgrove," he told her, "and when I saw your light I guessed that you couldn't sleep."

"Thanks, Mark," she said gratefully. "I'm glad of the company. What do you think of the whole thing?"

"She won't change her mind," he told her. "Martha is never wrong and Martha never changes her mind."

He was not criticising his sister; he was simply stating a fact. It was one of the things that had always endeared him to Kate: he was totally non-judgmental of people. Part of it was that he had very little interest in what went on in the parish, as he was preoccupied with his music and drawing, but he was also very tolerant, and what people did was their own business.

"I brought you your picture," he told her, opening his bag that he had hung on the back of the chair.

"Oh, I'm so happy to have this," she told him appreciatively as she looked again at Ned planting the young beech along the ditch of Mossgrove.

"Never thought the day I drew it that there would be so many changes so soon," he said.

"Our whole world is turned upside down."

"Ned was so solid it was as if he held us all together."

"You're right there," she agreed. "Did Ned know that you were sketching him?"

"Oh yea," he told her. "Ned was one of the few people whom I could draw and it didn't make any difference to him. A lot of people become very self-conscious."

"I think that I'd be like that," Kate admitted.

"Look at this one now," Mark said, drawing another out of his bag.

"Well, isn't that just perfect!" Kate gasped in admiration. She was looking at a picture of Jack sitting by the fire wearing Nellie's old glasses and reading the paper with his feet up on the hob and Toby and Maggie stretched out on the hearth. It was a view from outside the window, which was lightly sketched into the foreground.

"Jack didn't know?" she asked.

"No," he said simply. "I did it from outside the window one night. Pictures seen through a window are fascinating; most of us have no curtains, and it's almost as if the window is the frame of the picture. People in those situations are completely natural. Wonderful pictures!"

Kate was amazed and amused. Nobody but Mark would think of doing something so outlandish and see nothing extraordinary in it. He did not look in windows out of curiosity. Mark simply saw them as interesting pictures. If anyone else went around looking in windows she would have been horrified, but because it was Mark it was different – innocent.

"I've a picture in here," he said tentatively, patting his bag, "and it worries me."

"Would you like me to look at it?"

"If you wouldn't mind," he said anxiously, "but then that would be passing the worry on to you, and you've so much trouble on your shoulders now that I hate bringing more."

"But maybe I could do something about it," she suggested.

"Well, yes," he agreed, his normally tranquil face distressed. "You're about the only one who could, though how I don't know."

"Let me see it so, Mark," she suggested, "and then we'll decide what to do."

Slowly he drew the picture out of his bag, as if the very act was painful to him, and he handed it across the fire to her. When she looked at the drawing she recoiled in horror. The fear in the picture was palpable. Little Kitty Conway was sitting up in bed with a look of absolute terror on her face and the palms of her hands pressed forward as if pushing away something hateful. In the candlelight the menacing shadow of Matt Conway was sketched beside the bed.

"When did you do this, Mark?" she asked in a choked voice.

"A few nights ago," he whispered back, "but I didn't know what to do with it."

"What did you do that night?" she asked.

"I rattled the window to frighten him, and then I ran,

because that way he didn't know who it was in the dark, and someone unknown might scare him more than me."

"It probably would," she agreed.

"When I got home the scene haunted me and I couldn't rest. I nearly went crazy, so I had to draw it. It was the only way to get it out of my head. What are we going to do, Kate?" he asked in desperation.

Poor Mark, she thought, who lived in a world of music and painting where there was no place for the sordid things of life. He was a free spirit and should not be fettered by this horror.

"Mark, listen to me," she told him firmly; "try to put the whole scene out of your mind and leave it to me. I'll look after it – and leave that drawing with me because it could get you killed."

"What about you, Kate?" he asked in a worried voice.

"It's my job to look after these kind of things," she assured him, "so leave it with me and I'll look after it."

"I knew that you were the only one who could help," he said. "I came by last night as well but there was someone here."

"Oh, that was David Twomey, the Doc's son," she told him. "He is hoping to start a secondary school here and he's running into problems."

"Isn't life full of problems?" he sighed.

"Mark, that's not a bit like you," she protested. "You're to put all this out of your head now and go back to your music and sketching and leave the problem to me."

"Thanks, Kate," he said, rising and putting his bag over his shoulder. "If I could influence Martha about Mossgrove I would, but she never took any notice of me. My sister thinks that I'm a fool."

"What a mistake!" she said, shaking her head and going out into the hall before him.

"Good night, Kate, or should I say good morning?" Mark smiled down at her. "You've taken a huge load off my mind. I couldn't think the last two days with the upset of that." He slipped out the door and disappeared down the street into the grey misty dawn.

She returned to the room and sat down heavily in the chair beside the dying fire. What a bloody awful start to the day, she thought. She picked up the picture and looked at it. It sent revulsion coursing through her. She went over to the sideboard and put it face down in one of the drawers. She had thought earlier in the night that there could be nothing worse than the sale of Mossgrove, but this needed immediate action. It was her day for visiting old Mrs Conway, and she determined that by the time she did she would have something worked out. I'll call to see Sarah Jones later on, she thought, because she's the only one to have her finger on the pulse of the Conways. But for now she decided that she would get a few hours rest because all of a sudden she felt drained and exhausted.

Hours afterwards a loud knocking on the door woke her. She sat up in bed and knew straight away by the light in the room that it was late morning; a glance at her watch told her that it was ten o'clock. She jumped quickly out of bed and ran down the stairs, wrapping her dressing gown around her. Doc Twomey stood on the doorstep with a surprised look on his face.

"Kate, I thought that you'd be pacing the floor with anger and frustration."

"I was doing that at three o'clock this morning," she said grimly.

"I never heard it until Hannah showed me the *Eagle* this morning," he said, "otherwise David or I would have been over to you last night."

"Come in, Robert," she said; "I've another problem besides Mossgrove."

"God, Kate," he said in surprise, "I thought there'd be room for nothing else but Mossgrove in your mind today."

"I thought that too, early last night," she said, taking the drawing out of the drawer, "but this came later."

As he looked at it wordlessly his jaw muscles tightened and he rubbed his hand across his forehead in agitation.

"Tells its own story, doesn't it," he said grimly, and then, as an afterthought: "An amazing piece of drawing – Mark's, of course."

"Yes, he was lucky that he didn't get himself killed, but at least now we know, thanks to him."

"Any ideas on how to handle it?" he asked.

"I'm going to discuss it with Sarah Jones," she told him.

"That's a good idea," he agreed. "Sarah is about the only one to have the measure of the Conways. But you be careful with that fellow: he's a bad egg in more ways than one."

"I know," she agreed; "he gives me the creeps."

"Anything I can do," he told her, "you know that I'm here."

"Thanks, Robert, I feel better that someone else knows," she said.

"Any chance of a cup of tea?" he asked hopefully.

"You put on the kettle, and I'll get dressed."

As she ran up the stairs the shocks of the previous night were replaced by a determination to tackle the Conway problem as soon as possible. When she came back down he had the tea made and the table set for two.

"You're handy to have around the house," she told him. "I might keep you."

"You could do worse," he smiled.

As they had breakfast they discussed the Conways, Mossgrove and David's new school.

"You had David, Thursday night," he said.

"That's right. We discussed the school."

When she had answered the door on Thursday night and found David standing there, a sudden awkwardness had overcome her. They had not come face to face for a long time. He had seemed equally unsure. We are both being wary of each other, she had thought. But later as they had chatted some of the lost easiness had returned. She had looked across at the dark, attractive face and thought how readily she could slip back into the old feeling. Careful, Kate, she had warned herself, you walked down that road before.

"David is finding the old P.P. awkward enough," Robert said now.

"But does he have to have his approval?" Kate asked.

"You spent too long in England," he told her. "If he is against it some of the parents won't send their children, and that's it."

"We're a strange crowd, aren't we?" Kate mused.

"Well, strange or otherwise, that's the way we are, and now I suppose we'd better get moving. Will you start with Sarah?"

"I will," she said, "because I can't concentrate on anything else until I have a start made on that problem. I'm due to dress old Mrs Conway's leg this morning anyway, so that gives me the chance to get inside Conways'. Only for her leg, there isn't a hope in hell I'd get in there."

"Or me either," he told her.

As she pushed her bike back along the village a few neighbours who obviously did not know what to say smiled sympathetically to her instead, and she knew that the word had gone around about Mossgrove. People would find it hard to understand that she had anything other than Mossgrove on her mind this morning. When she cycled close to Nolans' gate she hoped that Betty would not be out in the yard because, if she was, there would be no getting away from a lengthy discussion on the sale. Thankfully there seemed to be nobody about and she kept going. Betty would think it very peculiar that she did not call in the circumstances, but she could make some excuse later. She felt guilty passing the gate of Mossgrove, thinking about Jack and the turmoil that he must be going through. Did the children know yet? she wondered. As she cycled past Ned's young beech trees, she thought ruefully, little did he think when he was planting them that there would be a for sale sign on the gate before they were well rooted.

She was glad to arrive at Sarah's gate and she hoped that she would be at home. Relieved to find the front door open, Kate stepped into the sunlit hall that smelt of Mansions floor polish. The door into the kitchen was open and Sarah was sitting at the table inside the window reading the paper.

"You had no idea about this before it appeared here?" she asked, tapping the *Eagle*, and when Kate shook her head she nodded.

"Jack and I thought so last night," she said. "I went over to him when I read it because I was afraid of what the shock would do to him."

"How was he?" Kate asked anxiously.

"Knocked sideways," Sarah said, shaking her head.

"What is that woman thinking of at all? I suppose she's still in shock. I always tell people to make no big decision for two years after a bereavement because they're not in control of their full faculties. That's after an ordinary death, if there is such a thing. Sure, what's happened down there would blow the head off you."

"There will be no changing her mind," Kate told her quietly.

"Don't I know," Sarah agreed; "always was as stubborn as a mule, like her father before her. But he'd never sell land. Martha was always a strange one, but then so is Mark, but he brought all the gentility of Agnes, whereas she has all the hardness of the Lehanes in her.

"Sarah," Kate interrupted her flow, "I want to discuss something else with you."

"Something else! Kate, girl, I thought you would have nothing on your mind today only Mossgrove. Jack and myself talked ourselves hoarse last night, for all the good that it did us. But I felt that Jack needed someone to talk it out with him."

"You were right, Sarah, as usual, and I'd have called to him just now but there is something that I must sort out first."

She sat on a chair next to Sarah and looked out the low window into her garden that was overflowing with flowers, vegetables and scratching hens. The garden is like herself, Kate thought, brimming with life and energy. It seemed a shame to blight the vibrant scene with her dark sketch, but she opened her bag and reluctantly drew it out and placed it on the table before Sarah. There was no reaction of surprise, only a narrowing of the eyes.

"So, he's at it again," she said bitterly.

"How do you mean, again?" Kate asked in astonishment.

"There was an older girl there – Mary," Sarah said.

"That's right," Kate said, "she went to Dublin to an aunt."

"Ever wonder why?" Sarah asked.

"Oh, God," Kate looked at Sarah in horrified realisation.

"That's right."

"But how did you find out?"

"The old woman," Sarah said. "And she helped to get her out as well."

"What about the mother?"

"Oh, Biddy," Sarah said dismissively; "useless – she's scared stiff of him."

"And the grandmother?" Kate asked.

"You couldn't frighten that one," Sarah declared.

"Wonder she didn't do something this time."

"Probably didn't know," Sarah said thoughtfully; "might have only started since she cut her leg and wasn't able to get around."

"So she's my best bet?"

"That's right, but let me think this out carefully and figure out the best way to go about things."

Kate sat quietly while Sarah did her thinking. Outside the window a pair of blackbirds darted back and forth beside the hedge, occasionally coming to a standstill with heads alert for any intrusion into their private corner. Nobody invaded their territory, so they continued their busy pecking, stopping now and then to make short swift flights into the hedge. Are they nesting? she wondered.

"Now, I think that this is the best way to do it," Sarah broke the silence. "No direct accusations or you'll be thrown out and they'll all clam up. Suggest that Kitty's bed be moved into the grandmother's room to keep an eye on the old lady. The old lady will know straight away what's going on, so she'll go along with it. That keeps Kitty safe for the present and gives us breathing space. Now, the old lady writes to Mary in Dublin, so I'll tell Joe in the post office to watch out for a letter and to copy the address. He might even have it in his head. Joe has done things like that for me before and no one was any the wiser. Then we'll take it from there."

Kate looked at her in admiration. This little woman with her small round face and soft clear skin probably knew most of what went on behind the closed doors of the parish but kept it all to herself.

"Thanks, Sarah," she said, getting to her feet. "Wish me luck."

"You'll be grand," Sarah told her; "just be fine and cool and remember that you have right on your side. That's always a help." And dipping her fingers into the holy water font hanging beside the front door, she gave Kate a good sprinkle.

As she cycled into Conways' yard the dogs came barking from all directions and Matt Conway appeared immediately with a triumphant leer on his face.

"So the Phelans are selling Mossgrove," he said, "and we'll be the highest bidders."

"How can you be so sure?" Kate asked.

"No matter what it goes to, we'll be there, because Conway money will come from America for this one," he gloated.

"We'll see," Kate said evenly and kept walking towards the front door.

"Oh, we'll see all right," he sneered; "we Conways have waited a long time for this day."

Kate did not rise to his baiting but opened the front door and went into the kitchen where Biddy Conway, with her thin red face and short hair pinned with a steel clip behind her ears, regarded her suspiciously. On previous calls Kate had attempted to make conversation with Biddy but had failed, so now she no longer tried. She went straight down to the grandmother's room.

"Ha, ha," the old lady greeted her, "so she's selling ye out. Ye got a cuckoo in the nest, as long as ye ran."

"Let's see that leg," Kate instructed, turning back the bedclothes and unwrapping the bandages.

"She was always an odd one: good-looking but odd," the old lady continued. "I knew when she got her claws into young Ned that he didn't stand a chance. Now she's going to have her own back."

"How do you mean, her own back?" Kate demanded.

"Odd ones like her always carry a grudge: they think that everyone is against them, and she always thought that ye had no time for her, so now she's going to get the better of ye."

"That's nonsense," Kate protested.

"Mark my words, my girl, but I'm right, and you'll find it out in due course," the old lady asserted nodding her head.

During her regular visits over the previous weeks Kate had developed a certain respect for the old lady. She was canny and calculating and tough as old leather, but she was a good patient and not a complainer. When she had the fresh bandage in place she stood over the old woman in the bed and looked down at her.

"I want you to do something for me," Kate told her.

"Why should I do anything for you?" she demanded.

"Because it's in your own interest. I want to bring Kitty's bed in here to your room."

The old lady went motionless in the bed and her piggy blue eyes narrowed in her flat flabby face.

"Why?" she rasped.

"Because if you wanted a drink or anything at night she could get it for you," Kate said casually, but their eyes locked and both of them understood exactly what was at stake.

"I'll get the boys to do it later on," the old lady said.

"We'll do it now," Kate told her decisively. "It's Saturday, so the boys are at home."

"Please yourself," the old lady agreed.

She went down into the kitchen where Biddy was clattering around in a pair of boots that were too big for her, and when she was asked about the whereabouts of the two boys, she pointed to the back door.

"I want to shift Kitty's bed into her grandmother's room so that she will be there at night if the old lady should want something," Kate told her, and knew by her furtive look that she knew the real reason for the move. She put her head out the back and yelled at the boys to come in. They came, big, beefy boys with close-cropped black hair and thick heavy Conway jaws, with puzzled looks on their faces. Small dainty Kitty with her red hair and pretty face was a total contrast to her brothers. They looked at Kate with mute, expressionless faces, but when she explained to them what she wanted done they got to work without question. In a few minutes they had the iron bed taken asunder and shifted across the kitchen into their grandmother's room.

Looking in the doorway, Kate recognised Kitty's room from Mark's drawing and felt chilled.

Just as they had the bed reassembled Kitty came in the back door dragging a dog behind her and looked uneasily at Kate. "Where's my bed gone?" she asked in surprise as she looked in through the open doorway at the empty room.

"We've moved it into Nana's room," Rory, the biggest of the two boys told her, " 'cause Nurse Phelan wants somebody with her at night."

Kate watched Kitty's face closely and saw a fleeting look of surprise wiped out by an overwhelming wave of sheer relief. She's off the hook, Kate thought, the poor little mite. Feeling Biddy's eyes on her, she looked across the kitchen and knew that Biddy too was aware of her daughter's relief. What a mess, she thought, feeling suddenly angry, but Sarah's words of warning came back to her. *If you get yourself kicked out you'll be no help to Kitty.* So she smiled at Kitty and told her, "Tidy up your bed, now, and look after Nana for me, and I'll be back next week."

When she went back out into the yard Matt Conway was waiting for her. "What kept you so long?" he demanded.

"We were moving Kitty's bed into her grandmother's room," she told him, feeling a glow of satisfaction when she saw the unease in his eyes. She let the silence hang between them and looked him in the eye until he dropped his glance. He knows now, she thought, that I know. Then she said casually, "She needs somebody to be with her at night." And getting on her bike she cycled out of the yard without a backward glance.

CHAPTER TWELVE

On the way home Kate decided that she would call to see Mark to tell him that she had taken things in hand. He had been deeply distressed last night and she did not want him to be worrying needlessly.

Everything about Lehanes' house made it different from their neighbours because Agnes had allowed Mark's flair for colour run riot. He had painted the long, low, thatched house a blazing yellow with a bright red door, and as she walked up the short path it peeped out at her through overgrown greenery like a mischievous child.

Mark must have seen her coming and he whipped open the door with a welcoming smile. His clothes always intrigued Kate because they looked as if they had been knitted on him. Agnes loved knitting, and his long, muted-coloured sweaters, threadbare and worn, poured down to his knees. She had often smiled to hear Agnes complain that once he got into a sweater she could not get him out of it until it almost fell apart. His trousers suffered the same fate because they were soft and bleached from over-washing and they skirted his long legs down over soft leather boots. The overall impression was in total contrast to the house because Mark himself looked like a grey shadow.

Now his warm brown eyes beamed out at her from the midst of soft, flowing, dishevelled hair and put her in mind of a wren peering out of its all-encircling nest.

"Kate, come in," he smiled in welcome, opening the door wide so that she stepped straight into the kitchen.

"I can't stay a minute," she told him, "but I thought that I'd let you know that I'm working on that problem and things are o.k. now."

"That's a relief," he sighed. "Since it happened I haven't been able to concentrate on anything. It's blocked off all my thinking."

"Well, that's why I called," she told him, taking his hands and looking up at him. "I've taken steps to keep Kitty safe, so you have no need to worry. You can go back to your own doings and forget about it." Then she smiled up at him and said admiringly, "Mark, you're like a tall, willowy tree."

"And you, Kate," he replied, "are like a small, dark, thorny, well-rooted bush that could not be blown over no matter what way the wind blew. A big storm could topple me!"

"I'm not sure, Mark," she laughed, "whether that's a compliment or an insult."

"It's a compliment, Kate," he assured her, putting his arms around her and drawing her close to him. "There is something so solid and sane about you, Kate, and you make me feel good about myself, whereas some people around here make me feel crazy."

"People always feel threatened by things that they cannot understand," she told him gently; then, putting her nose against his sweater, she sniffed and said, "You smell of Lux flakes."

"Kate, there is no romance in your soul!" Holding her back from him and laughing down at her, he asked, "Have you no time for tea?"

"No," she answered as she looked around. "Where's Agnes?"

"Gone over to Mossgrove," he told her ruefully. "She's dreadfully upset by the sale. She thinks that she can change Martha's mind, but of course she can't."

"Poor Agnes," Kate sighed, "I suppose she's worried about the future of the children too."

"What about this new school?" Mark asked. "That would be a great help to them if it came."

"Hopefully it will work out. Did you ever regret, Mark, that it was not there in your time?" she asked.

"Maybe I did, because there were so many things that I wanted to find out about. But then Tady Mikey came along and taught me to play, and that was the first ray of light. But it was the Miss Jacksons who really opened doors for me. When they took me on their trips they pretended that it was to help with their luggage, but of course that was only to make me feel good. They changed my life. Then, of course, I had Ned, who was always there for me if the other fellows tried to rough me up."

"You were good friends even going to school," Kate said.

"I sometimes think that I was the one who brought himself and Martha together, because he used to spend so much time here with me. Looking at how things are turning out, I think that I did him no favours," he said ruefully.

"Mark, will you stop it," Kate demanded. "Ned wouldn't have married Martha if he had not wanted to. Men were always fascinated by Martha because she was so lovely, and when Ned married he was the envy of every man in the parish."

"They didn't have to live with her," Mark said simply.

"She loved Ned a lot."

"I suppose so," he agreed, "but I hated it when she was not kind to Nellie."

"How did you know about that?" Kate asked in surprise.

"Ned and I discussed it often."

"Did you really? Ned never discussed it with me, or with Jack either."

"That was because he felt so guilty; he felt he'd let you and Jack down," he told her quietly.

"Oh, I never knew that," Kate said sadly. "Poor Ned, he was caught in the middle."

"He loved Martha but he wasn't blind to her faults, and the fact that I was her brother made it possible for him to talk with me about it. He didn't feel disloyal discussing it with me. Ned had a strong sense of loyalty but he had a stronger sense of justice, and he felt that Nellie was being wronged, which she was."

"She was indeed," Kate agreed, "but because of her sense of loyalty to Ned she never discussed it with me. I knew what was going on and I would have tackled Martha myself, but she would have taken it out on Ned and I didn't want to make things difficult for him. Family relationships are something else, aren't they?"

"That's for sure," Mark agreed. "She's my sister, but I could never understand her. She always thought that other people had it better than her."

Kate thought of old Molly Conway and wondered if maybe indeed she had Martha read right. But she decided that they could spend the day analysing Martha and be none the wiser, so she smiled at Mark and said, "Now, you're not to replace one problem with another. You can do nothing about Martha and Mossgrove, so forget about it. You have such wonderful gifts, Mark, that you owe it to yourself, and indeed to us less talented mortals, to follow your star, and that's the thorny bush advising you now."

"Right, mam," Mark said in mock submission, giving her a military salute.

"Well, I'm off," she told him. "And tell Agnes not to worry, it's bad for her asthma."

"Right, nurse," he smiled.

As she cycled along the road she thought back over her conversation with Mark. She was glad that Ned had discussed the problem of Martha and Nellie with him. She was very fond of Mark and at one stage when she was younger, before David came on the scene, she had imagined herself in love with him, but she had got over that phase and he had become a second brother in her life.

When she reached Sarah's cottage she was standing at the gate waiting for her.

"Well, how did you get on?" she asked anxiously.

"Did just as you said," Kate told her, getting off her bike, "and I think that it worked well."

"Thank God," Sarah said fervently. "At least we are all right for another while. I've been thinking since that it might be no harm to mention this to Fr Brady."

"Why so?" Kate asked in surprise.

"Well, he's fairly sound and he's pretty tuned in to what's going on around, and sometimes it's no harm to have a few reliable people in the know, because you'd never be sure when you'd want a bit of a back up."

"That sounds reasonable," Kate agreed, "and I'll be meeting him one of these nights about the new school."

"I heard rumours about that," Sarah said. "How far has it gone?"

"Not very far really," Kate told her. "David is waiting to hear from the Miss Jacksons' nephew to know if he would rent the old house in the village."

"Well, it would be better if the nephew did something with that house, because it's no good having it standing there idle," Sarah said.

"Hopefully he'll think of it like that as well," Kate said, "but apart from that there is a problem with the P.P."

"What's the problem with him?" Sarah asked in surprise.

"Well, apparently there was an old parochial agreement with the nuns over in Ross that there would be no school opened in the parish in opposition to their commercial school over there."

"But that's daft," Sarah protested.

"I know," Kate agreed, "but Sarah, I sometimes think that we're all half daft."

"Speak for yourself, my girl," Sarah told her briskly, and they both smiled.

"But the P.P. might use that agreement as an excuse because, as you know yourself, the Doc and himself had a bit of a run-in after Joan's funeral, so the Twomeys are not exactly his favourite parishioners."

"You had better watch yourself as well, if you have good-looking men calling late at night," Sarah teased.

"Aha, you were gossiping with Julia!" Kate smiled. "The Doc was saying that she was probably on duty that night."

"And what about handsome young David on Thursday night," Sarah smiled.

"Hope to God that she was asleep at about three o'clock this morning when Mark called."

"Oh, I'll hear it if she wasn't."

"How do you hear everything and tell people nothing?" Kate asked curiously.

"The easiest thing in the world," Sarah told her, "because most people are only interested in the sounds of their own voices."

"Probably most voices in the parish are talking about the sale of Mossgrove today," Kate said regretfully.

"More than likely," Sarah agreed, "but I haven't been to the village yet, so I haven't been in the way of meeting people to talk about it."

"Typical of Martha not to tell anybody, isn't it?" Kate asked. "She is so secretive."

"Maybe we should have smelt a rat when she went off in the pony and trap on Monday and was missing for most of the day," Sarah decided.

"Was she?" Kate asked with interest. "I didn't know that. But then I didn't meet Jack during the week."

"He told me last night," Sarah told her. "He said that she went away early in the day and was not back until evening. She probably went over to Ross and put the ad into the office of the *Eagle* herself."

"We always gave any ad for the *Eagle* to Joe in the post office," Kate said, "but she was probably afraid that Joe would say something to myself or Jack."

"He probably would have, too. Like most people around here he would hate to see Mossgrove go out of the Phelan name," Sarah said, then continued thoughtfully: "Strange, you know, though I never owned land myself apart from this acre, I still like to see the farms remain in the same families. It gives a sense of stability to the whole community. They're like trees that are allowed to reach maturity and to put down deep roots in the one place."

"Well, if this goes ahead the Phelan tree in Mossgrove is about to be cut down and a new Conway tree will be planted in there," Kate said bitterly.

"I was thinking that the Conways would be the front runners," Sarah said. "There's one of Matt's brothers in the buildings in England and doing well, and another ranching in America. Strange thing about the Conways, when they got out of that hole over there they seemed to blossom."

"Pity that Matt Conway did not go away and blossom somewhere else."

"He's about the worst of them."

"People don't come much worse than that creep," Kate said with venom, "and to think that he might actually own our house makes my skin crawl. If I went down to Mossgrove now I'd be afraid that I'd strangle Martha with my bare hands."

"It isn't sold yet," Sarah told her, "I've seen Mossgrove sail close to the wind before, but it got back on course again."

"But if they had sold then it would have been because they had no option, but now it's being done by choice. It's a betrayal!"

"I can understand how you feel," Sarah said comfortingly. "Jack was saying the same thing last night."

"Poor Sarah," Kate said bleakly, "we're all crying on your shoulder."

"Ah well, that's what I'm here for. Nellie and I often talked ourselves out of a tight corner together. She helped me and I helped her when times were tough. When all mine were small I hadn't much to put in the wind either, and my fellow liked his drop as well. Now that he's dead and all my crowd are working, I have it easier than I ever had it. It would be nicer if they were not all in England and America, but what else was there for them only the boat?"

"That's why this school is so important," Kate declared vehemently; "it would give them all a better chance, even if they still had to emigrate."

"I'd be very surprised if it didn't get going in spite of whatever problem there is about parochial agreements. The people here would only oppose the clergy for one reason, and that would be the future of their children, and the old P.P. knows that. I'd say that he won't push it that far."

"Well, Sarah," Kate said thoughtfully, "we'll find out over the next few weeks."

"He has someone to answer to too, you know," Sarah remarked enigmatically. "Will you be calling to see Jack?"

"Will you drop over to him when he comes up and tell him that I'll call back tonight to talk things over."

"I'll do that," Sarah told her.

"The other thing that is worrying me is Nora and Peter," Kate said. "Surely Martha will tell them before going to mass tomorrow because someone might say it to them. But whatever about tomorrow, they'll definitely have to know before Monday because the Conways will be bursting to ram it down their throats."

"Jack will know whether she told them or not."

"That's right," Kate said, getting on her bike, "and Sarah, will you say a prayer that I won't lose my cool and tear the head off Martha when I go to Mossgrove?"

Though she said it jokingly they both knew that she was half serious. Jack and the children would look to her to try to talk Martha out of her intention. But as Mark, who should know better than anyone, had so wisely remarked, that was not possible.

As she cycled along the road the whole problem of Mossgrove that she had pushed to the back of her mind returned like a reinforced black cloud. When she came to the entrance to the farm she leaned her bike against the stony ditch of Jack's cottage and climbed up on to the top of the gate. She sat there and looked down over the fields of Mossgrove. The big well field just inside the gate lay with its brown ploughed bosom turned up to the warm spring sun. She closed her eyes and could visualise it full of waving wheat, barley and oats, and see the pale shades of cream and yellow stretching away across the wide field, different-shaped heads waving in the breeze. She could hear Ned's voice as he looked at the barley with its bearded heads.

There's music in my heart all day,
I hear it late and early;
It comes from fields far, far away,
It's the wind that shakes the barley.

He had often stood on the headland looking up the field and recited that poem when the barley was ripe and rippling in the wind. She was able to see over the ditches back into the Clune field. That, too, was ploughed, waiting for the potatoes, turnips and mangles that were meant to feed the people and animals of Mossgrove in the year ahead. Ploughed fields were places full of promise. Jack had told her that when she was a child and she had never forgotten it.

In the fields below she could see the cows grazing and some of them lying down chewing the cud. She liked to look at a field full of cows: they exuded contentment and wholesomeness. In the field beyond them the sheep were dotted around like soft white cushions and she could see that some new lambs had arrived. The chimney of Mossgrove was barely visible in the trees and the smoke was coming straight up, like the spray from a fountain, and diluting into the clear blue sky.

She remembered days like this when she had come home on holidays while training in England. She remembered sitting on top of this gate just as she was now, staying there for a long time and simply absorbing the fact that she was back in her own place. There was no place else where she felt as complete as when she walked the fields here. Phelans had lived here for generations and when she came inside the gate she felt encompassed by them. Her grandfather had been so proud of Mossgrove. Even as a very young child, when he had taken her by the hand and led her out to walk around the farmyard and down the fields, she had sensed his feeling for the place. And yet her father did not have it. Maybe it skipped a generation. Was that why the old man wanted to implant it in his grandchildren? But then Nellie had loved this place too, and that had been a great bond between the old man and herself. When his relations came to visit him, Nellie had entertained them as if they were her own, and indeed she regarded them as such. That was the attitude that had kept Mossgrove going for so long. Great women marrying in here and setting their standards and keeping things going.

She thought of the women whom she visited around the parish. In many cases those country women were stronger than their menfolk. They handled childbearing and hard work, and many of them managed the money of the farm. Those who were afflicted with troublesome husbands made their own money from the eggs and the fowl around the farmyard. Some of them endured living with difficult mothers-in-law and domineering fathers-in-law. When they married into a house they became "the woman of the house", but sometimes the title conferred responsibility without authority. But they stuck together and helped each other out.

She remembered Sarah spending long hours talking to Nellie when she was young, and she had always felt a sense of security when they sat across the fire from each other in the kitchen and she was told to play in the garden. She knew that no matter how drunk her father would be when he got home, these two women were equal to it.

Then of course there was Jack. What would they have done without Jack? He seemed to have an infinite capacity for holding things together. He had been there like a secure anchor all through her childhood. When her father had died she had been heartbroken, because she had loved him despite all his faults, and Jack had understood and comforted her, and he took his place in many ways. She had sensed as a child that he loved Nellie and she took it for granted. When she grew up she realised what he had done for all of them. Ned and himself had been like father and son – maybe closer, she thought, because she knew of many father-son relationships that were fraught with disagreements. Now Ned was gone and Jack was still here. It was extraordinary to think that he had seen three owners of Mossgrove die before him, as well as Nellie. Well, the old man's death was natural enough, because he was a good age, but her father had been a young man and Nellie had only been in her early sixties, the same age as Jack himself. And now Ned, the generation after him. Jack, she thought, had endured great suffering here.

She sat there for a long time, her mind suffused with many thoughts until Toby, waking from his midday sleep, barked for attention.

"You're right, Toby," she told him, "it's time to get a move on, and as well as that I'm stiff from sitting up here like a crow on a branch."

She wheeled her bike along the road, not wanting to get back quickly into the village because she needed more time on her own. She felt as well that she could not pass Nolans' without calling in, and she knew that Betty would be turning over every possibility to prevent the sale of Mossgrove, and she felt that it was a pointless exercise because, short of a miracle, she could see nothing to prevent the sale of Mossgrove.

CHAPTER THIRTEEN

AS HE GOT out of bed Jack decided that he felt every day of his sixty-five years, and maybe a few with it. A grey cloud had moved into his mind. It was almost too much for his brain to take in that Mossgrove was for sale. Since Ned's death it had been tough, and there had been days of despair, but always deep down he had a gut instinct that they would succeed. The return of Kate had confirmed that. She had straightened things out, and slowly they were getting on top of the work. Only last night he had walked home with a new confidence. With the ploughing finished, he was sure that they had turned the corner in Mossgrove.

The weather was good now and the crops once sowed would soon catch up. There was the additional ease of having Davy to help wherever he was needed. He was a good lad. Then Martha was back in action in the house and around the yard. That was good! He had been so sure that she had decided to do her best to keep Mossgrove going, and he had felt a new appreciation of her. It was great to see her up and about and keeping things in order. When he had told the children that she would not stay down for long he had been pretty certain that he was right. In his opinion some people had the habit of lying down under trouble and he secretly called them "the all-fall-down brigade", but she was definitely not one of them. All these thoughts had run through his head as he had walked home last night. It had never crossed his mind that she intended to sell out the whole place and turn her back on it. It was hard to take that in. For the first time in his years at Mossgrove he felt that he was up against a stone wall. There was no way out of this one.

He walked down the boreen by the well field and looked across the ditch at his ploughing of the previous week. As he had walked home last night the sight of it had given him much satisfaction. This morning there was no joy in it.

He turned into the field above the house and rounded up the cows to take them down to the yard for early morning milking. Some of them were grazing and raised questioning heads as he approached, others were lying down chewing the cud and rose reluctantly, leaving flattened pools of grass where they had lain. Slowly they turned their heads towards the bottom of the field and the bulk of them came together and headed in that direction. The stragglers dribbled along behind. He had always enjoyed bringing in the cows for milking, walking slowly behind as they ambled at their leisurely pace. It was usually a soothing start to the day, but this morning it only filled his mind with the question of how long more.

Bran bounded in the gap to help with the round-up.

"Good boy, Bran," Jack praised him automatically, and he darted around the field to round up the slow movers. When they saw him their cloaks of lethargy slipped from them and they strode quickly towards the main herd. As Jack walked slowly behind them he looked over the bawn and viewed them with pride. He could remember most of their mothers and grandmothers. You did not build up a herd like this overnight. It had taken years of breeding and culling to bring them up to this high standard. They were the finest herd in the parish and he took great pride in them. Ned had been a good judge of an animal and knew what to keep and what to sell, and it had paid dividends. He wondered if they would be sold off or would the new owner buy them with the farm. They would probably make more money if sold in ones or twos. It would be a sad day for Mossgrove the day that this bawn of cows went out the gate. The cows were the heartbeat of the farm, and it would be dead without them. He could hardly bear to think of the possibility. There was a pain of defeat and hopelessness in his heart.

The cows found their own way into their stalls and waited patiently to be tied up for milking. He had just started milking the first cow when Davy came in rattling his bucket. But milking cows was the last thing on Davy's mind.

"Jasus, Jack! Did you see the shagging *Eagle* last night?" he demanded angrily.

"I did, Davy," Jack said evenly.

"What in the name of Christ is that one thinking of?"

"Easy, Davy," Jack soothed.

"Easy! How do you mean, easy?" Davy said angrily "Wasn't it only yesterday that you told me that there was a job here for me. I don't want to take the boat again."

"Davy, this is just as big a shock to me as it is to you," Jack told him quietly.

"Do you mean to tell me that you read it in the *Eagle* like me?"

"That's right."

The wind taken out of Davy's sails, he stood looking at Jack, an incredulous expression on his face.

"Well, she's one lightning bitch, and that's all that there is to it," Davy declared. Then another thought struck him: "Do you think that she's right in the head?"

"Well, whether she is or she isn't, she has got the power to make the decision," Jack told him sadly.

"God, didn't the Phelans take on trouble the day that they took her on board," Davy said with feeling.

"Well, they say that it's for better or worse," Jack reminded him.

"Jasus, Jack, it couldn't be much worse than this. You'll have no job, I'll have no job . . . what about the two small ones?"

"She surely told them."

"Peter didn't know last night. We were planning something for the summer," Davy said. "Peter wouldn't do that if he knew that I wasn't going to be here. Peter is as straight as a die."

"They'll have to be told then, before someone outside the house tells them," Jack decided, "but it's no one's place to do it but their mother's."

"Someone had better tell her that," Davy said, "and while you're at it, Jack, you might tell her that we would like to have known as well."

"I don't think that it would bother her a whole pile," Jack told him bitterly.

"Do you know something," Davy said, standing in the channel of the stall with a bucket in one hand and the milking stool propped on his hip, "I'm so bloody mad that I can hardly sit down to milk."

"Come on, Davy, and get started or we'll be here all day," Jack told him wearily.

Davy rattled the bucket in annoyance and, catching the milking stool firmly, he banged it on to the floor beside the cow with such a thud that it caused her to jump sideways in fright and nearly knock Jack and his bucket of milk off his stool.

"Christ, Davy, will you cool down or you'll be the cause of killing me," Jack protested as he pushed the offending cow back from him.

Soon afterwards he heard milk dance like rain off the base of Davy's tin bucket and knew that Davy was working off his frustration, much to the consternation of the cow, who looked back questioningly and moved protestingly from side to side. But gradually Davy slowed down, and then Jack could hear the even tempo as he got back to his normal calm rhythm of milking. Nothing like this to calm the mind, he thought, and he even felt a bit better himself. While he milked Jack decided that for today he would try to keep going as if they were not up for sale. It was the only way that he could survive in this present dilemma. By the time they had the cows milked they had both cooled down a little.

As they walked towards the back door Jack advised Davy: "Now, don't lose the head when we go into the kitchen and get yourself sacked. Mossgrove isn't sold yet, you know, and while it isn't you still have a job."

"Do you think it mightn't be?" Davy asked hopefully.

"I have no idea," Jack told him, "but sometimes in life worries can be overcome by events."

"What the hell does that mean?" Davy asked.

"Wait and see," Jack replied, opening the door and going into the back kitchen. When they had their hands washed they went into the kitchen where Martha had the breakfast ready. She dished out the porridge with an expressionless face and silently put the boiled eggs on the table. I suppose I had better say something, Jack thought.

"The two are still in bed?" he asked.

"They're having their Saturday morning sleep in," she said evenly.

Now, where do we go from here, he thought. If I don't mention the sale she is not going to mention it and that will keep us all in the dark. . .

"Why are you selling Mossgrove?" Davy blurted out.

"That's my business," she told him firmly, her face discouraging further questions as she poured milk on to her porridge. Jack could see Davy's face darkening in temper, so he cut in hurriedly.

"Have you told Nora and Peter?"

"That, too, is my business," she replied icily.

"God blast it!" Davy shouted angrily. "Are you telling me that it's none of my business if I don't have a job in a few weeks' time?"

"Well, that's certainly none of my business," Martha told him. "You both read the paper, so I presume you both know that Mossgrove is for sale, and that is the end of it as far as I'm concerned."

Davy opened his mouth to protest, but before he could say anything a step of the stairs creaked and the door at the bottom of it opened slowly and Nora's small pale face peered out at them.

"Are we selling Mossgrove?" she asked in a strangled voice. They all looked at her in shocked silence. Martha was the first to recover.

"We'll talk about it later, Nora," she said, but Nora was not listening.

"So Kitty Conway was right," she whispered, staring at her mother; "you're going to sell Mossgrove and we'll all be out on the road like tinkers."

"Nonsense," Martha said briskly. "You know better than to listen to Kitty Conway."

"But she was right, wasn't she, so now I do believe her!" Nora cried.

"Come here and have your breakfast," Martha told her.

"No, no!" Nora shouted. "I'm going to tell Peter what you're doing," and she ran up the stairs crying. They heard her running along the corridor and the door of Peter's room banging shut behind her.

You could hear a pin drop in the kitchen. Without a further word Martha rose from the table and swept up into the parlour.

Davy looked at Jack in consternation. "You told me to keep my mouth shut, but of course I couldn't," he said, his big honest face full of regret.

"Well, it was better that they hear it this way than in the village or in school," Jack told him.

"I suppose so," Davy said doubtfully.

"Well, eat up anyway because we have a long day ahead of us," Jack said briskly, "because no matter what upheavals come our way the animals must be fed and the land kept going. I'm going to oil the corn drill after breakfast," he finished decisively, even though the thought had only just come into his head. It was better to be doing something.

"Jack, you're one mighty man!" Davy said appreciatively, "and of course you're right, so we'll keep on going and maybe whatever it was you said about our worries being overcome by events might happen."

I wish to God that I could honestly believe that, Jack thought, but in order to encourage Davy he said, "Fair play to you, you grasped that one."

"I'm not as thick as I look," Davy told him, stretching across the table and picking up the egg that Martha had left uneaten.

Later that day, as Jack was oiling the corn drill, Peter came and sat on the shaft. They were in the back of the cart-house behind the trap where the corn drill lay from spring to spring gathering dust. Peter said nothing for a long time and Jack let him alone with his thoughts. It was usually Nora who came to chat with him. Peter had always gone to Ned and then to Davy since he came. But now for some reason he felt the need to talk to himself, and Jack wished that he had answers but knew that he had none.

"She's making a mistake, isn't she?" Peter said finally.

"Well, I don't know what she's thinking," Jack told him. "Maybe she feels that she couldn't manage."

"But we are managing," Peter said.

"Well, I thought we were too," Jack admitted.

"I want to stay here," Peter said simply.

"Did you talk it over with your mother?"

"She talked and I listened," Peter said: "a lot of bullshit about education and a better way of life. I don't want what she calls a better way of life. I want to stay here with Davy and you and Bran."

At least, Jack thought ruefully, I made it before Bran on his list. Poor Peter, his heart went out to him, but he knew that what he wanted right now was somebody to just listen to him.

"When my grandfather died you ran Mossgrove with Nana Nellie, didn't you?" Peter asked.

"That's right."

"Well, it's no different now," Peter said.

That's where you're wrong, Jack thought; it is different, because we have a different woman of the house. Nellie loved Mossgrove and Martha doesn't, and that's the difference. But if she would only give herself a chance, Jack felt sure that she would grow to love it too. Martha had points that he had often admired, but there was some devil driving her and she could not rest easy. But selling Mossgrove was not going to solve that problem. If for some reason she had to stick with it he felt that things would come right, but there was no talking to her. When she got a notion she became hell-bent in that direction, and at the moment that notion was to sell Mossgrove.

"Listen to me, Peter," he said firmly, "there is no good in arguing with your mother. It will only back her into a corner, because she has a very stubborn streak. Our best chance is to take it easy and try to coax her around to our way of thinking, and you and Nora are the best to do that."

"Well, I'm after having a blazing row with her just now and Nora is crying inside in the kitchen. I don't feel like taking it easy, I feel like kicking her in the shins," Peter told him bluntly, a mutinous look on his face.

"It's hard to blame you, I suppose," Jack sighed, "but we'll only have to hope for the best."

He could see that Peter was not getting much comfort

from their conversation. Soon afterwards he got up silently and, with his hands thrust deep into his pockets and his shoulders hunched, he strode up the boreen with Bran on his heels. Probably going down to Nolans', Jack hoped, because maybe Betty Nolan would be more of a help to him, and Jeremy and himself would be able to thrash things out between them.

Soon afterwards Nora arrived, tear-stained and bedraggled. "I don't want to go to school on Monday," she said tearfully.

"And why so, Nora?" he asked sympathetically.

"Because Kitty Conway will be all talk about Mossgrove and saying horrid things about us," Nora said, wiping her eyes with the back of her hand.

"Maybe she mightn't."

"She will, Jack; she's always at me every chance she can get."

So Ned had been right, he thought: one of the Conways was at Nora. But he decided that he had better tread carefully in case she'd shut up like a clam if he showed too much interest.

"Why is she at you?" he asked casually, pouring oil carefully into the axle of the wheel.

"Well, it's better now," she told him, "since I'm not sitting with her and I'm with Rosie Nolan."

"How did you manage that change?"

"I thumped Kitty's head off the desk," she told him proudly.

"You did what?" he said in amazement, all pretence of not being interested gone.

"I did," she said, proceeding to outline in detail the events of her first day back in school after the funeral. He listened with interest, thinking that Miss Buckley was a fair bit of a bitch to treat a child like that after all she had been through.

"You handled that well," he told Nora when she had finished her story.

"Do you think that I did, Jack?" she asked in delight, all sign of tears disappearing.

"You did so," he said admiringly, "and you'll handle Monday as well. When it comes to it, you won't be afraid."

"Do you think I won't, Jack?" she asked doubtfully, "'cause I'm afraid of the thought of it."

"Sometimes that's the worst part of it," he reassured her.

"Could be," she agreed slowly, but then her eyes filled up with tears again and she sobbed: "I don't want to leave Mossgrove. I want to stay here with you and Bran and Davy."

He put down the oil can and sat on the shaft of the corn drill, where she climbed on to his knee and put her arms around his neck and cried into his shoulder. He let her cry for a while, patting her head as he would Bran. Then he unwound her arms from around his neck and, taking her by the shoulders, he held her back so that he could look into her eyes.

"Listen, Nora, it is now the beginning of April, and the sale is not until the end of May, so that's a good few weeks away. A lot can happen in that much time. I'm not saying that it won't be sold, but I'm hoping to God for all our sakes that it won't happen."

"I'm praying to Dada," she confided, "since the day Kitty Conway said it. But so far he hasn't done anything about it only to let it happen," she finished disconsolately.

"Well, we can't lose heart," Jack told her, "or if we do

we're finished. So you keep praying and I'll keep running the place, and who knows: maybe this time next year we'll be still here."

He wished that he could feel as confident as his talk, but he hated to see her so dejected. She brightened up and smiled at him and then slid off his knee.

"You're nearly as good as Dada was for making things all right," she told him as she dried her eyes and straightened her shoulders. "And now I think I'll go down to look at the tadpoles in the frog spawn in the Glen and see if they've come out."

As she ran out of the haggard Jack thought that it was great to be ten and to be able to forget your troubles in the pursuit of tadpoles. He wondered if it was fair to be encouraging her to think that Mossgrove might not be sold when in his heart he did not really believe it.

Do you know something, Jack, he said to himself, you'd want to be God to do the right thing here today.

He sat there looking around the old cart-house. In here was stored the square timber butt that was used to shift the big dung-hills from outside the cow stalls and stables. He had been planning to do that soon. Parked behind and almost under the butt was the low mowing machine with its back-slung iron seat. When that came out the hay rakes and the pikes had to be taken down from the rafters above. Beneath them the wheel raker and the swath turner that came out for the hay making. Hanging off the wall were the slatted timber sidings that went on to the creamery cart when the bonhams were taken to the fair. The big shed was full of the machinery that kept the farm going, and the old man had trained him well in the care of it.

The birds made this open-fronted shed their own, and he had to throw an old sheet over the trap to keep it free of their droppings. Anything else in there did not have to be protected as it all belonged to the open fields anyway. In this shed he had spent many a long winter day doing repairs. There was great satisfaction in cutting a piece of timber and planing it to the exact size to fit snugly into a portion that was showing wear and tear. There was a sense of achievement in a job like that well done. He had many hours of deep-rooted satisfaction in here. Now he walked around and ran his hand lovingly over the long shafts and the cool iron seats. He had enjoyed looking after them and was proud of their condition. But what was to become of all his well-cared-for farm machinery?

Later, as he walked home up the boreen, he decided that it had been an unreal kind of day. When he had got engrossed in something he could almost forget that they were for sale, and then it would hit him like a ton of bricks and nearly take the heart out of him. He had thought that Kate might have called, but as the day wore on and that hope faded, he felt more disheartened.

Maybe Kate would stand aside and let Martha go ahead without protest. Why should she bother anyway; it was no skin off her nose. Kate had her good job, and maybe now with Ned gone Mossgrove did not mean as much to her. After all, it was Martha's responsibility, and Nora and Peter were her children, and she would be very quick to tell Kate that.

As he opened the back gate Toby went wild with delight and Jack stooped down to pat him on the head.

"Glad to see that someone is in good humour anyway," he said. Looking around the little yard he was pleased to see the henhouse closed. God bless you, Sarah, he thought, you're a great neighbour. Just then she appeared around the side of the cottage.

"I lit the fire for you, Jack," she told him; "it's after turning chilly. Kate said to tell you that she will be back to you later on."

"Oh, will she?" he said with relief, his face breaking into a smile. "I was half expecting her below all day."

"Well, something turned up," Sarah told him, "and maybe it was just as well not to call today. Things might get said that were better left unsaid."

"Maybe the time for talking out has come," Jack told her grimly. "A few people have taken more than their due from our woman below. It could be that it's time to take the bull by the horns. We have nothing to lose now, and there is no one to be hurt."

"Jack, you're in fighting form!" she said in alarm.

"Do you know something, Sarah, I'm beginning to think that maybe it's bad to put up with too much, because then people will give you plenty to put up with. The old man put up with nothing, and by God no one trod on his toes and got away with it."

"Could be that you have a point," she admitted slowly, "but that was never your way, Jack, and you're a bit long in the tooth to be changing direction at this stage."

"Sarah, you're a great one for keeping things in perspective. Will you come in for a cup of tea?"

"No, yourself and Kate need time to thrash things out between you, so I'll be off. I might call back to Agnes – this is not easy on her either."

He tidied up the kitchen quickly and put extra turf on the fire. He was so glad that Kate was coming. For a bit there, coming up the boreen, he had lost heart, thinking that she no longer cared about Mossgrove. He should have known better. You could always depend on Kate to be there when you wanted her. Look at the way she had got Martha out of the bed, though on second thoughts maybe they should have left her there. But of course that was no solution either, because they could not have kept going on that way. He was delighted that she was coming because no one else could understand the situation like her. Even though Sarah had been great last night she did not share his feeling for Mossgrove. Kate knew exactly how he felt about the place because she felt the same way. There was great comfort in talking to someone like that. He sat by the fire, eased off his heavy boots and stretched his toes out to the fire. It was not yet dark and he liked to sit in the half light by the fire.

He must have dozed off because when he opened his eyes again Kate was sitting across the fire from him with the Maggie on her lap and Toby stretched out at her feet.

"Didn't like to wake you," she said gently; "you probably needed the little sleep."

"Old age must be catching up with me at last, Kate," he told her, straightening himself up, "to be dozing off in the chair like an old man."

"The upset of this sale is enough to put years on all of us."

"What do you make of it?" he asked wearily.

"She intends to go ahead with it," Kate said, "but we'll give it a fair try to make her change her mind anyway."

"Do you think it's possible?" Jack asked.

"No, I don't," Kate admitted, "but we can't give up without a struggle of some sort. We're not beaten until the hammer goes down on the day of the sale. Then the Conways will move in."

"Christ, the old man will turn in his grave." Jack shook his head in desperation. "Of course they're interested and the money will come from over the water."

"That's right," Kate told him; "had it all for nothing from Matt Conway this morning. Delighted to tell me, of course."

"Dear God! Did I ever think that I'd see this day, that the Conways would move in to Mossgrove. If it weren't for them we could hold it, because if we sent out the word that we didn't want it sold, no other neighbour would bid. But of course we can't do that now, because that would mean that the Conways would get it for half nothing."

"I had thought of that too," Kate said, "because in actual fact Martha is in no fit state to make a decision like this right now. She could be sorry next year."

"Too late then," Jack sighed; "you can't unsell the sold."

"It was the one thing that Nellie said after reading *Gone with the Wind,*" Kate remembered. 'Don't ever sell land. Because when all else failed, Scarlet still had Tara.'"

"I think that if our Scarlet has her way there will be no Tara left," Jack said bitterly.

"Now Jack, don't let it get you down; we're not out in the road like the tinkers, as Kitty Conway told Nora. By the way, do Nora and Peter know?"

"They do indeed," he said and explained how it had happened.

"Strange woman," she commented when he had finished. "I've been thinking, and I decided that some morning next week when they're gone to school I'll call on Martha and try a persuading job. It would be better if they were not there in case I get carried away."

"Maybe it's time that someone got carried away."

"God, Jack, that's a change of approach coming from you," Kate said in surprise; "your policy was always a bit like Nellie's – don't rock the boat."

"Maybe I was wrong, and maybe we've been tiptoeing around Martha for far too long."

"So you think, Jack, that it's time to take off the kid gloves?"

"I do," Jack said with conviction.

"I'll remember that when I go to Mossgrove."

CHAPTER FOURTEEN

FR BURKE, A large, red-faced man, stood with his back to the altar. A rosary of chins cascaded down on to his white alb. He was busy turning the Blessed Trinity into a bigger mystery than it had ever been in the minds of his congregation. Most of them had parted company with him shortly after he had embarked on his complicated unravelling, and they were busy thinking of yesterday's activities or intent on tomorrow's plans.

We are a very tolerant people, Kate thought, to have put up with his pompous expounding for as long as she could remember. She sometimes wondered if he knew or cared that most of the parish slept open-eyed through his sermons. They were too polite to close their eyes and doze off in front of him, but if somebody found themselves comfortably placed behind a lady with a large hat they availed of the shelter she afforded them and blissfully closed their eyes. St Paul could never have anticipated that his instruction to the women of Jerusalem would in the course of history be a blessing to the suffering people of Kilmeen. Why was it, she wondered, that the priests who gave the most boring sermons felt the need to keep going. Fr Brady was interesting and never continued longer than your concentration span, whereas Fr Burke was like a cawing crow who could not find a suitable branch for landing so he kept circling.

Finally, with a heartfelt "Thanks be to God", the relieved congregation blessed themselves and hurriedly left the church. Outside in the general milieu she met David, who was immaculately groomed and looked so attractive that her heart gave a jerk at the sight of him.

"David, you look as if you have just walked out of a gentlemen's tailoring establishment," she smiled at him. "I never saw you so dressed up before."

"You haven't forgotten," he asked worriedly, "that we're going to meet his nibs at three o'clock, have you?"

"Of course not," she told him.

She had been surprised when David had asked her to accompany him on his visit to the parish priest to get sanction for the new school. David had already written to Fr Burke from Dublin but had heard nothing back, so he had arranged a meeting while on holidays. It was his father who had suggested that it might be a good idea to have Kate go along as well. The Doc thought that Kate, having no axe to grind, might strengthen David's case. The P.P. and Nellie had been good friends, so he felt that maybe the sight of Kate might soften the old boy. Kate had her doubts about that possibility, but when David asked her she felt that he, too, must have thought that she might be an asset. She was only too happy to do anything to help.

"You're coming back to our place for a bite to eat first, aren't you?" he asked.

"As I told your father yesterday, I can never say no to Hannah's cooking," she told him, "and Hannah doesn't give you a bite to eat, she packs you up to the gills."

"That's right," he agreed, patting his stomach. "I've even put on a few pounds since I came home."

"Well, that's no harm to you, you're just skin and bone."

"You can't fatten quality," he said smiling.

"What are the two of you sparring about?" Sarah Jones asked, joining them. She was neat and trim in a brown coat with a matching hat framing her white hair.

"We're going up to the P.P. after dinner," David told her.

"Well, I never thought it was that serious between you two," Sarah joked.

Oh God, Sarah! Kate thought, I wish you wouldn't say things like that.

"One thing at a time now, Sarah," David laughed. "We have our hands full at the moment. Kate has told you about the school?"

"She has indeed," Sarah said seriously, "and I wish you luck this evening, and let me know how things go. But now I must get moving and do my bit of shopping before heading home."

As she walked briskly away from them, Kate looked after her in admiration. "She's really an amazing woman for her years: she'd be in her mid-sixties now and she'd pass for twenty years younger."

"She was always full of energy," David agreed, "and so interested in everything. She's very keen for this school to get going, isn't she?"

"That's Sarah all out," Kate told him. "Maybe it's the fact that she delivered the most of them that she is so conscious of the welfare of the children. She has great interest in the school."

"Well, we'll keep her posted. But we had better get going or we'll be late for Hannah's dinner, and that would never do."

Just as she turned to go she felt eyes fastened on her and looked across the street to find Matt Conway staring at her with a malevolent look on his face. Never had she encountered such naked hatred. Feeling suddenly chilled, she shivered.

"Are you all right, Kate?" David asked with concern.

"I think that someone has just walked over my grave," she said.

"Ah, come on, Kate," he said, "there are enough daft notions around here without you adding to them."

"I suppose you're right," she agreed, pulling herself together and thinking that it was silly to be frightened by an ignorant lump like Matt Conway.

As they walked down the street she was happy to have David beside her and she could feel the old sense of excitement in his presence. She wondered if there was any romance in his life in Dublin. If there was somebody in Dublin he would hardly be planning to come back to Kilmeen. While these thoughts ran through her head she realised that he was talking beside her.

"I'm going over to see old Hobbs in Ross next week," he was saying. "I wrote to the address in America that you gave Dad. Hobbs would have an idea of the rent expected and it might be no harm to get in touch with him as well. You dealt with him about that house before, didn't you? Would you like to come with me? You might think of something that I'd forget," he finished.

"If this school gets going I'll be looking for my cut out of it," she smiled, "but of course I'll come. What day are you going?"

"Would Monday week be all right with you?" he asked. "Because I wrote to him and he wrote back, that that was the soonest he could see me."

"That's fine. Old Hobbs doesn't move in a hurry, and anyway during this week I'm going to Mossgrove and not looking forward to it."

"Dad was telling me about it," he said. "Any hope of changing her mind, do you think?"

"Very little, I'd say," she shook her head, "but at least I'll have a shot at it. It's really too soon after the shock of Ned's death for Martha to make a wise decision. If she goes ahead now she could be sorry in a few years time, and as well as that there are the children. They want to stay where they are and they need the security of Mossgrove right now."

"You've enough on your plate at the moment, haven't you, without my problems on top of it?" he asked as they turned off the pavement up the stone steps to his home. The brass door knob gleamed on the dark green door and David pushed it open and led her into the spacious black-and-white-tiled hall.

"Strangely enough," she told him, "I find it a distraction from what's happening in Mossgrove, so it's a good thing really. Otherwise the sale of Mossgrove might get on top of me."

"I'm glad," he said, taking her coat and hanging it on the tall hall-stand beside the stairs. "And now we're going to enjoy Hannah's dinner and forget all our troubles for an hour."

Hannah came bustling from the back of the hall, a navy blue overall belted around an ample waist and her snow-white hair caught back in a knot behind a round red face. She was a large woman with a heart to match, and her one aim in life was to make things easier for the Doc, whom she felt the entire parish were trying to kill with their night calls and constant demands. Kate was a favourite because she was deemed to lighten his load whenever possible.

"Kate, you're welcome," she smiled, pointing towards the door at the foot of the stairs. "Himself is inside reading the papers. David, you come in and take out the soup for me."

"At your service," he said, following her back the hallway to disappear under the curving staircase into the kitchen. Kate knew that the door beside her opened into the living room, which had a connecting door through to the kitchen.

As she pushed the door open the warmth of the fire swept out against her. It was a large, high-ceilinged room with a long table in the centre and sagging chairs and sofas overflowing with floppy cushions around the fire. The Doc was stretched out on the sofa nearest to the fire with a cat asleep across his knees and a stack of newspapers scattered on the floor around him.

"Kate, you're welcome," he said, smiling; he attempted to remove the cat but she stuck in her claws and refused to be disturbed.

"Don't upset her; stay where you are," Kate told him, settling into a small, deep chair by the fire. The white marble fireplace curved over her and the deep grate was full of glowing logs.

"Hannah believes in a good fire," she smiled.

"Always," he said. "It's great to come in here on a cold evening and stretch out before the fire."

"She has you spoilt."

"Don't I know, and it's great to have her."

Kate knew that Hannah had kept this house a home after his wife Joan had died. The two women had been old neighbours over in Ross, and even when Joan was alive Hannah was second in command, and indeed sometimes first if she did not agree with something that was being done. She had been like an aunt to his children, and when their mother died she had become more.

"Will everybody please be seated," David instructed, coming through from the kitchen bearing a tray of steaming soup bowls and placing them at the four places set on the table.

The Doc uncurled himself off the couch and eased the protesting cat on to the floor where she arched her back and headed underneath the table.

The soup was thick and creamy and Kate felt that it was a meal in itself, but Hannah followed up with laden plates of main course. When Kate remarked that the spring lamb was delicious, Hannah smiled and said, "Could be Mossgrove lamb: Danny the butcher and his father before him always bought from the Phelans, as you know."

"It tastes wonderful anyway," Kate told her, thinking that they might not be buying Phelan lambs much longer.

"This is a grand time of the year," said the Doc, sensing her train of thought: "lambs and daffodils and the first of the rhubarb. Isn't that right, Hannah?"

"You stole into the kitchen," she accused him, "and you saw the rhubarb."

"Have you got rhubarb already, Hannah?" Kate asked in surprise.

"I put an old iron bucket over it to bring it on fast," Hannah told her. "I wanted to have it for David for Easter. He always loved rhubarb since he was a small, bold brat."

"Oh, Hannah, you're a brick!" David said. "I can never remember an Easter that you did not have rhubarb and custard. To me nothing's better than rhubarb and custard at Easter."

Kate had to agree with him when Hannah brought a big bowl of pink rhubarb in from the kitchen.

"Do you know the Irish for rhubarb?" David asked Kate.

"No," she answered in a puzzled voice, "can't say that I ever heard it."

"Ah, David, for goodness sake," Hannah protested, "why do you always have to remind us of that every year?"

"What is it anyway?" Kate asked.

"Purgoid na manac."

"Does that mean what I think it means?"

"I don't know how good your Irish is," David said, "but it means the purgative of the monks. It was the only laxative they had long ago in the monasteries."

"Well, you learn something new every day," Kate said. "Will we take some of it up to Fr Burke?"

"Oh, Kate, you're not the nice girl that I thought your were," David laughed, and the Doc and Hannah joined in.

They finished with cups of tea and light pastry oozing cream. Kate felt that she could lie down on one of the comfortable couches and sleep peacefully for the evening. But David had his eye on the clock, and as soon as the last plate was carried back to the kitchen he said, "We'll head up towards the presbytery now. He'll be looking for excuses to get the better of us, so we'd better start with a clean slate."

Kate rose reluctantly to her feet, thinking how pleasant it would be to spend the afternoon here with himself and the Doc, instead of facing up to Fr Burke, whom she had always found a bit hard to take. As well as that, she was a little worried that she might not say the right thing. She knew how important this was to David and she wanted to do everything she could to help him. Maybe I'm trying to impress him, she decided.

As they walked up the street with the Doc and Hannah's good wishes ringing in their ears, she could sense David's tension. This school is very important to him, she thought, which had the effect of making her feel even more nervous.

The avenue to the parochial house curved in behind the church. It was a large, imposing house with bare green lawns and no flowers. When David lifted the heavy black iron knocker, the bang seemed to thunder through silence.

"Good God," he whispered, "I never thought it would make such a racket – 'twould wake the dead."

"Never mind," Kate assured him, "it's probably faint enough from the other side," and she had to make an effort to stop herself from giggling.

Then they could hear bolts being drawn back; the door opened slowly, and Lizzy the housekeeper's nose came around the edge. A tall, thin woman with black sparse hair, her nose was her dominant feature, and she sniffed the air around her as if nothing about it pleased her.

"Good afternoon, Lizzy," David greeted her pleasantly, "we have an appointment with Fr Burke."

"Not finished yet," she informed them in disapproving tones.

"Can we come in and wait?" Kate asked as Lizzy made no attempt to open the door further.

"I suppose so," she said grudgingly, and slowly opened back the door just wide enough for them to get in sideways.

"Wait here," she told them and disappeared back a long brown corridor.

Kate looked around and realised that, even though she had not been in here for years, nothing had changed. Everything was brown. The lino on the floor and running up the stairs was a dark brown with white linking along the sides. The stairs themselves wore many coats of varnish that did not fit snugly on top of each other but bubbled up along the handrail in foxy protest. The walls were covered in beige wallpaper and the picture rail bore brown, sad-faced saints who could not muster up a smile between them. On the huge hall-stand carved gargoyles snarled at each other under Fr Burke's hats.

"He should get Mark in here to brighten up his colour scheme," she whispered. "I never saw anything so drab."

"Kate, we're not here to redesign his house," David said severely, but he smiled in spite of himself. "I feel as if I'm back in boarding school waiting outside the headmaster's door to be reprimanded," he added.

Just then they heard shuffling footsteps and saw Lizzy's shadowy figure reappear.

"He's ready now," she told them in a prim voice, and they followed her thin form back the corridor.

"In here," she said, knocking so timidly on a heavy door that Kate thought nobody on the other side could hear.

Nevertheless, a big voice boomed through.

"Come in," it instructed with authority.

Lizzy inched the door open very slowly, and gradually the room inside came into view. The entire wall straight opposite the door was book-lined from floor to ceiling, and in front of it behind a large desk sat Fr Burke, his huge pudgy fingers interlaced and resting on the green leather top. A tall, north-facing window let in a grey light and there was no heating in the room.

Looking at his overheated face it was obvious that he had just vacated a much warmer room. We were brought in here to be intimidated, Kate decided.

"Sit down," he instructed. Two straight-backed chairs were already in position, well apart, directly in front of him.

"Well, now, what's all this about?" he enquired.

"I wrote to you about it, Father," David began with determination. "It's about starting a new secondary school here in Kilmeen."

"For what reason?" Fr Burke barked, his folded chins shaking in annoyance. He was glaring at David, his purple lips pursed.

"The children around here need education," David told him quietly.

"Are you saying that what the good nuns over in Ross are doing is not education?"

Careful, David, Kate thought, he's going to turn this into a battle of wits and is trying to trip you up. But David said calmly, "The nuns are providing a very good commercial course, but it's mostly girls who go there, and. . ."

"You can't blame the nuns for that," Fr Burke cut across him.

"It's no fault of the nuns," David agreed, "but even for the girls who go there it would be better for them to do their Inter and Leaving certificate before going on to Ross."

"So you're saying that what the nuns are providing is only second-rate stuff," he barked.

"No I am not," David told him firmly, "but there is need for more educational facilities here. Our children are emigrating uneducated, and it's only manual jobs that are available to them wherever they go."

"So you think that manual labour is beneath them? There's nothing wrong with earning your bread by the sweat of you brow, my boy. Many a good Irishman did it before them."

"I'm only saying that they should have the choice," David told him.

"And you would take the bread out of the mouths of the nuns in Ross, who started their school here on the understanding that theirs would be the only school in this parish?"

"Things change, Father."

"And some of them not for the better," Fr Burke asserted. "You have a job in Dublin: why can't you stay up there? Do you not know when you're well off with a fine comfortable pensionable job. Your school here could fall through, and then where would that leave you?"

"It won't fail," David told him, "and even if it did I could always get another job."

"Nobody likes to employ a failure," Fr Burke observed.

"That would be my problem," David said sharply, annoyance creeping into his voice. "And . . ."

"Well, the setting up of this school is my problem," Fr Burke cut in, "and my first duty is to the nuns in my parish.

They are under my protection, and that's the end of the matter as far as I am concerned."

You arrogant old toad, thought Kate, I would not like to be depending on you for protection. She had planned to say very little in case of saying the wrong thing, but as she listened she could feel the school slipping away and her irritation mounting. She decided that they had got nowhere and that the time had come to get a few facts straightened out.

"So apart from the opposition of the nuns, you have nothing against the school," she interceded.

For the first time he turned his small, piercing blue eyes on her, giving her his full attention.

"What do you mean?"

"You say that your only opposition to the school is the protection of the nuns, is that right?" she shot back at him, sitting on the edge of her chair and looking him straight in the eye.

"Well, what of it?" he asked angrily.

"Is that the only objection that you have?" she persisted.

"That's my business," he told her. "I don't have to explain myself to anybody."

"Well, I can tell you," she said, "that the nuns have no objection to the new school. As a matter of fact, they think that it will be good for their school, which it probably will."

"Do you mean to tell me that you went behind my back about this?" he blustered.

"I did not go behind your back. I never went behind anyone's back in my life," she said, rising to her feet and striding to the front of his desk. "I went to school in Ross and loved the nuns there, and now I visit them regularly, and yes, I have discussed this with them, as I was quite entitled to do. They are enlightened, forward-thinking women and want to see the children of this parish getting the best start that they can get in life. So they have no opposition to this school."

"You had no right," Fr Burke gasped but got no further, because Kate threw caution to the wind.

"I had every right because now we know! *You* are the only opposition. *You* are the only one standing in the way of progress."

Fr Burke put his two huge hands on his desk and jumped to his feet with such speed that his chair tilted backwards and crashed to the floor behind him.

"How dare you speak to me like this!" he spluttered, choking with rage. "To think that a daughter of Nellie Phelan's would come in to my house and. . ."

"Leave my mother out of this," she said fiercely. "She was a lady who listened to your self-opinionated, pompous meanderings all her life and never criticised you. But if she knew what you're doing now she'd turn in her grave."

"Get out!" he shouted, pounding the desk with his ham fist. "Get out of my house!"

"You don't need to tell me," she replied, pounding the desk with her closed fist and pushing her angry face close to his. "And may God forgive you for your narrow vision, because I never will and neither will a lot of this parish." And before he could say another word she marched across the floor and whipped the door open, nearly falling over Lizzy, who was standing there with a bemused expression on her face.

Kate banged back the big iron bolt of the front door and strode out on to the crunching gravel where she stood with her fists clenched in anger, and then headed for the gate. As she cooled down she was aware that David had caught up with her and was walking silently beside her. She was afraid to look at him because she knew that she had burnt their boats behind them. Whatever hope he had had before, she had now put paid to everything. As they walked in silence around the side of the church, she sneaked a sideways glance at him. His face was white and his jaw was tight with anger.

"I blew it, didn't I?" she admitted miserably.

"No, you didn't," David told her quietly. "He was against it anyway. I had hoped that he'd have been some way reasonable, but he was impossible. There is no way that he is going to agree to the school. He must really have it in for Dad. But, God, it was something to watch the two of you. It was like a terrier and a bloodhound in attack."

"I lost the head totally," Kate admitted.

"You did."

"Are you angry with me?" she asked tentatively.

"Angry? There was enough anger in there to set fire to a hay barn, not to mind me adding to it, and the best part of it all was that you and Dad had warned *me* to keep cool."

"I was a fine one to talk, wasn't I, but he just drove me mad with his patronising attitude towards everything."

"As soon as you started I knew that you were going to let him have it. I could feel it coming like a thunderstorm."

"He's been irritating me for years with his boring sermons and his overbearing attitude," Kate declared, "but I never realised how much I had it in for him until I started."

"Lizzy will have a great time telling the whole village what Kate Phelan said to the P.P."

"Oh my God," Kate gasped. "I never thought of that, and of course she'll make me out to be a real demon."

"Never mind. You only said what a lot of us are thinking."

"But thinking it and saying it are two different things."

"Well, maybe it needed to be said. He's always got away with murder."

"You must be very disappointed," she said.

"I suppose I am," he agreed.

"I wish to God that I had stayed out of it. You'd have had some chance without me."

"If you hadn't done it I might have lost my cool myself," David admitted, "but I don't think that I would have been as dramatic as you. I'd forgotten that you were so fiery."

"Where do we go from here?" she asked.

"He's going to make an announcement next Sunday off the altar," David said. "He told me that after you stormed out, but I think that we've had it as far as he is concerned."

"I think you're right," Kate agreed bleakly.

"It's a shame, because our whole future hinged on his decision."

Later that night, as she prepared for bed, Kate thought back over David's words. What exactly had they meant?

Better not read too much into this, my girl, she told herself as she drew back the curtains before getting into bed. Suddenly she noticed someone move in the shadows of her back garden. She stepped back from the window and watched in the darkness, and just as she was beginning to think that she had imagined the whole thing, Matt Conway slunk out from under the hedge and disappeared through the gate. She crept downstairs and checked that every window and door was securely locked, but she did not sleep too well that night.

CHAPTER FIFTEEN

NORA LAY IN bed and wondered if she could get out of going to school today. The thought of it nearly made her sick. Could she pretend that she was really sick? She was feeling terrible, but she knew that it had really nothing to do with being sick in the usual way, and it would be very hard to convince Mom. Especially when Mom already knew that she did not want to go to school. Mom did not understand that she dreaded going to school because all of them would be talking about Mossgrove being for sale. She never remembered anyone in school with their home for sale. Nobody that she knew had ever sold their house and farm. They would be looking at her as if she had two heads or something. She was not like Rosie Nolan, who loved being the centre of attention. She hated it.

It was bad enough after Dada had died, but at least people died in other houses too, but nobody sold their farm and moved away. Most of her friends had their grandparents living with them or near them. She did not want to move away either. At least she supposed that they would be moving away, because why else would Mom be selling. She did not really know what was going to happen. Mom did not seem to know what they were going to do either, only that she was going to sell Mossgrove. It was all such a muddle. She could hardly believe her ears when she had overheard Jack and Davy talking about the Conways buying Mossgrove. The thought that the white worm would be sleeping in her bedroom nearly made her sick. The whole thing from the first minute that she had heard Davy shouting at Mom about it made her miserable.

Peter was in a silent rage and would not talk about it, and she knew that Davy felt uneasy talking to her about it. Mom just told her that it would be all for the best, but she did not believe that. Jack was the only one who understood, but she sensed that he was more upset that he was letting on. If only Aunty Kate would call. She was the only hope. Maybe she might be able to do something. Aunty Kate loved Mossgrove the way Dad and Jack did, so she would try to stop Mom if she could. But would she be able? Mom did not like Aunty Kate, and she had not liked Nana Nellie. Was that why she was selling Mossgrove, because they all liked it and she did not. Why didn't Mom like Mossgrove? She could never understand that, but then there were a lot of things she could not understand and it made everything very complicated.

She wished that Dada could come back and straighten it all out. Everything was upside down since he went. He had kept everything straight, and you could talk to Dada and he understood. Why did he have to die? God was mean to take him away. If he wanted somebody, why did he not take Nana Lehane. She had heard Nana herself saying that and it had surprised her. But maybe Nana was right. Uncle Mark could manage without Nana, but they could not manage without Dada. They had been in a terrible mess at the beginning before Aunty Kate came back, but now they were worse than ever again. She prayed to him every night but he did not seem to be listening. Where was he anyway? she wondered for the hundredth time since he had died. Surely if he could hear her he would not let Mossgrove be sold. Maybe nobody would buy it. If the neighbours like the Nolans knew that they did not want to sell, maybe nobody might buy, but then that would not stop the Conways. Nothing could stop the Conways.

She looked around her familiar room with the sloping ceiling and the window above the farmyard. She sat up in bed to look out and she saw Jack bringing a bucket of milk out from the stalls and pouring it in over the top of the churn. She could even see the white strainer cloth that Mom had tied around the top of the churn. If she lent sideways and hung out over the side of her bed, she could look out through the other window and down over the valley to the river and see Conways' farm on the hill opposite. But she did not want to look out that window this morning. Instead she raised her eyes to the picture of St Theresa above her bed. It had been Nana Nellie's picture and she had called it the Little Flower. Nora liked looking at her because she looked calm and serene, as if she had no worries.

Mom had wanted to put Nana Nellie's pictures into the back of the old press in the landing, but Dad had asked herself and Peter if they wanted to hang any of them in their rooms and she had taken the Little Flower. When Dad had suggested that they give the rest of them to Aunty Kate, Mom had frowned at him and said "they belong here", and that had been the last she had ever seen of the pictures.

She wondered if the Little Flower ever had problems like she had. Then she looked over at the Child of Prague on top of the orange crate. He always looked happy, as if he did not have a care in the world, and yet look what happened to him. On the back of the door her green coat was hanging under an old coat to keep the dust off it. Mom had got it cleaned a few weeks ago, and it was as good now as it had been the night that she had finished making it. That night seemed like a long time ago.

She had felt like a princess that night in her bright green coat, and Mom had been so pleased. When Dada came in he had pretended not to know her, she looked so grand, and he had told Mom that she was a great woman. Mom was always delighted when Dada praised her. She loved the coat, and even though Kitty Conway had mocked it and made her feel bad about it for a while, she had got over that and now she loved it again. She did not wear it now because she wore the black coat that Nana had so miraculously produced the day of the funeral. But on Sundays after coming home from mass she sometimes put it on and walked around the room in it, and if she closed her eyes she could hear Dada's voice saying, "I don't know this grand stranger."

Mom said that she could wear the green coat again when they came out of mourning for Dada.

"Nora, will you get out of bed, you lazy lump, or we'll be late for school," Peter burst in the door, his face full of annoyance that she was still inside in bed.

"Pete, I don't want to go today," she protested tearfully; "they'll be all asking questions and I'll hate it."

"What about me?" he demanded. "Won't it be the same for me?"

"I know," she agreed, "but you won't have. . ."

"Yea, yea, Kitty Conway," he said impatiently, "but I'll have the lads lording it over me. Can you imagine what Rory Conway will be like?"

"But you're bigger than me."

"Listen, Norry," he advised, "it will be easier if you go today because if you don't, tomorrow will be harder."

"I suppose you're right as usual," she agreed, reluctantly turning back the bedclothes and sliding on to the floor.

"Move fast now," Peter told her, "because if we're late 'twill look as if we're afraid to come, and if we're early we'll have the Nolans with us."

"Right, I'll be down in two secs," Nora told him, whipping off her nightdress and starting to drag on her clothes in high speed.

Later they walked together silently up the boreen, each busy with their own imaginings of the day ahead.

"What does she want to sell at all for?" Peter burst out angrily. "It's not fair."

"I know," Nora sighed. Then, thinking of Kitty Conway, she added, "I wish that we were coming home."

"Norry, you're a great one for wishing things away, but that's no good."

"Makes me feel better, to think that in a few hours time we'll be walking down this boreen and that the first day will be over."

"Today is going to be the worst all right," Peter agreed, "and do you know something: they'll all be asking where are we going and what are we going to be doing, and I haven't a clue. Isn't that stupid?"

"Could we pretend?" Nora asked.

"Pretend what?" Peter demanded.

"Pretend that we know but that we can't say," Nora suggested, brightening up.

"Norry, will you have a grain of sense – they'd know that we were only bluffing."

"Well, it was only an idea."

"And a stupid one," he told her, closing the gate behind them.

As he heard the rattle of the gate Toby came bounding across Jack's yard and put his head out between the bars of the gate to lick their hands in delight.

"I'll miss Toby if we won't be coming in and out this gate," Nora said mournfully.

"What about Bran?" Peter asked.

"I'd die after Bran," she told him, "but surely we'd take Bran with us?"

"Depends where we're going," Peter said darkly.

"'Tis true for Kitty Conway," Nora said tearfully; "we'll be out on the road like the tinkers."

"Nora, will you shut up! We won't be out on the road like the tinkers."

"Do you think that Aunty Kate might try to stop Mom from selling?" Nora asked hopefully.

"She doesn't seem to be making much of an effort so far," Peter said bitterly. "She never even called after seeing it in the paper."

"She called to Jack," Nora said.

"Did she?" Peter asked eagerly. "Is she going to do anything?"

"She's calling some day while we are at school."

"That's because she's expecting a row and she doesn't want us to hear," Peter decided.

"I never thought of that," said Nora.

"But of course there will be a row: Mom wanting to sell and Aunt Kate trying to stop her."

"I hope that she can stop Mom."

"I doubt it."

They walked along the road beside Ned's young beeches.

"The leaves are out on Dada's trees," Nora said with excitement.

"They're out with a bit," Peter said dismissively.

"I know, but they look all there this morning," Nora said, and Peter laughed. "They're sort of big enough to move in the breeze, aren't they?"

Just then they heard a shout from behind and looked back to see the Nolans running to catch up with them. Rosie arrived puffing with exertion.

"You said that you'd be early," Jeremy told Peter, "and you meant it."

"He nearly rushed me off my feet," Rosie protested.

"The exercise is good for you," Peter told her.

"Cheek of you, Peter Phelan," she said, sticking out her tongue at him. "I could beat you in a race any day."

"Right," said Peter, "race you to Sarah Jones's gate." And the two of them took off, school sacks flying behind them.

"I hope she'll beat him," Nora said with feeling.

"Are you and Peter having a fight?" Jeremy asked in surprise.

"He won't talk since the thing in the paper and he's awful snappy," Nora told him.

"He was down with me on Saturday and we talked of nothing else," Jeremy told her.

"Well, he won't talk to me about it," Nora declared.

"That's because he's afraid you'd cry," Jeremy told her.

"I would too," she admitted.

"Crying is no good Nora," he said, "and whatever you do, don't cry in front of the Conways today."

"So you know about the Conways buying Mossgrove as well," Nora said.

"Everybody in Kilmeen knows that; the Conways love boasting. Although my father says that normally when people are buying land, they tell nobody, but then the Conways are not normal."

"I hate the thought of Kitty Conway sleeping in my room," Nora told him sadly. Jeremy was good to listen and she could tell him about most things that bothered her.

"It might never happen," he assured her; "my father says that land is never sold until you have the money in the bank, and ye're a long ways from that yet."

"Will you fight the Conways with Peter today if they have a row?" she asked him.

"Of course," he said, "Peter and I always fight the Conways together, but other times we can be friends with them too."

"Kitty and I are never friends," she told him.

"Rosie says that she really has it in for you."

"And I never did a thing to her," Nora told him as they arrived at Sarah Jones's gate where Rosie and Peter were sitting on the wall.

"Who won?" Nora asked.

"Do you mean to say that you weren't watching?" Rosie demanded.

"I beat her sick," Peter asserted.

"You did not, Peter Phelan," Rosie declared. "I beat you with inches to spare."

"It was only an old race, and you started ahead of me anyway," Peter told her.

"Come on, Peter," Jeremy said, "we'll go on ahead because the two of them are too slow for us."

"We could pass ye out if we wanted to," Rosie called after them, "but we have important things to discuss."

"Oh, we have indeed," Nora told her as the two boys went ahead. "I'm dreading Kitty Conway today – she's bound to get me in a corner at some stage."

"Now, you listen to me, Nora," Rosie instructed, "you will have to face up to Kitty Conway and stop being afraid of her."

"Look what happened the last time I faced up to her – I nearly killed her."

"She got what she deserved, and since then you've been avoiding her, so from today on no more avoiding. Just stand your ground."

"Rosie, today is going to be hard enough without taking on Kitty Conway as well."

"It's your chance not to back down. Once she sees that she'll leave you alone," Rosie instructed with an air of authority; then, softening a little at the look on Nora's face, she finished: "I'll be there as well to back you up if you need me, but it would be better if you did it on your own."

"But Rosie, I might not be coming to school here much longer anyway," Nora protested.

"You will. My mother says that Mossgrove will only be sold over Kate's dead body, whatever that means exactly.

But it sounds as if it might not be sold after all."

"Oh, wouldn't it be just great," Nora breathed. "If only that could happen I'd never again be lazy, and I'd be out of bed like a shot every morning."

"My mother says that your mother and Kate never got on and that Kate will tear strips off her about Mossgrove."

"Oh, Aunty Kate wouldn't do that," Nora protested, "and I wouldn't want Mom to be hurt."

"Oh Nora! My mother only meant that Kate would argue with her about not selling Mossgrove."

"Oh, that would be all right," Nora said in a relieved tone.

They arrived at the school to find that the yard was empty and everybody had gone in.

"Oh, we were too slow," Nora said in dismay; "the boys were right."

"We're not late," Rosie said firmly; "we were often later than this."

Nora knew that this was true, but she did not want to be last in today so that they'd be all looking at her. Rosie strode in ahead of her, and as Nora followed her to the front seat Miss Buckley turned around with a frown on her face.

"Nora Phelan, you can go back to your old seat now," she said. "I think that you've learnt your lesson."

Nora could hardly believe her ears. How could this be happening to her today of all days? She slouched over to the back seat and perched on the very edge of it, as far away from Kitty Conway as she possibly could. Kitty looked straight ahead and gave no reaction to Nora's return. All morning Kitty never looked in her direction and Nora began to wonder if she were invisible. Kitty never acknowledged her return one way or another. Nora was amazed and relieved, but she was afraid to relax as she thought apprehensively that there was a long day ahead.

At the break, when the rest of the children gathered around curiously asking questions, Kitty sat in the far corner of the playground eating her lunch by herself.

Rosie asked, "Did you say something to Kitty?"

"No, nothing," Nora told her, "but she's never said a word all morning. I can't believe it."

"What's come over her?" Rosie wondered.

"Don't know," Nora said, "but the sewing class is this evening. She'll murder me then."

When the tin boxes were distributed along the desks they all took out their pieces of sewing and knitting. Nora was endeavouring to turn the heel of a sock, a complicated procedure which required all her concentration. Kitty had a grubby piece of pleated cotton which she was trying to top-stitch as neatly as possible. Both kept their heads down, intent on their work, and when the girl at the other side of Kitty attempted to chat to her she was ignored.

What's come over Kitty, Nora wondered, but she was afraid to say anything in case she might trigger off the usual torrent of criticism and abuse. She decided that she would leave well alone, keep her mouth shut and give all her attention to her knitting.

At first she thought that she imagined the whisper beside her, but then it came again a little louder.

"Your Aunty Kate is very nice," Kitty whispered.

Nora was so surprised that the knitting almost dropped from her hands. Kitty was looking at her with such a changed expression on her face that she looked like a different person.

"When did you meet her?" Nora asked, gathering her wits about her.

"She calls to our house to look after Nana's leg," Kitty told her, "and I'm helping her because I sleep in my Nana's room now, in case she would want something at night."

Nora thought of big, heavy Mrs Conway who always smelt as if she needed a knickers change, and thought that she would not like to share a room with her. But she was Kitty's Nana, so she was fond of her, and that was different.

Nora was not sure what to say next. This new Kitty was such a change from the old one that she was afraid that any minute she would dissolve and the old one slip back into her place. But a bigger surprise was yet to come.

"I hope that your mother won't sell Mossgrove," Kitty said.

"But your father wants to buy it," Nora exclaimed.

"I know," Kitty said, "but I hope he wont get it."

"So he won't bid for it?" Nora said hopefully.

"Oh, he'll bid all right," Kitty said bitterly.

Nora was finding the conversation a bit confusing, but there was no doubt but that Kitty had changed towards her and it had something to do with Aunty Kate. Kitty, who had always looked at her with such dislike, was now actually smiling at her. Nora felt a great sense of relief: she had never wanted to have Kitty as an enemy, but Kitty had been hell bent in that direction. Now, for some reason, it was all changed, and Nora wanted to keep it that way.

"Will we be friends from now on, so, Kitty?" she asked.

"I'd like that," Kitty told her quietly.

"It was like a miracle," Nora told Rosie later as they walked home together. "She wanted to be friends and that was it."

"When I looked behind me in school I could see the two of you talking and smiling and I could hardly believe my eyes," Rosie told her.

"It must have been Dada," Nora decided. "No one else could have sorted all that out so well. This morning I had my doubts about him, but now I'm sure again. Now I have only one more job for him and this is the big one. He must stop Mom from selling Mossgrove."

CHAPTER SIXTEEN

THE DISPENSARY WAS always quiet on Tuesday mornings. People seemed to find Monday difficult, but by Tuesday they had decided that they were sufficiently recovered to face the week. So Kate decided that she would go to Mossgrove that Tuesday morning. The children would be in school, Jack would be at the creamery and Davy would be busy with the yard jobs. There would be nobody in the house but Martha. She felt that for the first time she would be facing Martha with no fetters attached. But she did not relish the thought of confronting her. The stakes were high: the future of Mossgrove.

She knew that Jack and the children, and even Davy, were depending on her. So she had to get it right, or at least as right as possible. It might make little difference to Martha's decision in the end. But at least she wanted to come out of it feeling that she had done her best and not lost her head as she had done with the old P.P. David, despite his disappointment, had been very gracious about the whole thing. But then she would not have expected anything else from David: he was his father's son in every way. Sarah had listened grim-faced while she had related the story, and then she had told told her, "There is no doubt about it, but you're not Edward Phelan's granddaughter for nothing."

When she arrived at the gate of Mossgrove she decided to leave her bike against Jack's wall and walk down the short boreen. The walk would help to steady her nerves. The sun warmed her face and lit up the entire countryside. Some of the brown ploughed fields were fringed around by whitethorn hedges, and on the steep hill across the river the grass was spattered with splashes of yellow furze. On the broad ditch beside her the young leaves swayed in the breeze and the birds, though in a fever of nest building, still took time to sing. It should be a good day to be alive, she thought, no matter what the problems.

She decided to go to the front door of the house in case it annoyed Martha if she walked in the back door. She knew that Betty Nolan would call this pussy-footing around Martha, but she desperately did not want to get off to a bad start. After knocking on the front door a few times she tried turning the knob, but as she expected the door did not open. Just as she was about to go around and try the back door, Martha's voice from inside ordered, "Go around to the back door."

Here we go again, Kate thought, as she went around to the back and found that door bolted as well. She stood waiting patiently and after a while the door opened and Martha stood there with a questioning look on her face.

"What do you want?" she asked coldly.

"I want to talk to you, Martha, please," Kate said.

"What about?" Martha demanded.

"Can I come in?" Kate asked, feeling that they would get nowhere standing on the doorstep.

"Very well," Martha said with a sigh of annoyance, opening the door just wide enough for Kate to fit through sideways.

That's twice in one week, Kate thought. She went into the kitchen and sat at the table, while Martha turned her back and busied herself at the fire.

"Martha," Kate began, "can we sit down and talk this out?"

"What is there to talk about?" Martha demanded over her shoulder.

"I want to discuss the selling of Mossgrove," Kate said quietly.

"I don't want to talk about it," Martha told her firmly, turning around and standing with her back to the fire.

"There is no harm in talking it over. . ."

"Oh, I know what your talking it over means," Martha said, her hands on her hips. "You want to talk me out of it, but you're not going to succeed."

"Why are you selling?" Kate asked.

"That's none of your business," Martha told her.

"Maybe not," Kate agreed, "but this was once my home and. . ."

"Well, it was never mine!" Martha cut in, her face suffusing with anger.

"But why not?" Kate asked.

"Because you and your mother made damn sure that it never was!" Martha spat.

"But how?" Kate asked in bewilderment.

"Because it was always more yours than mine." Martha walked across the kitchen and faced Kate. "Phelan furniture, Phelan pictures, Phelan everything in every damn corner!"

"But what else did you expect?" Kate protested. "We lived here."

"I know that, but even when ye were dead ye still lived on."

"But how?"

"Take that old dresser," Martha said bitterly, pointing to the bottom of the kitchen, "that Grandfather Phelan made, and Ned thought was perfect. I could not even think of throwing it out in the shed where it belonged. We had to keep that old hearse of a dresser that filled the entire wall of the kitchen. Just because it was made by Grandfather Phelan! Phelan pictures everywhere, and your mother with a pained look on her face if I even moved one of them half an inch, and even her bloody roses outside the front door that I could have cheerfully dug up and flung out on to the dung hill. All Phelans, Phelans, Phelans! I'm shit sick of Phelans and everything belonging to you!" she shouted, striding up and down the kitchen.

"But Martha, we had no idea that you felt like this," Kate protested.

"Oh, of course not," Martha said angrily, "because you were so bloody busy thinking how perfect you all were and how wrong I was. I could do nothing right. I was not good enough for the Phelans. The perfect bloody Phelans."

"But we never thought we were perfect."

"Don't you be trying to fool me," Martha shot at her,

standing now with her hands on the table, glaring down at Kate. "From the first day that I came in here I was second best."

"But nobody ever said that."

"There was no need to say it. It was made clear from the beginning."

"But I wasn't even here at the beginning," Kate said. "I was working in England."

"You mightn't have been here but you were always talked about here," Martha told her, "and when the letters arrived your mother had to read them out at the table for Ned and Jack, and you'd swear to God that she was reading the gospel. I sometimes felt that I should be standing up for the reading. We had you for breakfast, dinner and supper until I was tired of the sound of your name."

"I could hardly help that," Kate said in exasperation.

"No, but your mother could, and she never lost a chance to sing your praises and to belittle me."

"I don't believe that. My mother wouldn't do that."

"Oh no, your mother wouldn't do that," Martha said fiercely; "your mother was perfect. But let me tell you that from where I stood she was far from perfect. Her husband might be dead but she turned her son into a substitute husband, and of course she had Jack, who was blind to her faults because she had him wound around her little finger. The sainted Nellie who behind it all was a right bitch. Living in the same house as her was like living in a bloody shrine. The shrine of St Nellie. Why do you think your father drank? He couldn't stand it, so he buried himself in a whiskey bottle."

Kate felt a slow rage beginning to simmer in the pit of her stomach. Old Molly Conway was right. Martha hated them all, and it was part of her reason for selling, if not all of it. How had the old woman worked it out so astutely?

Martha had gone to the window and was breathing heavily, looking down over the fields.

"The Conways can have it," she said bitterly, "but they'll pay dear for it. They'd pay any price to get Mossgrove and now is their chance, and by God I'll make them pay dearly for their chance to get even with the Phelans."

"And what about the Phelans?" Kate asked bitterly. "Your children are Phelans."

"Only in name," Martha pronounced, still looking out the window. "Your mother tried to come between me and my children, but she failed because I knew what she was at even though I could not make Ned see it."

"Maybe there was nothing to see."

"Oh yes, there was plenty to see, but she knew that I was clever enough for her and in the end she gave up and withdrew to the parlour entirely, where she should have been put the first day I came here."

"So you got your way in the end," Kate said. "Did that make you happy? She is dead with two years and you're still full of bitterness. What do you want from her? Do you know that she never once complained about you to me even though I guessed what was going on."

"Do you expect me to believe that?" Martha swung around from the window and stood glaring down at her. "As soon as she got sick you were back snooping around here. I had no privacy, my children were not mine any longer. . ."

"You wanted to possess your children," Kate told her angrily. "You were married to a Phelan on Phelan land and you had Phelan children, and yet you wanted to wipe out any trace of Phelan in them. You wanted the impossible. You were the outsider and we were ready to welcome you, but you wanted to make us the outsiders. You had no welcome for us. When you married Ned you became one of our family, but you never wanted that. We never knew what you wanted, and I'm beginning to think that neither did you."

"Well, now I know what I want," Martha told her vehemently, "and it's to get rid of this place as fast as ever I can and to move away from this hole where everywhere you go everybody knows your business."

"You're full of bitterness, and wherever you go you'll take it with you," Kate told her, "because you're not running from the Phelans or Kilmeen, you're running from yourself."

"So, you're coming clean at last and laying all the blame with me," Martha challenged.

"Maybe that's where it belongs!" Kate asserted. "Once you got your legs in the door here you were determined to cause trouble, and by God but you caused it. My mother was a saint, so she put up with you. Above all else she wanted you and Ned to be happy, so she was prepared to sacrifice her own dignity or anything else that was necessary to achieve that end. But nothing would satisfy you! You wanted to make her crawl. And you used your emotional blackmail on Ned to bring him to heel. You're a pathetic bitch with a warped power complex."

Kate was standing now facing Martha across the table with all the buried frustration of past years boiling to the surface. So often had she suppressed her unspoken thoughts because she had not wanted to upset Nellie and then Ned. Now there was no more need for restraint. Martha could not damage the dead!

"Oh, it's all coming out now," Martha taunted her.

"Yes it is," Kate told her fiercely; "for so long you had the whip hand because you were prepared to hurt Nellie and Ned with anything that I said. You were even prepared to twist it to do damage. But they're gone now, so I'm free from you petty tyranny. You can no longer hurt them, and by God anything that you say will certainly not hurt me now. I got immune to your jibes years ago, but it broke my heart to see how you hurt Nellie, and I will never forgive you for that."

"I don't need your forgiveness."

"Maybe you don't, but before you'll ever have peace of mind you need to forgive yourself for the way you treated my family. And selling Mossgrove is not the way to do it. You're just putting another nail on your martyr's cross, because that's what you always thought you were, a bloody martyr."

"I don't have to stand here in my own kitchen," Martha said angrily, "and listen to this ranting."

"Oh yes you do," Kate shouted at her, "because all this needs to be said. It should have been said a long time ago. Old Molly Conway told me that when we got you in here we got a cuckoo in the nest. By God, but she was right."

"So you're going around discussing me with the neighbours," Martha said.

"I wasn't discussing you." Kate told her. "Molly Conway was only too happy to voice her opinion when she saw that Mossgrove was for sale. It didn't surprise her that you were selling. She had your measure from the beginning, and now she'll have your farm as well. You played it right into their hands."

"Stop twisting everything," Martha cried.

"Oh, I'm not twisting anything," Kate told her, "but you don't want to hear the truth. You never faced the truth – it was always a made-up version of what you wanted to believe."

"Oh, and you are so smart, of course, that you could see it all clearly," Martha declared with rancour.

"I didn't have to be very smart to see what was going on. And now in your vindictiveness over your imagined wrongs of the past, you are going to deny your children their birthright. This land is their land. It was the land of generations of Phelans before them and Ned meant Peter to carry on when his time came. Have you no respect for Ned's wishes?"

"Ned is dead, dead, dead!" Martha cried. "I can't spend my life living for the dead. I saw enough of that here. Old Grandfather Phelan was dead and buried before I ever came here, but he was never allowed to die because every day here he was remembered. Ned never said that he wanted Peter to carry on."

"Of course he did: he told me the day before he died that he wished that Peter would have the love of Mossgrove that he had."

"Typical," Martha declared; "you poking your nose into the future of Mossgrove when it was none of your business."

"I wasn't poking my nose, as you put it; we were just talking and it came up in the course of the conversation."

"And what else came up in the course of that conversation?" Martha demanded.

"Nothing much, except that Ned wanted Peter to have more schooling than he had."

"Fat chance of that in this hole."

"If there was a secondary school started in the village. . ."

"You put paid to that on Sunday when you insulted the P.P."

"News travels fast around here."

"That's right, especially if somebody makes a fool of themselves," Martha remarked acidly. "You were not content with insulting the parish priest and messing up David Twomey's plans, you're trying to mess me around as well."

"I was only trying to make you stop and think before you do something that you might later regret," Kate told her and, suddenly feeling saddened by the whole upheaval, she sat down wearily on the chair.

"I won't regret it," Martha declared.

"What about Nora and Peter?"

"Nora and Peter are my responsibility," she said coldly, "and I will take care of them."

"But they don't want to leave here," Kate persisted.

"Don't you try to make trouble between me and my children. That was always part of your problem. You had none of your own, so you wanted to stick your nose into the rearing of mine. Why don't you get your hooks into David Twomey now, and get a man and children of your own. Was that what you were at when you offered to intercede for him with the parish priest? That was a laugh, to think that you spoiled whatever chance he had."

Kate sat looking at Martha as she strode up and down the kitchen, her normally pale face red with anger. It came into her mind that one of the Spanish nurses in the London hospital had a saying. She could not remember it exactly but the gist of it was that some people only came alive in controversy. It surely applied to Martha. Mark was right: she would not change her mind.

"It's been a waste of time coming here," Kate told her, wearily rising from the chair. "You have no vision of the future; you are blinded by your own narrow-minded prejudices, and there is no love of the land in you."

"And you are a self-righteous old spinster trying to live your life through your brother's children," Martha retorted. "You have no right to come here again. After the sale I doubt that you will want to come back. So get out now and stay out."

Kate walked slowly towards the back door. She stood there and looked around the kitchen and then walked out into the back yard. Martha banged the door shut behind her.

The yard jobs had been done and a satisfied silence hung over the whole place; only the hens were busy scuffling in the sunshine. The farmyard after feeding time always reminded her of a hospital ward after dinner when all the patients were resting. From here Grandfather Phelan had led her by the hand to see the new calves of the season and then down through the fields of Mossgrove He had done the same with Ned. He had wanted to nurture a love of this place in them and had succeeded. It all seemed so pointless now.

Suddenly she felt old and tired. There was no good, she thought, in fighting the inevitable any longer. Mossgrove was going to be sold and there was nothing that she or anyone else could do about it. She walked up the boreen feeling utterly dejected. The singing birds and the buzz of spring seemed a contradiction of her mood. How could it all have gone so wrong, she wondered. This place that she had thought about every day during her years in London. She had carried it around in her heart like a hidden garden, knowing that when she came back she would always be welcome here. She thought of Nellie, who had loved this place and sacrificed so much to keep it going. Had she ever thought of selling after Kate's father had died? She had asked Jack that question once and he had looked at her in surprise. "Nellie sell Mossgrove? The thought never even crossed her mind. The only reason she'd have sold was if we'd gone bankrupt and we had to, but we scrope our way out of that one, thank God."

She would have to tell Jack that she had failed, might even have made things worse. That was two things that she had messed up in one week. Martha had heard about the other one pretty fast, but of course Lizzy would have been delighted to spread that news around. Martha had a point about everybody knowing your business around here, she thought, but she preferred it to living somewhere where nobody was interested in you.

When she reached Jack's cottage she decided that she would go in and sit down for a while. Jack never locked the door. She sat in the quietness of his small kitchen and tried to accept the fact that she would never again walk down the boreen to Mossgrove. It would take her a while to get used to the idea. Jack would have to retire, and maybe the time had come for that anyway, though he had always proclaimed that he wanted to die in harness. But that was not to be. Davy would have to go back to England. Poor Davy, he so badly wanted to stay at home, and he was happy in Mossgrove where he got on well with Peter. He was good for Peter right now because Davy understood how he felt, having walked that road himself. Peter is like my father, she thought; if he is not handled properly there will be trouble there yet. Whereas Nora was different: she was like

Nellie, always the peacemaker, but she also had the inner resilience of her grandmother.

Foolish Martha to think that they were Phelans only in name. How could she be so blind? But was she right in other ways? Am I trying to live my life through them? Because if Martha was blind to her own faults there is no reason, Kate thought, why I could not be blind to mine. Should I leave Kilmeen and go away and lead a life totally separate from this place? Am I too wrapped up in Mossgrove and Kilmeen, in the children and Jack, in David and the school?

The door opened quietly and Jack stood there. Suddenly the sight of Jack was too much for her, and she felt tears course down her face.

"It was no good, Jack," she told him tearfully, rising and walking across to him. "There is no more to be done."

"I know that you did your best, Kate," he soothed, putting an arm around her and patting her head as if she was once again a child. "Even the Lord himself advised that having done all we should, then stand still. Maybe we have reached that stage."

CHAPTER SEVENTEEN

KATE HEARD THE tapping at the door as she slowly surfaced out of the depths of sleep. Who could it be at this hour of the night? she wondered. She had gone to bed exhausted after the trauma of the day and fallen into a deep, deep sleep. Now she tried to pull herself up out of it and to get her brain turning over again. She slid out of the bed and pulled her warm dressing gown around her.

When she had come back to Kilmeen to take up her job here, Sarah had advised the purchase of the warmest dressing gown that she could find.

"It's one of the requirements for this job," Sarah had told her. "There is nothing like the comfort of a heavy wool dressing gown to ease the pain of dragging yourself out of a warm bed on a cold night. It wraps itself around you and makes you feel human when the rest of your fellow creatures are sound asleep."

It was wise advice, Kate thought, as she ran down the stairs to find out who was in trouble at this hour of the night. When she opened the door fear clutched her. Matt Conway was standing there. He looked more dishevelled than usual in a huge overcoat with the collar reaching up over his ears and strings of foxy hair hanging down over it.

"The old woman is dying and wants to talk to you," he told her abruptly.

"She was fine a few days ago," Kate said stupidly, trying to recover from the shock of seeing him.

"Well, she's not now."

"Did Dr Twomey see her?"

"Yea, and he said she's had a stroke. I was up with Fr Brady now and he said to tell you that he'll collect you in a few minutes and bring you out to our place," he told her in an expressionless voice before simply walking away.

She ran upstairs, got dressed quickly and packed extra towels into her bag, together with anything else that she thought she might need. If Molly Conway died she would have to be laid out, and Biddy Conway did not strike Kate as the kind of woman that would have anything put by for such an emergency.

She had just opened the door when Fr Brady's black Hillman pulled up outside. He reached across and opened the car door for her. An extremely tall, thin young man, he was curved over the steering wheel, and his dark hair looked as if he had combed it with his fingers. As Kate got into the car he finished his dressing by fastening his collar at the back.

"Good morning, Kate," he said pleasantly, moving his shoulders to settle more comfortably into his jacket. "As you can see I'm not at my best at this hour. We're having an early start to our day."

"We are indeed, "she agreed. "This is a bit of a surprise because she was fine a few days ago. I was tending her since she cut her leg badly, but of course they did not get it looked after in time. They don't like outsiders around the place."

"I've never been there."

"Very few have; it will be part of your rural education."

He was what Jack termed a "townie" and knew very little about the country.

"What about Kitty?" he asked.

"Sarah told you?"

"She did, and I'm glad," he said. "It's better to know what's going on because then you're not walking in the dark."

"Sarah said something like that when we found out," Kate told him, "and of course she was right."

"Messy business," he said quietly.

"Makes you sick in your stomach," she agreed, "but if Molly dies there is pressure on us to move fast."

"Molly Conway knows that you know?"

"She does," Kate said, "and so does he."

"How did you manage that?" he asked in surprise.

"Without opening my mouth."

"I could understand the need for that," he said, "but it was a fair achievement in the circumstances."

"It just fell right for me on the day."

"Hope that it falls right for us tonight as well."

No barking dogs heralded their arrival. He must have them all locked up, Kate thought.

The whole family were gathered together around Molly

Conway's bed. Kitty's was the first face that Kate saw, and it was ashen and terrified, a replica of Mark's drawing. Kate suddenly felt chilled. When she looked at Molly Conway's face and checked her pulse she knew that it was only a matter of time. The old lady was grey-faced and breathing heavily. When she felt her hand being held she opened her eyes and forced herself to focus.

"Kate Phelan," she rasped.

"Yes, it's me," Kate told her, bending close to her in the bed, "and Fr Brady is here as well to anoint you."

"He can wait," she said, struggling for breath. "There is something more important." She closed her eyes again but took another breath and they fluttered open. "Send them down to the kitchen," she gasped, looking around the room at her family before sinking back on the pillows.

"Leave us for a few minutes," Kate said quietly, and they trooped silently out of the room.

Fr Brady stood in the shadows by the window, out of Molly Conway's line of vision. Kate was glad of his presence in case she needed someone to witness what Molly wanted to say.

"What is it, Molly?" she whispered into the old woman's ear.

"Are they gone?" she asked with an effort.

"They are."

There is very little left in her, Kate thought. She could hear the death rattle deep in the old woman's throat, but still Molly struggled against it. Suddenly, with a determined effort she rose up in the bed and grasped both of Kate's hands in a vicelike grip. She struggled for breath and the words came out in gasps.

"Kate Phelan?"

"I'm here, Molly. Tell me what's bothering you."

"It's Kitty," the old woman breathed painfully. "Look after Kitty for me."

"What do you want me to do?" Kate asked.

"I have money left to Mary. . . to look after Kitty. . . a lot of money." The words came in gasps with rasping breaths in between. "In the bank in Ross. . . in her name. . . a letter too. You are to get Kitty out of here. . . up to Mary."

"I'll do that," Kate promised her.

"Tonight," Molly gasped. "You're to get her out tonight."

Kate hesitated for a moment, wondering how on earth she was to get the child out of the house that night. In the shadows Fr Brady moved slightly and nodded his head.

"He'll help," the old woman said clearly. Even at this stage Molly was perfectly lucid in her thinking and aware of what was going on in the room.

"I'll do that, Molly," Kate promised. "You've nothing to worry about now, because I'll look after Kitty. She'll be quite safe."

"Thank God," the old woman sighed and sank down into the pillows. Kate stepped back into the shadows and Fr Brady, with the anointing oils in his hands, moved over to the bed.

She looked out the window over the valley towards Mossgrove and saw the dawn breaking on the far horizon, and ever so gently a bird chirped, the first note of the dawn chorus. Behind her she could hear the murmur of Fr Brady's voice and Molly's breathing getting more laboured. What is it like to die, Kate wondered; to know that you are leaving everything behind and facing into the unknown. She had seen many people die and had never lost her wonder in the presence of death. She had felt the same sense of wonder in the presence of birth. The beginning and the end.

Fr Brady joined her at the window. "She is sinking fast," he said; "they'd best come in." He opened the door and beckoned to the family who were hunched together around the fire. They filed slowly into the bedroom: Matt, Biddy and the two boys who had moved Kitty's bed, and two older boys whom Kate just knew were Conways when she saw them. They stood awkwardly around the bed, not quite sure what was expected of them, and Kate went out quietly and closed the door behind her.

Kitty was sitting on a chair by the fire, her teeth clenched.

"Is Nana dying?" she forced out the words.

Kate went over to the fire and sat on a wide sugan armchair across from her.

"Do you want to sit here beside me, Kitty?" she asked, moving sideways to make room for the child. Kitty slipped into the chair beside her and Kate put an arm comfortingly around her thin shoulders.

"Your Nana is dying," she told her, "but she asked me to look after you, and I promised her that I would."

"She was always very nice to me, but I got a terrible fright tonight when she called me."

"She was lucky to have you with her. You were a great girl to be able to help her."

"Where will I sleep now?" Kitty asked fearfully.

"You're coming back to my house tonight."

"Am I?" Kitty asked in amazement. "Why so?"

"Because your Nana said so," Kate replied.

"Oh! Nana said that she would make everything all right."

"And she did," Kate told her, lifting Kitty on to her lap. She was rigid with shock and tension. Kate rubbed her hands and legs and gradually she warmed a little. She badly needs a bath, Kate thought, as she looked down at the matted hair and dirt-ringed neck. Poor little mite, she is worse off than Nora. A dead father is better than the monster in this house.

The bedroom door opened and the family filed down into the kitchen. The boys looked bewildered but there were no tears. Their grandmother had helped to rear them, Kate thought, so they must have felt something for her, but there was no evidence of it.

"She's gone," Matt said, looking at Kate and his daughter with an expressionless face.

"Will you go over for Sarah and we'll lay her out?" Kate asked him.

"Sarah will do it by herself," he told her sharply.

Kate was about to protest, but Fr Brady, coming up out of the room, said quietly to Matt, "We'll call to Sarah on our way past to spare you the bother of going over, because you will have a lot to do here preparing for the wake."

"That's right," Matt agreed with a triumphant glare at Kate.

"Your mother wanted Kitty to come with us," Fr Brady added quietly. "She is after a bad shock for one so young and might be better out of the house. Death isn't easy for any of us, but it's a terrible shock for one so young."

"If that's what the old woman wanted," Matt agreed hesitantly.

"That's what she wanted," Fr Brady told him firmly, "so we'll be going now and I'll call back in the morning to make funeral arrangements. When you've had a chance to sort things out between yourselves."

Kitty walked out of the kitchen holding Kate's hand without a backward glance. She has more courage than I had yesterday, Kate thought. As she passed Matt Conway she barely heard the hiss, "I'll get you for this yet." She cast a sideways look at Kitty and knew that she had not heard.

As they drove up the road, the early morning sun shot beams of light across the landscape. It's a new day and a new start for Kitty, Kate thought, and suddenly her heart lifted and she felt a great surge of admiration for the woman who had just died. Molly Conway had her faults but was a force to be reckoned with even in death.

Kate tapped on the window of Sarah's bedroom and then went to the front door to wait. After a few minutes Sarah opened the door wrapped in a long wool dressing gown.

"Who's dead?" she asked simply.

"Molly Conway," Kate told her, and added: "a stroke. You'll have to lay her out on your own, Matt didn't want me around."

"What about Kitty? Sarah asked quickly.

"In the car with us," Kate told her, nodding towards Fr Brady's car.

"How did you manage that?"

"Molly's instructions, and Fr Brady helped."

"And where from here?" Sarah asked.

"Up to Mary – she left money for it," Kate told her.

"I knew she had money," Sarah said. "I'll send a telegram to Mary as soon as the post office opens, telling her that Molly is dead."

"Have you everything that you need for over?" Kate asked, nodding across the valley to Conways. "I'd say Biddy hasn't even a clean towel in the house."

"Ah, Kate," Sarah told her, "I've walked down that road before. There are a good few like Biddy knocking around. But not to worry – I'll manage."

"I'll leave you to it, so, and I might see you later on."

"Would you like to come in for a cup of tea?" Kate asked Fr Brady when he pulled up in front of her door.

"It won't be too much trouble?" he asked, uncoiling himself out of the car.

"Not at all," she assured him. "I'll be making it anyway and I'm sure that Kitty would like something too."

She ushered them into the hallway, then led them into the kitchen.

"What a lovely warm kitchen," Fr Brady said admiringly.

"The range is great," Kate told him, putting on the kettle and then rattling up the fire with the long poker between the bars, "especially if you have to go out on a night call."

Kitty stood looking around her in awe.

"Would you like a cup of warm cocoa?" Kate asked her, and she nodded her head.

"I'd like that too," Fr Brady told her; "there is something very comforting about cocoa and toast."

"Cocoa and toast it is, so," Kate said, putting cuts of bread on top of the still-warm range and three mugs on the side where she spooned the cocoa into them and mixed it with sugar and milk, adding water then from the boiling kettle.

"Now, sit down here," she told them, putting the mugs of cocoa on the table, "and this will put hair on your chest, as Jack used to tell me when I was small." Kitty giggled as she drank the cocoa down and chewed the toast with satisfaction.

"You're a fast eater," Kate told her as she drained the cup. "Would you like another one?"

"No," Kitty mumbled, packing the last of the toast into her mouth.

"Come with me, so," said Kate, holding out her hand. "I'll be back in a minute," she told the priest as she and Kitty left the kitchen.

She led Kitty up the stairs and into her small spare bedroom at the back of the house. "Now, Kitty, you can sleep in here, and now I'll show you the bathroom."

Kitty looked at the big white bath in admiration. "Mary told me that she had a bath like that in Dublin, but I never was in one."

"Would you like to go into it now?" Kate asked in surprise. She had been tempted to suggest it but had not wanted to hurt Kitty's feelings.

"I'd love it," Kitty said with excitement.

Aren't children wonderful, Kate thought, as she turned on the taps. She put in expensive bath oil that she had bought in London and spared for special occasions. This is definitely a special occasion, she thought, as she ran her hand through the warm water and bubbles foamed up. She eased Kitty's clothes off over her head and then lifted her into the bath where she squealed with delight.

"Now, Kitty, I'll wash your hair and then you can soak for a while and enjoy yourself."

It took two rounds of shampooing before she felt that Kitty's lovely red hair was clean, and then she soaped her down with a big soft sponge.

"Now you're squeaky clean, so we'll run off that dirty water and fill the bath up again with clean warm water."

Kitty laughed with delight as the water gurgled out of the bath and then the steaming taps filled it up again.

"Are you all right now?" Kate asked her.

"Grand," Kitty grinned up at her. "I love the warm water. I feel like a fish."

"Stay there as long as you like. I'll be up to dry you off, or if you want to do it yourself the towels are there."

"Can I lock the door when you go out?" Kitty asked timidly, fear lurking at the back of her eyes.

"Of course you can, and I'll knock when I come up," Kate told her.

Downstairs Fr Brady had refilled their cups with cocoa.

"I'm an old hand at this," he told her. "My grandmother loved cocoa and got me into the habit of it, so now I make it every night. I heard running water – were you giving Kitty a bath?"

"She asked for it herself and is having a good soak above now. She's a grand little girl and I hope that she'll recover from what she's been through."

"What are you going to do about her now?"

"Sarah is going to send a telegram to Mary, so she'll probably take her back with her after the funeral."

"It will be a huge change for her," he reflected, "and a big responsibility for Mary, who cannot be that old herself."

"There are aunts up there as well," Kate told him, "and Mary has a good job. Molly sent up money to send her to school."

"She was an amazing old woman, wasn't she?"

"She was indeed," Kate agreed. "The better I got to know her, the more she surprised me."

"That sometimes happens with people, but not often,"

he reflected. "You had a bit of a run-in with the P.P., I heard."

"The whole parish probably knows it at this stage."

"Probably," he agreed, "but I think that Lizzy was secretly very impressed by your performance."

"Really?" Kate smiled.

"The P.P. is not an easy man to work for, and I think she might have enjoyed seeing him get his comeuppance," he said grinning.

"I think I may have blown David's chance of getting his approval for the school, though, and I do regret that."

"But his opposition is ridiculous!" he said vehemently.

"I knew that you'd be in favour."

"Any right-minded person would be, and if you want to go against him I'll back you up."

"Thanks," she said gratefully, "but we could never put you in that position. He'd make your life a misery afterwards."

"He probably would; he's acting very strange at the moment, and for some unknown reason the bishop is calling tomorrow."

"Does that happen often?" she asked in surprise.

"It's the first time he's visited outside of confirmation," he told her, "and your man is all in a tizzy about it."

"Does he know what's bringing him?"

"I don't think so."

"Will you meet the bishop yourself?"

"Hardly," he said rising, "I'm only the boy. Now, I had better get moving or Kitty will be after going down the plug hole upstairs."

"I'm glad you were with me tonight," she told him as they went out into the hall; "it made it easier. Matt Conway might have been more difficult if you had not been there."

"Thank God it worked out so well," he said. "At least now Kitty will get a chance of a normal life."

Upstairs Kate knocked on the bathroom door. "Kitty, you're going to turn into a duck if you stay in there much longer," she called out to her.

"I'm coming," Kitty shouted back, and after a few minutes she opened the door wrapped in a big towel. Kate lifted her up and carried her into the spare room where she rubbed her dry and slipped an old nightdress of her own over her head.

"In you go now," she told her, turning back the bed clothes, "and sleep like a bug in a rug."

Kitty snuggled down, her face flushed from the warm bath and her red hair glowing like a furze bush against the white sheets. She is going to be a beautiful girl in a few years time, Kate thought.

"Will my Nana be all right?" she asked in a worried voice.

"Your Nana will be fine," Kate assured her. "You had a wonderful Nana and she has arranged that you will go back to Dublin with Mary when she comes down for the funeral."

"For good?" Kitty asked in amazement. "To stay with Mary and my aunties in Dublin for good?"

"That's right."

"Nana fixed all that up?" Kitty asked in wonder.

"She did."

"She was a good Nana," Kitty declared.

"The best," Kate told her.

When she looked in a few minutes later Kitty was fast asleep, her lovely hair flowing out across the pillow.

She decided that it was not worth her while going to bed, so she went out into her back garden. She sat under the apple tree and watched the cobwebs glistening in the early morning sun. After a while she got up and walked around the garden looking at her flowers and plants.

"You're doing well," she told them, then decided that she would do some gardening.

An hour later she stood back to admire her work. Suddenly she heard a suppressed cough at the other side of the hedge and she froze to the ground. She remained motionless for what seemed like a long time and then gently eased the greenery of the thick hedge apart with her hands. Matt Conway was walking away from her, along by the ditch towards the gap at the bottom of the field behind her garden. She felt fear tighten in her stomach.

The quicker I get Kitty out of here, the better, she thought, and at least then I'll only have myself to worry about.

CHAPTER EIGHTEEN

When Kate opened her front door on her way to the first mass on Sunday, Sarah was passing by.

"I'll be with you," Kate told her, closing the door behind her.

"Well, Kitty went off in great form," Sarah remarked.

"It's supposed to be for a holiday," Kate said.

"Easier for them all that way."

"Mary is a grand girl, isn't she? I had kind of forgotten her, because she grew up while I was away."

"Both girls have a lot of old Molly in them, but the boys are all Conways through and through," Sarah said as they turned the corner towards the church.

"It's a relief to have Kitty gone. Matt Conway has been hanging around the back of my place lately."

"I don't like the sound of that at all. He tried that on me after we shifted Mary, but one night two of my fellows were home from England and they beat him solid. He's a bully, but a coward too."

"He mightn't come any more now with Kitty gone," Kate suggested.

"Keep your doors and windows firmly locked at night anyway, because with Molly gone now there is no control on him any more."

"Where did Molly get her money?" Kate asked in a puzzled voice.

"She had her own sideline," Sarah said.

"What sideline?"

"Ever wonder where Jack and all the rest of us got the cure from?"

"Molly Conway!"

"Had been doing it for years, and her mother before her. They made the best in the county."

"How come I never knew that?" Kate asked.

"Only the old stagers like myself know these things," Sarah told her smiling.

"This is a strange place: there are layers upon layers of hidden things that nobody talks about."

"Why should they?" Sarah said. "There is no virtue in having your business on the top of every tongue in the parish."

"There are people around here," Kate decided, "and their right hand hardly knows what their left hand is doing."

"And there's nothing wrong with that, because there will always be the likes of Lizzy and your neighbour Julia to balance things out. Everybody's business is their business."

"Martha was complaining about that the other day, saying that nobody had any privacy around here."

"Well, if ever there was a closed book, she's one. Jack told me that you drew a blank."

"That's right," Kate sighed. "I think that I've given up hope of Mossgrove at this stage."

"Never give up, Kate; life is full of surprises."

"At the moment all mine are unpleasant, and the reason I'm going to first mass today is that I don't want to be listening to old Fr Burke shoot down the school at second mass."

"Will he shoot it down?"

"Be in no doubt about it," Kate asserted; "he even had the bishop over during the week to back him up."

"Was the bishop over?" Sarah asked in surprise.

"Fr Brady said that he was coming and that Fr Burke was all in a tizzy about him."

"That's very interesting."

"You could say that I suppose," Kate said bitterly as they went up the steps at the church gate. "Thanks be to God that I don't have to listen to him this morning. At least Fr Brady talks about things relevant to the world we live in."

"I'll see you later," Sarah whispered as they joined the stream of people going in the door.

Kate dipped her finger in the stone holy water font and filed in behind a large man who smelt of cows. He must have been milking before leaving home and that special smell of milking cows still clung to him. She smiled to see that Lizzy and Julia had taken up their usual position in the back seat under the gallery, from where they had a good view of everybody coming in. Sarah went up the aisle ahead of her to her usual seat. She always sat six seats from the back on the right hand side; Kate had never seen her sit anywhere else in the church. Nellie used to sit on the left by the confession box, and now Kate sat in the same place. We're a bit like the cows, she thought, all going to our own stalls.

The church had just one aisle with a gallery overhead at the back and stained-glass windows along the sides and behind the altar. The altar had elegant white turrets of marble which contrasted vividly with the richness of the windows. The early morning sunlight poured through the stained glass and cast coloured shadows over the seated congregation.

She watched others file in. Betty and Con Nolan with Rosie and Jeremy in tow went up the aisle. Betty looked flamboyant in a fur coat that her sister had sent her from America. Some women would have toned down the glossy fur with sedate accessories, but not Betty, who had dressed it up with a dashing red hat. Kate always thought that Betty's clothes reflected her personality, and Rosie was going to be a carbon copy of her mother, whereas Jeremy, like Con, was quieter and more restrained. She had always thought that the Nolans were an ideal couple. They were two strong personalities but neither dominated. If she ever got married, that was the one thing that she would need, the independence to be herself. She saw Ned's and Martha's relationship as claustrophobic. Martha was what Betty Nolan termed a "grow-off-the-arm job", and Kate knew exactly what she meant. Martha wanted to be inside in his head, and she had seen Ned lose a lot of his freedom to accommodate Martha's demands. I could never put up with that, she thought.

Just then the bell rang and Fr Brady swept out of the sacristy ushering a cortège of altar boys ahead of him. There was exuberance in his entry as if he was the bearer of good news.

He launched into *"Introibo ad altare Dei Ad Deum qui laetifiat juventutem meum"* with fervour.

When he climbed the altar steps and started the mass, Kate felt that it was a celebration of joy, and his movements on the altar were almost a dance of delight. Will his enthusiasm and idealism survive, she wondered, or will he be crucified along the road and have the spirit knocked out of him? The stained-glass window above the altar depicted the last supper. The same celebration, she thought. Jesus the enthusiast and his fishermen, and beneath him today his successor and his congregation off the land. Both peoples close to nature. Are people in touch with nature closer to reality, she wondered, and was that why Jesus started with the fishermen? Had they the joy of creation locked in their hearts?

At the consecration she thought of her parents and Grandfather Phelan, and now Ned as well. They had all been so close to her in life, and now in death they were so untouchable, and yet at the most unexpected times she had felt her mother's presence, although during the struggle to save Mossgrove there had been no sense of that comforting presence. Now she closed her eyes to better experience the miracle of what was happening on the altar.

"Dear Jesus," she prayed silently, "help me to bear with courage the loss of Mossgrove and comfort Nora and Peter, and help me not to feel bitter towards Martha, because at the moment I am finding that very difficult."

After the consecration the congregation sat down to listen to the sermon. Because it was Fr Brady they were alert; he usually said very little, but what he did say was always interesting. But today, instead of standing with his back to the altar, Fr Brady went down the steps and sat on a chair to the side. A ripple of surprise went through the congregation.

The sacristy door opened and Fr Burke emerged purposefully and strode slowly up the steps of the altar. He wore a long white alb belted tightly at the waist, and his ample proportions swelled out above and beneath it like billowing hills. He stood silently and viewed his curious parishioners. He's enjoying this, Kate thought; he should have been an actor! She felt a knot of apprehension tightening in her stomach. This had to be about the school. She would not put it beyond him to name names off the altar and to tell how he had been insulted in his own house by a parishioner. She felt her mouth go dry and perspiration come out on the palms of her hands. Still he stood there silently with his hands clasped across the rise of his stomach. His eyes swept over the seats until they came to rest on her. He stared malevolently down at her and she stared back, determined that she was not going to be cowed. Then he noisily cleared his throat and raised his eyes to the gallery overhead.

"My dear brethren, for many years as your parish priest I have sought to do the best thing for this parish. I have always put the needs of you the people before every other consideration. I have given this parish the best years of my life. The nuns in Ross have also served this parish well and educated your children when there was nothing else available to them. When they came here twenty years ago, I gave them to understand that theirs would be the only school in this parish and I have honoured that agreement."

Here it comes, Kate thought, wishing that she was anywhere else but sitting in the church in Kilmeen. She had come to the first mass to avoid this. He never said the first mass. Then she became aware that he had started again.

". . . Things change, and an agreement made in good faith so many years ago is no longer applicable today, and that is why I took it upon myself to ask the good nuns to release me from that agreement and to allow me to give permission for a new secondary school in the village. This secondary school will bring education to your children and give them choices that are not now available to them. I give it my approval and my blessing."

Kate could hardly believe what she was hearing. What on earth had happened? He looked benevolently over his congregation and lumbered down the altar steps and disappeared into the sacristy.

Fr Brady came lightly up the steps and smiled down at them. "This is wonderful news," he told them; "let us praise the Lord." He concluded mass for a bemused congregation.

Outside the church people stood around in groups avidly discussing the news. It was the first that some of them had heard about it, and since what the others had had mostly come from Lizzy, the approval of the parish priest was the last thing they had expected. It just went to show, they decided, that you could not believe everything you heard.

Kate made a beeline for Sarah. "You are coming home with me for the breakfast," she told her, "because if I don't talk this out with someone I'll simply explode."

"You got a bit of a surprise," Sarah said smiling.

"A bit of a surprise!" Kate gasped. "I'm absolutely thunderstruck with amazement. I simply can't believe it. It's just great!" And she did a little dance around Sarah.

"Come on home quickly," Sarah told her smiling, "or word will go out that Kate Phelan was drunk after mass and was dancing outside the chapel."

As they walked down the churchyard the Nolans caught up with them.

"Great news, Kate," Con told her, his normally serious face breaking into a smile.

"Good for you, Kate," Betty declared; "about time someone backed that fellow into a corner that he couldn't get out of."

"Who did Kate back into a corner?" Rosie wanted to know, and Con put his hand in his pocket and handed her some coins with instructions to get herself some sweets.

"Neither David nor his father were at mass," Betty said, "so they won't have heard the news yet. They'll be delighted."

"Hannah was there, so they'll know soon," Sarah remarked.

Betty and Kate walked ahead and Betty said in a relieved voice, "Well, the school solves our problem of what to do with Jeremy next year, and I suppose Peter will go as well."

"If he'll still be here," Kate said.

"Where is he going to be gone to?" Betty wanted to know.

"Your guess is as good as mine," Kate told her, "but with Mossgrove sold the Lord only knows where they'll be."

"Is she planning to leave Kilmeen as well?"

"I don't know and I doubt if she knows herself," Kate said.

"Bloody woman!" Betty fumed.

"Don't let's spoil the joy of today's good news by talking about Mossgrove," Kate pleaded as they waited at her door.

"Do you want a lift home?" Con asked Sarah as they came abreast.

"I've been invited for breakfast by my old neighbour to

help her to digest the good news," Sarah said. "I think that she is finding it hard to believe."

"Well, we'll leave you to it, so," Betty told them as they parted company, "and we'll see you during the week, Kate."

Seated across the kitchen table from each other, Kate asked Sarah, "Did you ever have the feeling that everything did not quite add up?"

"Yes," Sarah smiled.

"Well, I feel that there is a missing link somewhere in this chain of events and I can't seem to find it. One and one does not quite make two in some way. Betty thinks that I bulldozed the old P.P. into this, but I know that she could not be further from the truth. He does not tick like that. The more you'd oppose him the more you'd get his back up. It was not me, of that I'm sure. So there is some other factor here that we're not taking into the reckoning."

"What about the bishop?" Sarah asked.

"I thought of that, too, but the only reason that he could have known was if Fr Burke told him, and I doubt that he did that."

"Maybe someone else went to the bishop," Sarah suggested.

"No, no," Kate said with conviction, "the people around here would not dream of doing that. As well as that, he lives miles away and no one here would know him well enough to chance visiting him.

"I would," Sarah told her quietly.

"You would!"

"I wasn't going to say anything about it," Sarah began, "but I can see now that you're like a dog with a bone and you're going to keep chewing until you arrive at some conclusion, so it might as well be the right one."

"But how did you do it?" Kate asked.

"Well, it all goes back a long time ago," Sarah told her. "When I was young there was a big crowd of us there, and when I left national school I was sent working to the local presbytery. That was all of fifty years ago. There was a young curate there at the time: it was his first job and my first job and he was one of a big family as well. We were both lonely and maybe a bit out of our depth. He was a Fr McGrath.

"The bishop," Kate breathed.

"That's right. Over the years we did not keep in close touch, but always at Christmas we wrote."

"You went to him about the school?"

"Yes," Sarah said; "last Monday I hired Joe's hackney car. Joe is a good man to keep his mouth shut. I went over to the bishop's house and we discussed the whole thing, and he just told me to let it with him."

"He must have moved on it straight away," Kate said thoughtfully, "because Fr Brady told me on Tuesday night that they were expecting him."

"I knew that I could depend on him to do whatever was necessary," Sarah said with assurance. "The only problem now is that Fr Burke might think that you were the one who went to the bishop."

"I can live with that," Kate told her with relish. "It might be no harm if he thought that I had a leg in with the bishop. Keep him on his toes."

"Now that you know," Sarah told her, "we will leave it between ourselves."

"But what about David? He'll think that I swung it with Fr Burke, and I don't like him thinking that when it didn't happen. It puts me in a false position with him – he'll think that I helped more than I really did."

"You're too honest, Kate. Many a woman would be delighted to have that string to her bow in the circumstances."

"What circumstances?"

"Kate Phelan, don't be playing the innocent with me! You never wore your heart on your sleeve, but I always saw that when David Twomey was around you had a special glow about you. I wanted him back in Kilmeen for the school, but I also wanted him back for you as well."

Kate looked across at Sarah and shook her head in wonder. "Sarah, you're a wise old owl," she said gratefully, reaching across the table and covering the older woman's hand with hers. "I have hardly admitted it to myself."

"Well, you've a better chance with him here under your eye than up in Dublin where you wouldn't know what would come his way."

"Oh, Sarah," Kate laughed, "but you're some dark horse. To think that you had all this worked out and not to say a word about it, and to never mention all these years that you were friendly with the bishop."

"As I told you before mass, there is no virtue in broadcasting some things. One of the problems of life today is that there are too many people saying too many things."

"Well, you're not one of them: you're one great woman!"

"Just one other thing now," Sarah instructed, "before we put this conversation behind us for good."

"What?" Kate asked with interest.

"David will be employing teachers for this new school, and some of them could be pretty young women. You have a long summer ahead of you before they come to Kilmeen. Make good use of it."

"They might be all settled matrons and men," Kate said smiling.

"Don't depend on it."

Just then there was a loud knock on the door and Kate rose reluctantly to her feet.

"The last thing that I want now is someone with a pain," Kate said, but when she opened the door David swept in and swung her around the hall in delight.

"Kate, isn't it just wonderful! I might have chanced going ahead with the school, but this takes all the hardship out of it. I knew that you got to him last Sunday."

"There's more to this than meets the eye," she told him. "Come in and Sarah will fill you in."

"Is Sarah here?" he asked in surprise.

"She is indeed," Kate told him, "and we wouldn't be dancing in delight today but for her."

Kate watched David's face as Sarah filled him in briefly on the happenings of the past week.

"Kate said that you showed a special interest in the school from the beginning," he said.

"Well, I had that ace up my sleeve all the time," she told them, "but I didn't want to use it except all else failed."

"Well, all else had failed," Kate assured her; "there was no way he'd have given in but for the pressure put on him by the bishop. When I heard him say that he was giving it his blessing, I knew that there had to be a hidden factor."

"They'll all think now that you went to the bishop," David told Kate.

"Well, let them think it," Kate smiled.

"I'd best be going," Sarah said, "and thanks for the breakfast, Kate."

"I'll run you back," David said. "I've Dad's car outside and it's just starting to rain."

As they went out the hallway he told Kate, "Dad said to come up for the dinner."

"This is becoming a habit," she said.

"Well, we've something to celebrate today," he smiled.

As they drove away Kate stood at the door and looked along the village street. It was always very quiet between the masses on Sunday. There was no movement but for a brown terrier and a black sheep dog trying to outdo each other in sprinkling the base of the light poles along the street. Across the road Julia's curtain moved and Kate smiled to herself as she went in and closed the door.

She tidied up after the breakfast and then walked out into the garden where a light mist was falling. She went over to the old seat under the apple tree and sat there listening to the birds singing. She wished that she felt joyful. It was great news about the school and she was delighted for David, but he had given her no firm indication that she was part of his plan. Maybe Kilmeen was the obvious place for him to start his own school and it had nothing to do with her. Could she stay on here without being part of David's plans? Sarah was right about her feelings for David, and it was best to admit it to herself. But as well as David there was the question of Mossgrove.

Could she live here with Mossgrove sold? The thought of the sale and the auction at which everything would be sold off frightened her. Had she failed Nellie and Ned and Grandfather that she had not succeeded in persuading Martha? Should she have understood Martha better and talked things over with her? But Martha was determined to prove that she was the one in control.

The drizzle dried off and the sun shone out, sparkling off the moisture-laden leaves. It's going to be a lovely day, she decided, rising with determination from the seat. I'm going to enjoy Hannah's wonderful cooking, and being with David, and tomorrow we will have the evening together going over to Mr Hobbs in Ross.

CHAPTER NINETEEN

PEOPLE ALWAYS REFERRED to Mr Hobbs as old Hobbs, even though there was no young Hobbs. He was extremely tall, thin, bald and courteous, and as soon as one entered his office it seemed clear that hurry had no part to play in his life. His softly spoken, unassuming and slightly bewildered air clothed a brilliant legal mind that sometimes annihilated an unsuspecting arrogant young barrister in court. The people of Ross and Kilmeen knew that if they were going into court it was better to have old Hobbs with them than against them. For the drawing up of wills or other legal documents free of loopholes, Hobbs had been tried and tested over the years. As well as that, he had the ability to listen carefully to his clients, and sometimes he read from their voices what it was they wanted to say rather than what they were actually telling him. He gave visitors to his office his undivided attention, and his secretary was under sentence of sacking not to interrupt under any circumstances.

This place is like a confessional, Kate thought; some great stories must have been told in here.

"Now, Mr Twomey," Mr Hobbs began in a precise voice, his long, thin fingers opening the file on his desk, "regarding the Jackson property in Kilmeen, tell me exactly what you have in mind."

He must know that already, Kate thought, when she saw the correspondence on his desk; nevertheless Mr Hobbs listened attentively to David's plans for the house.

"Sounds a very commendable plan," he commented mildly.

"I have sent a detailed account of it to Rodney Jackson in Boston," David told him.

"Well, that certainly helped things on," he remarked, "because Mr Jackson lost no time in getting back to me."

"Is he in favour of the idea of letting the house for a school?" David asked. Kate could feel the restrained urgency in his voice.

But Mr Hobbs was not to be hurried. He put a pair of small silver-rimmed spectacles on top of his thin nose and picked up a flimsy sheet of paper and ran his eye over it. Then he laid down the document and looked at David over the top of his half spectacles and cleared his throat delicately.

"Mr Jackson actually sent me a cablegram and made a phone call," he smiled thinly. "Not at all necessary in the circumstance, but then the Americans are a fast-moving people."

"And what did he say?" David asked with barely suppressed impatience.

"Actually, he's very enthusiastic," Mr Hobbs announced, nodding his head in approval.

"Well, that's great," David sighed in relief.

"Yes," Mr Hobbs agreed; "it is the only place in Kilmeen suitable for what you have in mind."

"That was my problem," David agreed, "but now with Mr Jackson willing to rent I'm home and dry."

"Not quite," Mr Hobbs informed him calmly.

"But why?" David asked in alarm.

"Our Mr Jackson has made a stipulation," Mr Hobbs said.

"What kind of a stipulation?"

"A rather unusual one really," Mr Hobbs told him, putting his hands together in a praying position. "It would appear that Mr Jackson has a great interest in the arts, and he wants the walls of this school to be adorned with paintings and drawings so that the children will develop an appreciation of such things. He is very specific about this requirement and there will be quite a number of pictures required; he will make a bequest to cover the cost."

"How extraordinary," David said.

"I rather thought so too," Mr Hobbs agreed.

Kate, however, was not so surprised. "I remember his great-aunts the Miss Jacksons; they were interested in art and often spoke about the lack of any such facilities in Kilmeen, so they obviously had spoken to him about it."

"Well, he took their opinions seriously," Mr Hobbs said, "and he is prepared to be very generous in the pursuit of their wishes. But it still puts you in a bit of a dilemma, Mr Twomey, because he will not sign the contract until he is guaranteed that the pictures will be hanging for the opening, which I assume will be at the beginning of the school year in September. Not a lot of time to acquire a specified amount of drawings and paintings. He also wants some of them to be of local interest, as he feels that this would be good for the children."

Kate looked at the two men on either side of the desk. David wore a puzzled look on his face and Mr Hobbs was waiting for a response.

"Mark, of course," she burst out. "His stuff would be ideal."

"That's the solution," David sighed in relief.

"Excuse me," Mr Hobbs intercepted politely, "but who is this Mark?"

"He lives in Kilmeen," Kate explained; "he's an artist, and his pictures are excellent."

"I would have to see them," Mr Hobbs said cautiously, "because Mr Jackson would expect a high standard."

"Of course," Kate assured him, "and by a strange coincidence it was the Miss Jacksons who encouraged Mark as a child. They took him to exhibitions and arranged classes for him, and I think that there is a family connection there. I can let you have some pictures within a few days and you will see for yourself how good he is."

"That sounds satisfactory enough," Mr Hobbs agreed, "and if everything goes according to plan I believe that Mr Jackson intends to come over for the opening."

"That's wonderful," David said with enthusiasm. "But what about the rent: are we talking big or small money?"

"Very modest, I would say," Mr Hobbs informed him, mentioning an amount that Kate knew was less that David had expected to pay.

She felt a great surge of appreciation for the absent Rodney Jackson. What an amazing stroke of good fortune! She wondered had his great-aunts told him about Mark and was he giving him an opportunity? His aunts had been lovely old ladies and he was obviously influenced by them. It would be interesting to meet him when he came over in September.

"Was Mr Jackson ever in Ireland?" she asked Mr Hobbs, who was busy making notes.

He finished what he was writing and laid down his pen. "As a child he came once with his father, and it must have made a lasting impression on him. He is an only child and born, it would seem, with the proverbial silver spoon in his mouth."

"So that's why he didn't need to sell the house," David said.

"That's right," Mr Hobbs agreed; "he seems quite attached to it, really, because his grandfather was born there. He is delighted with the idea of it being turned into a school."

"Lucky for me," David smiled.

"Yes, indeed," Mr Hobbs agreed. "Now we have covered everything and I will be in touch with you at your Dublin address, so I think that completes our business."

As they both rose to go, Mr Hobbs turned to Kate. "Miss Phelan, could you stay for a few minutes: there is something that I would like to discuss with you."

David shook hands with him and told Kate he would wait in the car. Mr Hobbs carefully returned everything to David's file and put it in a drawer beside him. He then took down a much thicker file from a shelf above his head and opened it on his desk.

"Your sister-in-law Martha Phelan is proposing to sell Mossgrove?" he queried.

"That's right," Kate said in surprise; "it was in the *Kilmeen Eagle.*"

"I do not get that particular publication," he told her. "So she has come to you about it?"

"Not quite, but her solicitor has been in contact with me."

"Her solicitor?" Kate said in surprise. "But you have always been our family solicitor."

"Correct," he agreed, "but Mrs Phelan has chosen to go elsewhere. Not always a wise decision."

"She probably went to someone else," Kate said thoughtfully, "because what she is doing is against our way of thinking."

"I take it from that that you are not in agreement with the decision to sell?" he asked.

"Totally against it. I have tried to persuade her not to, but it's no good. I can't stop her."

"Yes, you can," he told her simply.

Kate looked at him in amazement. "I can what?" she gasped.

"Mrs Phelan cannot sell Mossgrove without your agreement," he told her slowly.

"But why?"

"Because years ago your mother and I made provision for such an eventuality."

"My mother," she said in surprise. "What has my mother got to do with it?"

"Shortly after your father died, when your brother Edward and you were both children, your mother came in here to me and drew up a will," he told her.

"And she left Mossgrove to Ned," Kate filled in.

"That's right," he agreed, "but she gave you the right of residency."

"The right of residency," Kate echoed.

"Yes, the right of residency."

"But what does that mean?" she asked in bewilderment.

"It means," he said slowly, "that you have the right to reside in Mossgrove for as long as you live and, more important still in the present situation, it cannot be sold unless you waive your right to residency."

"Good God!" she declared.

A slow joy started at her toes and spread throughout her whole body. She looked at Mr Hobbs with naked gratitude. It was simply incredible. She felt as if a huge weight had been lifted off her back. Mossgrove was safe!

"My mother made that provision in her will when we were both children?" she asked in amazement.

"That's right, and when she came in here to fix up her affairs in later years we decided to let the original will stand. You had your own job by then and did not need to reside in Mossgrove, but I pointed out to her that the only time the clause in the will would cause a problem was if Mossgrove was to be sold."

"That was very far-seeing of you," Kate concluded.

"We solicitors have to cover all eventualities. We need to protect the wishes of the dead, the rights of the living and the interests of the unborn. It is a formidable task, but one a good legal man will always strive to perform for his client. Your mother was guided by me."

"But she never mentioned it," Kate said in wonder.

"There was never any need to," he told her. "Usually these things never come up until somebody decides to sell, and then they are an impediment to the sale. In this particular case, rightly so."

"Does my sister-in-law know about this?"

"Well, I wrote back to her solicitor last week informing

him of the right-to-residency clause, so I would imagine that she has heard from them by now."

"But you would not in normal circumstances have written to me?" she asked him.

"Not unless her solicitors requested me to do so," he said.

"So as far as Martha is concerned, she could think that I know nothing about the right-to-residency clause?" she asked.

"That is probably correct."

"I'd like to leave it that way."

"Very wise," he said.

"I never thought to look for a copy of my mother's will," Kate said thoughtfully.

"People don't."

"Thank you for telling me," she said. "I'm very grateful: it takes a huge weight off my mind."

"Your family have always been valued clients of mine, and if your sister-in-law had come to me in the first place she would have been made aware of the situation and spared herself a lot of unnecessary trouble."

"She knows that now," Kate said.

"She does," he agreed, rising from his desk, "and if you have any problem you can come back to me."

"Thank you," she said as they shook hands. "I'm sure you have seen the Phelans through a few sticky patches over the years."

"And my father before me," he told her evenly. "He represented your grandfather in that famous case against the Conways. We should have lost that one, I think, but they were lucky on the day. The gods smiled on them."

"And on me today."

When she got outside the door Kate stood and closed her eyes better to absorb what she had just been told. She could hardly believe it. It was almost too much to take in. She felt that she could explode with relief and happiness. When she opened her eyes she saw that David had wound down the window of the car and was viewing her with an amused look on his face.

"Kate, have you gone into a trance?"

"I feel as if I'm in a dream," she slipped into the car beside him; "a good dream. So many things are coming right today."

"I feel the same – everything is coming together for the school. It's none of my business, but old Hobbs must have told you that you have come in for a fortune judging by the look on your face."

"I have," she told him. "Martha can't sell Mossgrove."

"Good God, why not?"

As she explained a look of understanding came over his face. "God, Hobbs is a wily old fox," he said, starting up the car and taking the road back to Kilmeen.

"He is all of that," she agreed "He says that a family will has to protect the wishes of the dead, the rights of the living, and the interests of the unborn."

"That's some challenge."

"It is," she agreed, "but my mother and himself did just that when they drew up that will."

"Wonder would Martha agree?"

"Maybe not now, but in a few years time I think she might."

Kate looked out at the passing countryside. Everything looked better and brighter than it had a few hours earlier. The sunny day was in perfect harmony with her mood.

"This visit has been a great success for the two of us," David said.

"And for Mark. I'm so delighted for him. It's a wonderful opportunity, and to think that it is the Jackson family again who are opening doors for him."

"You're very fond of Mark, aren't you?" David asked thoughtfully.

"Oh yes," Kate declared. "I've always felt that Mark is someone special, and it drives me mad when people around here dismiss him as an eccentric."

"Well, I suppose in a small country village like ours someone like Mark is bound to stick out a bit; even to look at him you'd know that he didn't spend his days piking hay."

"I suppose so," Kate smiled, "but he is such a gentle soul that he always makes me feel good. He was so understanding about Mossgrove, and it was not easy for Mark, being Martha's brother."

"I'd say that as far as Mark is concerned, what you think is far more important than Martha," David said ruefully. "I've always been jealous of your relationship with Mark."

"There was never need for you to be jealous of anybody, David," she told him honestly, then asked hurriedly: "What time are you leaving this evening?"

"Dad is taking me to catch the six o'clock train."

"You'll just have time for a quick cup of tea when you get home," she said looking at her watch. "Thanks for today, David. If I had not gone in with you I might never have found out what I did."

"You have been such a help to me with all this business about the school," he told her with feeling, "that I'm glad you benefited in some way out of it."

"We'll call it quits, so," she smiled as they pulled up in front of her own door.

"I'm looking forward to the summer," David said as she got out of the car. "It will be great fun painting and doing up the school."

"It will indeed," she agreed, wondering if that was what she had to look forward to – a summer painting walls in order to be with him.

"Goodbye," she said as she closed the door of the car. But he leaned across and wound down the window and grinned out at her.

"Kate," he asked, "might we go for a walk across the bog again this summer?"

"We might indeed," she beamed at him.

"And this time there will be no Jack to haul us home," he told her, and she knew then that she was part of his plan in returning to Kilmeen.

When she got inside the door she kicked off her shoes and shot them back along the hall and danced into the sitting room until she stood in front of Grandfather Phelan's picture.

"We've made it," she told him joyfully. "We've made it!"

Then she got a strange feeling that she was not alone. She turned around slowly, and Matt Conway was sitting in a chair in the corner by the window. A cold chill ran down her spine.

"How did you get in?" she demanded.

"You should lock your back door."

"What do you want?" she breathed, and she could feel the fear crawling up her legs and along her hands.

"Just to settle a score. Did you think that you could come into my house and do what you did and get away with it?"

"It was your mother's dying wish," she told him.

"It was you who planted the idea in her head, and now you're going to pay for it."

"What do you want?" she asked, her voice shaking in spite of herself.

"Just a little bit of fun."

"You'll never get away with this."

"Oh yes I will," he said, "and one scream and I'll bury this in you."

She saw the glint of steel in his hand. I mustn't panic, she told herself, but her mind refused to function. Play for time, she thought. He was still sitting in the chair, but he was nearer to the door than she was, so if she made a dash for it he would bring her down. She needed something heavy to defend herself. Her mother's footstool was solid, and it was just beside her.

"Don't try to be smart," he threatened.

As he bent forward to heave his bulk out of the low chair she dived for the footstool and flung it across the room at him. It got him on the side of the head. He roared with rage and fell back into the chair. Just as he hoisted himself out of it again, she grabbed Grandfather Phelan off the wall, bringing hook and all with her, and as Matt Conway rose she crashed the big picture over his head and, with a splintering of glass, the frame came down over his shoulders. She ran for the door and he lunged after her, blood pouring down his face, but the frame held his arms. She dragged open the door and ran out into the street just as Julia Deasy dashed across the road.

"Who's inside there?" she demanded. "I saw shadows inside the window."

"It's Matt Conway," Kate gasped; "he was waiting inside for me when I came home."

Julia dashed in the door and shouted out to Kate: "Run down to the barracks and bring up one of the guards. This fellow won't go far – he's bleeding like a pig."

Kate ran down the street, but suddenly the face of old Molly Conway came back to her and she stopped. If this goes to court, she thought, Kitty and Mary will be dragged into it. All of a sudden she was icy calm. She would handle this her way.

She walked slowly back to the house where big hefty Julia was parked at the door of the front room armed with an old walking stick of grandfather's.

"If you move," she was threatening Matt Conway, "I'll floor you."

Slumped in the chair, his face covered with blood and the picture frame still around his shoulders, he did not look as if he could cause much trouble to anybody.

"Take this shagging thing from around my neck," he yelled.

"You had better be careful how you move or you could get your throat cut," Kate warned as she viewed the long slivers of protruding glass. She eased the picture carefully out over his head, but despite her care pointed edges of broken glass scraped his still bleeding face. He bellowed in pain.

When he was clear of the frame, she instructed Julia, "If he causes any trouble use that stick."

"Without a doubt," Julia said fiercely. "I've been wanting to do it for years."

Kate stood in front of Matt Conway with a determined look on her face. "You listen to me now," she told him grimly; "you're only getting away with this on account of your mother, who was a superior specimen of humanity to you. But you try anything like this again and you'll finish up in jail."

"I didn't touch you," he growled.

"Only because you didn't get a chance," Julia told him.

"Apart from today," Kate said, choosing her words carefully on account of Julia, "there is the other affair. Fr Brady and Sarah Jones know about that."

"Wonder you didn't put it in the bloody *Eagle,*" he muttered.

"That's exactly where it will be if you come near this place again, or if I find you skulking around the back."

"Are you going to let me bleed to death?" he demanded.

"I'll get my bag," she told him, "and stitch you up."

Half an hour later Matt Conway was cleaned and bandaged without a sign of blood in sight.

"Now you can get yourself home," Kate told him, "and don't you ever show your face in here again, or the next time you will bleed to death."

"Will I be able to walk home after loosing all that blood?" Conway protested.

"You can crawl; it would be more suitable for you."

"When we have Mossgrove," he snarled as he lumbered towards the door, "you'll never set a foot on it."

When he was gone Julia looked at Kate with concern. "That was a nasty ordeal. Are you all right?"

"Fine," Kate assured her. "I never enjoyed stitching anybody so much."

"There wasn't much old guff out of him while that was going on," Julia said with relish.

"No," Kate agreed; "this little visit might keep him quiet for a while – and thanks, Julia, for all your help. You were the right woman in the right place."

"I enjoyed the excitement," she said, and Kate knew that Julia had further delights in store with the telling of the story.

"Now, we'd better see if there is much damage done to Grandfather Phelan," she said.

"Not as much as he did to Matt Conway," Julia smiled.

"That would have given him great satisfaction," Kate said gleefully, examining the picture and deciding that it could be repaired with a certain amount of patience. Then she got a sudden idea that she would get Mark to paint a portrait from the picture. Why had she never thought of it before?

"Well if you're sure you'll be all right now," Julia broke into her thoughts, "I'll be off."

"I'm grand," Kate assured her, knowing that Julia wanted to get going with her exciting news.

When she closed the door behind Julia she noticed a note on the ground that had been pushed back into the corner. She picked it up and smoothed it out.

Please call tomorrow evening around four o'clock.

Martha.

[illegible]

[illegible]

[illegible]

[illegible]

[illegible]

[illegible]

[illegible]

[illegible]

[illegible]

[illegible]

[illegible]

CHAPTER TWENTY

THE FRONT DOOR of Mossgrove stood open and sunshine poured into the small square hallway. The door into the parlour was also pushed back to reveal the long table covered with a flowing white damask cloth that skirted it to the ground. It was set for a meal and laden with the best of Martha's baking. Behind the closed kitchen door to the right Kate could hear the murmur of voices. As she wondered what she should do, the kitchen door opened and Martha stood there. Kate looked at her, waiting for the next move. Martha held out her hand.

"Welcome, Kate," she said quietly as she opened back the door, and Kate saw that Jack, Nora, Peter, Agnes and Mark were already in the kitchen.

"I have good news, so I thought that we would have a little bit of a get-together," Martha told her.

"Mossgrove could do with good news for a change," Kate said evenly, just as Nora ran across the kitchen to her.

"We're having a party, Aunty Kate!" she almost sang with delight, a pretty dress on her and a happy smile lighting up her face.

"Norry, it's not a party," Peter protested, "and anyway we don't know what it's all about yet," he finished with a dark look in his mother's direction.

The adults, Kate saw, looked apprehensive, and she realised that she was the only one present, apart from Martha herself, who knew that the sale would not now take place.

"Come on now, everybody," Martha announced, "up into the parlour and we'll get started." She led the way bearing a large teapot in her hands.

Taking her place at the head of the table, Martha looked at Kate, who sensed that she was going to be directed to the bottom.

But Agnes intervened: "I think as the only grandparent here I'll take the other end of the table," she said smiling, and she slipped into her chair. Peter sat to the right of his grandmother and Jack took the seat opposite. That had been Jack's seat as far as back as Kate could remember. He liked to be able to sit at the table and at the same time to look out the window down over the fields of Mossgrove. She sat beside Jack for the same reason and Mark and Nora sat opposite to her. She smiled happily at Mark, thinking of the delight that the news about his paintings would bring him.

"Where's Davy?" Peter demanded.

"He'll be here in a minute," Jack assured him. "He's gone down to put out Conways' cows. They're after breaking in again."

"It might not be worth his while putting them out,"

Peter muttered under his breath.

"Shush, Peter," Agnes whispered.

They were all seated now, but for Martha, who remained standing, a fixed smile on her face.

"Before we start eating," she began, "I have an announcement to make."

"Shouldn't we wait for Davy?" Peter protested.

"This is a family matter," Martha told him.

"Davy is better than family," Peter said mutinously.

"It's all right, Peter," Jack assured him, "Davy won't mind."

"But I mind," Peter insisted.

"Are we to sit here looking at each other until Davy drags himself up from the Mear na hAbhann?" Martha asked.

"I'll see if he's coming," Peter told her, getting up and moving to the door. "I can see him coming," he shouted back, and they heard him calling to Davy to hurry.

"Hurry is not Davy's strong point," Jack smiled.

"No," Agnes agreed, "slow and sure was the way of all the Shines, and despite Ellen's best efforts she failed to put speed into them."

"Can't change generations of back breeding I suppose," Jack commented.

He and Agnes had their Sunday clothes on, and Kate realised that Martha had impressed on them that they were going to have tea in the parlour. As Sunday and Monday were the same to Mark, he wore no special clothes to mark the day. Davy came puffing in the door and came to a standstill when he saw them all around the table.

"Jasus! Nobody told me that we were having tay in the parlour."

Peter shot a murderous glance at his mother.

"Let your dirty boots at the door," Martha instructed him, and Davy dutifully complied while she went to the parlour press to fetch another setting, then laid it beside Kate. Davy arrived back in his stockinged feet and minus his working jumper and sat down heavily in the chair next to Kate. He grinned across at Peter.

"I want to sit at the other side of the table with Jack and Davy," Peter announced.

"Good God, Peter," Martha protested, "is there no satisfying you?"

"You can switch places with me," Kate told him, going around the table and slipping into the chair between Mark and Nora. As Peter sat in between Jack and Davy, Kate knew that he wanted to be with the working men of Mossgrove.

"Now, are you all finally settled and sure that you are in the right place?" Martha asked in a voice tinged with annoyance.

"I think that everyone is happy now, Martha," Agnes assured her quietly.

"As you all know," Martha began, "I decided to sell Mossgrove a few weeks ago, and you have all been very much against that decision."

"And we were right too," Peter blurted out angrily.

"Well, I have changed my mind," Martha announced, ignoring the interruption. "Mossgrove is no longer for sale."

For a few seconds there was a stunned silence, followed by gasps of delight.

"Jasus, Missus," Davy asked, "what made you change your mind?"

"The new school," she said evenly. "Ned had wanted the children to be educated, and that was impossible with no school here, but now with the school the problem is solved and it's better for the children to be here."

"Better for you too and all of us," Agnes told her, and Kate realised that Agnes did not want her grandchildren to feel that their mother was sacrificing herself for them. Then bedlam broke out, Peter and Davy cheering in delight and Nora running to the top of the table to hug her mother. Mark put his arm around Kate and hugged her, and she saw Jack and Agnes smile at each other and shake hands with joy. Then she felt Jack watching her across the table, put her hand across to him, and he grasped it warmly.

"Mossgrove is safe again, Kate, thank God," he said with feeling.

She closed her eyes and felt the unseen presence of Grandfather, Nellie and Ned. On so many family occasions she had sat with them around this table, and now they were surely here to celebrate. Nellie had saved Mossgrove with her foresight. In life she had never taken from the dignity of another person, and now it would be her wish that Kate would not take from the dignity of Martha's decision..

Jack's voice broke into her thoughts: "I want to slip out for a minute," he announced with a smile on his face as he rose from the table and left the room.

"Where's Jack gone?" Nora asked in alarm.

"He won't be long, I'm sure," Kate assured her, thinking that Jack probably felt that they should celebrate the occasion in fitting style.

He was back straight away carrying a dusty bottle wrapped in torn newspaper. He whipped off the newspaper and rubbed the bottle down the side of his jumper.

"We must have a drop of the good stuff to honour the occasion," he declared, "and I haven't forgotten the young ones either," he told them, pulling three bottles of red lemonade from a bag behind his back.

"Jack," Nora squealed with delight, "you think of everything!"

"Glasses, Martha," Jack ordered, and a surprised Martha rose from the table to bring glasses from the parlour press in the corner and place them in front of Jack. He poured the sparkling lemonade into the tall glasses and placed them in front of Nora, Peter and Davy. When Davy raised a questioning eyebrow at the lemonade, Jack told him, "You're only a stump of a young fellow yet, lad; you need a few more growing years to handle the hard stuff."

"Kate," he asked as he spooned brown sugar into the smaller glasses, "will you go down to the kitchen and bring me up a jug of hot water."

Kate smiled as she went down to the kitchen, thinking that this was Jack in full flight as she had not seen him for years. Martha's announcement had rejuvenated him, and she knew that Martha had probably never before encountered this side of Jack. He had always been careful in her presence, but now he was exhilarated with delight that Mossgrove was safe.

When she brought back the hot water he ceremoniously mixed his concoction and handed around the glasses with a flourish. Then he announced: "Let's drink a toast," and they all rose to their feet.

"To the Phelans of the past, the Phelans of the present and the Phelans of the future," Jack announced as they raised their glasses. The adults sipped their brew carefully, because Jack in this frame of mind could have a heavy hand, but the three younger ones slugged back the lemonade with relish.

"Can I do a toast?" Nora wanted to know.

"You don't *do* a toast," Peter told her, "you propose it."

"Well, whatever you call it, can I do it?" she wanted to know.

"Jack seems to have appointed himself master of ceremonies," her mother told her.

"Sure, Nora," Jack told her with enthusiasm, "we'll drink to whatever you want to propose."

"To Dada," she said, raising her glass of lemonade, "'cause I prayed to him not to let Mossgrove be sold and he heard."

"He sure did," Jack declared, raising his steaming glass, "and I'll certainly drink to that and to our other absent friends."

"Who are our other absent friends?" Nora wanted to know.

"Your grandmother Nellie Phelan and your great-grandfather old Edward Phelan," Jack told her warmly, "the great people in whose footsteps we are walking today."

"Do you know something, Jack," Peter laughed at him, "I'd say that the cure is gone to your head."

"Not a bit of it, boy," Jack assured him grandly. "I'm drunk with relief of the occasion that's in it. This is a great day for Mossgrove, and in years to come when I'm growing daisies down in Kilmeen cemetery, Peter, you remember this day and the joy that is in it. Because a lifetime of living only throws up a few days like this, and when they come they must be savoured and appreciated and recorded on the back pages of the mind, never to be forgotten. This is what living is all about, lad, celebrating the good days, and the memory of them will keep you going when things get rough. Because if you have good days once there is no reason why they will not come again. The secret is that when they are good you should say that they are good."

"By God, Jack, that was some speech," Mark told him appreciatively. "I didn't think that you had that many words in you."

"This is what you might call rising to the occasion," Jack assured him, rubbing his hands together with relish.

"Would it be possible to have our tea now?" Martha asked coolly.

"Certainly, Martha," Jack told her with a flourish; "pour away, my girl, and we'll sample some of your splendid baking."

Martha did not enjoy being termed "my girl", but her annoyance was lost on Jack who handed around cups of tea as if they were golden goblets.

"Jack, I never saw you in such good humour," Nora smiled at him.

"Good humour is a great thing," Jack told her with enthusiasm, "and why wouldn't we be in good humour and we wining and dining like lords and enjoying your mother's fine fare."

"Your cakes are scrumptious, Mom," Nora said.

"They are superb," Jack pronounced with vigour, handing plates up and down the table.

As Kate looked at the faces around the table she decided that Jack was right. After all the trauma they had been through it was good to celebrate this occasion. Peter, she had noticed, had not gone to his mother as Nora had done; it would take time for Peter to forgive Martha for what had happened. But she knew that Jack and Davy would get around him. There was no bitterness in either of them and they would encourage Peter to forget. If Martha had uprooted him out of Mossgrove, she would have had her hands full because he would never have forgiven her. Nora was different. Once the bad days were over Nora would let them go, and now looking at her smiling face Kate was thankful that she had handled Ned's death so well. She loved this little girl who had so much of Nellie and Ned in her, and she was glad that she would grow up here where they would have wanted. It would be good for her, too, to have Agnes and Mark near by, because they had the gentleness and kindness that Martha lacked.

Martha, on the other hand, had the determination to run Mossgrove and make a good job of it, because Martha was never prepared to be second best. Now that she had no other choice she would be hell-bent on proving that she was smarter and better than any Phelan. That could only be good for Mossgrove. There was no doubt but that now that she was not selling she would sort out the Conways pretty fast. Ned had held her back from being too drastic with them, but now there was no restraint. Matt Conway would meet his match. Kate smiled to realise that Martha was probably as tough as the old man Phelan, and maybe in the circumstances that was no bad thing. She would need to be tough to handle the Conways. It was ironic that they were celebrating the cancellation of the sale with old Molly's cure. She felt that it would have amused Molly Conway, who had had scant regard for her menfolk.

"Kate, you are away in a world of your own," Mark smiled down at her.

"Yes, I'm savouring the day, as Jack told us to."

"That was some speech coming from Jack, wasn't it? Never thought that he had it in him."

"I'm so happy for him that Martha changed her mind," Kate said.

"It's great for all of you," Mark smiled, "and I'm delighted for my mother as well. She would have missed them so much. The only problem she has now is me."

"You're no problem."

"Well, it would be nice if I earned a bit of money – not for my own sake, because I don't give a damn, but it would be nice for Agnes if I was turning over an honest pound. It would make her feel good in the face of Martha's criticism of me," he said ruefully.

"It's about to happen," Kate told him.

"Oh yea, and pigs will fly," he laughed.

"No, seriously," she told him. "I have an announcement to make."

Kate stood up and clinked her spoon against her cup. "I want to say something," she announced.

"This is great," said Nora. "I love when people make speeches. Will you be as good as Jack, Aunty Kate?"

"Couldn't be as good as Jack," Kate ruffled her hair; "he was on a runner."

"Norry, will you ever shut up and let Aunty Kate make her announcement," Peter said.

She could see Martha watching her. Bet she's worried now, Kate thought.

"This has to do with Mark," she began and saw a look of relief pass over Martha's face. "We all know that Mark has been turning out wonderful pictures for years. The problem was that there was nobody to appreciate them properly. Well, all that is about to change."

“Kate, what are you talking about?” Mark demanded.

“All will be revealed in due course. You all know that there is a new school coming to Kilmeen and that it will be in the Miss Jacksons’ old house. Well, their grandnephew in America is taking a great interest in it. He feels that there is no encouragement for the arts in Kilmeen, and how right he is. He wants works of art to hang on the walls to give the children an appreciation of such things. And guess who is going to do the pictures?” She paused for effect, looking around at the expectant faces. “Our Mark!”

“Where did all this come from?” Mark asked, a look of astonishment on his face.

“From old Mr Hobbs, and you are to take over some of your paintings for his approval during the week, but that is only a matter of form because they are the best there is.”

“But this is fantastic,” Mark breathed. “An opportunity to hang my pictures.”

“Yes, and when Rodney Jackson sees your pictures, Mark, it’s going to open doors for you.”

“I remember him coming once when I was a young fellow to visit his aunts,” Mark said.

“Old Hobbs said that he came, but I can’t remember him at all,” Kate said.

“Ah, you were too young,” Mark laughed; “I’ve a few years on you.”

“This is great news,” Agnes broke in. “At least now, Mark, you’ll get paid for all your hours of work.”

“Good man, Mark,” Jack proclaimed; “it was only a matter of time before you were valued. Not that I know anything about paintings myself, now, but Kate was always telling me that you were a genius and that we were all too stupid to appreciate you.”

"Ah, Jack," she protested, "I didn't put it quite like that."

"No," he agreed, "but that was the truth anyway, even if you were too polite to say so."

"So your pictures will be hanging in the new school, Mark," Davy said in an impressed voice; "that will be something!"

"I'll tell everybody that you are my uncle," Nora declared. "I can't wait to go to the new school."

"They'll all be all right kind of pictures?" Peter asked in a worried voice.

"Oh no," Nora told him in a mocking tone, "they'll be terrible! Don't be stupid, Peter, Uncle Mark only paints beautiful pictures, and if the Conways say anything against them you are to fight them with Jeremy Nolan."

"What's all this about?" Mark protested. "Talk of fights, and nobody has said a word against them yet."

"Well, the Conways are bound to be against them, because they are against everything," she said, adding loyally, "except Kitty."

"When were you over with Mr Hobbs?" Martha asked casually.

"Yesterday," Kate told her briefly. "Isn't it great news about Mark?"

"We'll have to see how it all turns out before we start getting carried away," she said.

"Oh, the sky is the limit now," Kate assured her airily. "With talent like Mark's all he needed was the opening, and this is it."

"We'll wait and see," said Martha coolly.

"Well, this will never keep white stockings on the missus, as the old man used to say," Jack announced. "So Davy, you and I had better get going and milk the cows."

"Davy and I will do them, Jack," Peter told him, rising from the table. "You're too dressed up to go milking, and as well as that you can't see too straight after that stuff you're after drinking."

"I could walk a straight line with the best of them," Jack protested, "but if you're generous enough to offer, I'll be generous enough to accept and go home early and give Toby a surprise."

"I'll walk up the boreen with you," Mark told him, and the four of them trooped out of the room

"Isn't it nice when the men are gone?" Nora observed as they closed the door behind them. "Now it's only us." And she looked around from Martha to Agnes and Kate.

"The women are left to do the washing as usual," Agnes smiled, "but who cares, because after all the good news we've had today I could wash up for a week."

"Things are coming together at last," Kate agreed.

"I'm so pleased for Mark," Agnes said with fervour.

"So am I," Martha said.

"Why didn't you say so when he was here?" Agnes asked her.

"That's not my way."

Later, as Kate walked up the boreen she thought over the day that was gone. Martha did not know if she knew about the will or not, and it was probably the best way to leave things. All her mother had wanted was for Mossgrove to be safe. Peter must never know that Martha could not sell Mossgrove. But it was amazing that Nellie had not told Jack about the will.

When she reached his cottage Jack was waiting for her at the gate.

"Come in, Kate," he invited, "and we'll have a chat. I'll find it hard to sleep tonight after all this excitement, but if we talk it over I might calm down a bit."

"It's great news, isn't it," she said when they were seated with Toby and Maggie by the fire.

"You knew, Kate, didn't you, before she said anything?" Jack asked quietly.

"What makes you say that?"

"I was watching your face," he told her, "and you were not in the least bit surprised when Martha told us."

"You're a wily old devil, Jack," she smiled.

"The mind is a strange thing," Jack mused, "but when Martha told me yesterday evening about the special tea it set me thinking. I knew that it could only mean that she had changed her mind, and there had to be a very good reason. Then I remembered something that Nellie had said years ago about taking steps to protect Mossgrove."

"You forgot all about it in the mean time?" Kate asked.

"I didn't understand what she meant; I asked her, but she wouldn't explain. It was one thing she kept private from me, and I put it out of my mind."

"Until yesterday."

"Until yesterday."

"It was all a long time ago," said Kate.

"Yea! But it was so important, and that was why she told me. She had something in the will, hadn't she?"

"That's right. She made it so that Mossgrove could not be sold without my permission. But we'll never tell anyone, Jack, why Martha changed her mind."

"I once told you that you were like the old man," he said reflectively, "but that's not one hundred percent correct.

He would have ground Martha under his heel with the power that Nellie's will gave you."

"Nellie would never have wanted me to humiliate Martha."

"Yes, that was her way. When she was the woman of the house here she did things well. But maybe our new woman will come into her own now."

"You could be right, Jack," Kate agreed.

OTHER BOOKS
from
ALICE TAYLOR

Alice Taylor

Quench the Lamp

"Taylor follows *To School Through the Fields* with these equally captivating further recollections of family life in pastoral County Cork, Ireland. Infused with wit and lyricism, the story centers on the 1950s when the author and her friends were budding teenagers. Taylor describes the past vividly and without complaint as years of hard labor for herself, parents and siblings, making clear that the days also were full of fun shared with neighbors in the close-knit community." *Publishers Weekly*

"What a lively, lyrical style of writing this author has. With warmth and vigour she tells all about growing up on a farm in the 1940s and introduces us to the many delightful characters (human and otherwise) that were around at the time." *Liverpool Echo*

ISBN 0 86322 112 2

The Village

"Ireland's Laurie Lee . . . a chronicler of fading village life and rural rituals who sells and sells." *Observer*

"Taylor has a knack for finding the universal truth in daily details." *Los Angeles Times*

"Taylor is in love with life, in love with family, in love with people, and in love with nature, and all this affection is evident in every page of the book. This is a book you should read if you are jaded with life and bored with your environment, because Taylor can find joy in any relationship and see beauty in every rural scene. . . . She uses imagery like a poet, creating scenes with a minimum of words and deftly transferring her sense of beauty to the reader." *Irish Echo*

ISBN 0 86322 142 4

Country Days

"A rich patchwork of tales and reminiscences by the bestselling village postmistress from Co. Cork. Alice Taylor is a natural writer." *Daily Telegraph*

"Like Cupid, the author has an unerring aim for the heartstrings; however, she can also transform the mundane into the magical." *The Irish Times*

"This is not a big book, but it has certain intrinsic values, not least the fact that it can be picked up and savoured in the odd spare moment and that it brings yet another breath of rural Ireland into our homes, all the while mixing the hilarious with the poignant." *Irish Independent*

"A work which will be received with delight and which will certainly enhance her reputation as a storyteller supreme." *Cork Examiner*

ISBN 0 86322 168 8

The Night Before Christmas

"*The Night Before Christmas* is a nostalgic and loving look back to a family firmly rooted in tradition and humour. Whether the reader is in the teens or is a senior citizen, this book will charm and captivate. It truly pulls back the curtain of time to the days when Christmas was really Christmas." *Irish Independent*

"Full of finely observed detail rendered with the misleading simplicity of a real craftswoman." *In Dublin*

"Alice Taylor has an unerring knack of bringing her readers into her home. Her stories of a childhood Christmas are rich, warm and amusing, and we are given a wonderful insight into life as it was. As with her other books, she writes in a very captivating manner in the old storytelling tradition." *People*

ISBN 0 86322 190 4

Going to the Well

"The selection of poetry is beautifully written; she gently and accurately writes about old age, death, the countryside and animals. Poetry that will bring a smile to the face of a reader, or leave them thinking about their own mortality. It is a book that can be dipped into quietly again and again because she exhibits an unerring sense of what is real, of what life is really like." *Examiner*

ISBN 1 902011 02 3

A Country Miscellany

Wonderful slices of country life, beautifully illustrated with photographs by Richard T. Mills. Irish cottages, the pleasures of walking in autumnal woods, a hens' hatching house and a country garden: these are just some of the elements in this varied patchwork quilt of views of rural life. Written with her own unique insight and wit, the text is complemented by a series of more than twenty full colour photographs of the Irish countryside in its many moods and seasons.

ISBN 1 902011 08 2